M000200484

Tower 2

Color Registration

———	1.5 mm
———	1.0 mm
———	0.5 mm
———	0.0 mm
———	-0.5 mm
———	-1.0 mm
———	-1.5 mm

Kaine Dragovich. I've brought down serial killers with just the power of my piss and vinegar. Don't test me, wench," Balthazar growled, giving a pretty excellent imitation of Kaine.

I fell out laughing. Watching Silvaria get arrested in front of all her rich friends after dealing with that shipping container and working underneath her felt good. Listening to Balthazar pretend like he could lip-read and give running commentary was just what I needed to get my mind off the fact that I hadn't heard from Bram.

Balthazar gave a dramatic hair toss and struck a sassy pose.

"Do you *know* who I am? I bought my degree at the Academy of the Profane and my seat on the board. I'll have your job for this! Everyone here will see I'm being mistreated."

Balthazar sounded a *lot* like Silvaria. I had no idea he was so good at this, but it didn't shock me. My eyes kept darting to Balthazar and my flat screen because he was *nailing* this.

Kaine gave a curt nod to someone, and then the entire bank was in chaos. Apparently, Silvaria wasn't the only person they were arresting today. Undercover agents sprang into action and started rounding people up. These rich people weren't going down without a fight, but a few tried to run.

He wasn't on my board or Ravyn's, but a fairly prominent warlock tried to run and got body tackled by what had to be a massive shifter. Felix and Gabriel were super into sports. Felix liked cricket, and they were both fond of supernatural dodgeball. Little Beyla told us all about human dodgeball, and we were all so confused. We didn't really see the point in it, and even I was offended.

Reyson was slowly getting into the world of contact sports on the television. They all sat up and started cheering the agents on like this was the world playoffs for dodgeball. Even Balthazar was into it and changed his commentary like he was some really bizarre sportscaster.

"And the warlocks are now fighting off the shifters and losing spectacularly. I think that big, beefy wolf may have dislocated something on that shifty warlock, but no one is throwing penalty flags in this game. The succubae are disarming the shifters by making them a little horny with a touch. I hope they know what they are doing because I've also had to fight off a randy werewolf with a boner, and it's so not fun.

"Oh, fuck. There's now a coordinated banshee attack. The home team we're all rooting for appears to be wearing jock protection for their ears because the shrieks didn't affect them. The bad team that we all know only won their awards because they are horrible cheaters and pay off the refs are dropping like flies.

"It's a beautiful sight, folks. The home team brought those cheating bastards to their knees. Literally. They look pretty dazed at their loss, and some of them are bleeding from the ears. Some of the spectators got a little too close to the action for their liking, but they are breathing a sigh of relief that the game is over and they aren't part of the casualties. I'm calling it, folks. The home team *destroyed* their opponents."

Felix liked to give Balthazar a hard time, but one thing Felix could appreciate was a violent sports match. He jumped up and gave Balthazar a standing ovation for turning this arrest into one. Gabriel and Reyson were clapping and whistling.

I had other ideas. Balthazar was so extra all the time,

and I knew other people gave him a hard time about it, but I loved every minute of it. I was sure all those people who got arrested with Silvaria at the bank also rented space at that warehouse. I was also fairly certain Kaine roped the bank into getting them all there to round them up at once.

I could appreciate that on a deep emotional level. The only reason we even got to watch this was Balthazar made damned sure it was entertaining. I flew off the sectional and practically tackled him with a hug.

"I love you!" I blurted out.

I'd never said that to a man before. It just kind of came out, but it was true. I meant it, and it felt good. All of this did.

"I mean it—all of you. We won something today. Yeah, I haven't heard from Bram yet, which worries me, but look what we did together. All those people had to have nasty shit at that shipping yard to get busted like that. Kaine wasn't fucking around. We make an *amazing* team, and I love all of you."

Reyson leaned back into the pillows with a smirk on his face.

"I told you, my witch."

I wasn't even mad at him for saying that.

"No woman has ever said that to me before," Gabriel said.

"You know I love you back, right?" Felix said.

Balthazar scooped me up and jumped on top of everyone with the both of us.

"Love fest cuddle pile!" he yelled.

"Your knee got my junk, and I'm not even mad about it," Felix said.

"Payback is a bitch. You threatened to curse mine."

"We need to celebrate," Reyson said. "Dorian isn't

happening until tomorrow. Bram has time to check his phone. Ripley is right. This is a victory. I'm sure Dorian Gray already took into account that his warehouse was compromised. Still, he couldn't know Balthazar had connections to the Paranormal Investigation Bureau, and the arrests would come this fast. He won't know until he checks his phone. Dorian might have had plans for Silvaria still that we messed up. It'll make him careless. We can use that. I want a feast, mead, and cake. I'm going to cook."

I wasn't wild about the idea when Reyson informed me I would be his wife, but the god literally cooked massive, delicious meals for any occasion, didn't leave the toilet seat up, was sexy as all fuck, and was just generally amazing to be around.

I wasn't mad at the idea anymore.

And yeah, shit was going to get real when Dorian landed. We weren't relying on Kaine and an entire team of trained agents. It was going to be all us, and our resident god was getting bad vibes about splitting up. And I still hadn't heard from Bram to give Dorian to him if we pulled this off.

I needed to forget about that and just celebrate our wins for now.

CHAPTER 9
BALTHAZAR

The guys were just so great, and Ripley just informed me she loved me. This was better than any illicit substance I may or may not have taken in my younger days at a club. I felt light and ready to party.

Most of the time, when I did this kind of stuff, I worked alone. Someone messaged me about a job, and if it was a shit job, I turned it down. I took all the information and usually worked alone in my apartment until it was done. I sent them a link to the information they wanted on an encrypted server I owned, and they wired me payment. We generally did everything via message.

The only person who ever spoke to me when they needed something was Kaine. He'd threatened to throw my ass in jail or burn me alive several times, but I knew he *really* loved me.

This was the first time I put my skills to work for people I actually liked and as a team. I was having *fun,* and they appreciated me. They didn't just throw money in my account and disappear until they needed something again.

I was going to help Reyson throw the best party ever.

Unfortunately, Ripley had to go back to work. Minerva Krauss agreed to watch her desk if Ripley promised to give her the good gossip when she got back. I knew Minerva meant a lot to Ripley and Ravyn, but I found her extremely awesome even before she gave us her diaries to help out.

She was this prim, buttoned-up witch with her hair in a tight bun, but once you started talking to her, she was anything but a prim, buttoned-up witch. She even made Reyson blush. I sat there as the two of them *graphically* discussed the werewolf porn in this library, and I was blushing too. I needed to read those books.

Reyson was cooking up a feast, and Gabriel was using his magic to help me decorate. Felix was where he always was—looking out for Ripley when we weren't there.

I liked Gabriel. I couldn't exactly make this a proper party unless I left for supplies. Or, I had an open-minded warlock willing to abuse their magic to make this place fabulous. Reyson was helping too in between oven duty.

Ripley painted all the walls in here black or purple, and she had this banging décor scheme going on, so there wasn't a ton of work to do. We just needed to dim the lights, hang some magical fairy lights, and light all the candles when Ripley and Felix returned.

I sat back and admired my handiwork. Was asking Reyson to conjure a smoke machine too much? Was Ripley even into raves? Reyson interrupted my thought process to hand me a plate with an absolutely gorgeous cake on it.

"Can you bring that down to Minerva if she's still here? I've got a bit of work left to do in the kitchen, and we all owe her thanks for relieving Ripley so she could watch the arrest."

"I'll go too," Gabriel said.

I knew why Gabriel was going. Minerva Krauss was a

highly respected witch, and she had been nothing but kind to Gabriel. But, unfortunately, the rest of the witching community wasn't like that for the most part. I got it. I wanted everyone to be nice to him.

Minerva was still there chatting with Ripley. I honestly didn't expect her to still be there since the library was going to close soon. I slid the cake in front of her and pulled a chair up.

"You should always eat it when then God of Chaos bakes for you. I think this is lemon," I said.

"It probably is," Ripley said. "He knows I keep lemon cookies here just for you when we are talking books."

A vampire was passing Ripley's desk on the way out and scowled at us.

"Oh, so *she* can eat in the library? You kicked me out last month for doing the same thing!"

"She's eating cake at my desk, Malik. You were trying to drink a succubus by the maps."

"Gross, dude. Don't drink people in public. If you have that kink, do it in a club like a civilized person," I said.

"Carry on," Ripley said, waving her hand at the vampire. "You know this library is sentient, right? Do that again, and it might ban you."

"Yeah, yeah," the vampire said, stomping out.

"This is delicious. Gabriel, Ripley tells me you killed a revenant. That's fascinating."

"It was in my family grimoire—bad family history. The spell is only good for one. That's what caused his downfall. He made an army of revenants to get out of his deal with a demon but trying to control all of them ended up killing him. If there had been more than one revenant at the warehouse, I wouldn't have been able to fight them off."

"Still, one day, you're going to have to entertain an old

witch with the story of how it's possible because I've tried to crack it several times. That particular magic was always going to be impossible for me without creating a revenant as a test subject. Ripley, go be with your men. The library should have closed five minutes ago. I'll take my cake to go. If Ravyn is getting that footage, I want it too."

Ripley slung her arm around my waist and pulled me into a hug.

"You'll miss Balthazar's *amazing* commentary, but it's still worth a watch."

"I'll get your email from Ripley and send it when I get it over to Ravyn."

"Thanks. Now, I believe you have a party to go to. Balthazar is already dressed."

So was Gabriel, but I'd save that comment for later. Gabriel took his man bun out and was wearing his hair down like one of the covers of the werewolf porn books in here. He was decked out in black leather and asked me to do his eyeliner for the first time. Wearing eyeliner for the first time was a big step for a guy, even if we looked amazing in it, and we all should. I made sure I did a damned good job.

The warlock drew the line at glitter. I was going to convert one of these assholes to glitter.

I went *all out*. I did a smokey eye with full rainbow eyeshadow. I broke out my best glitter and had my hair properly spiked up. I clapped my hands in glee when we got upstairs to Ripley's apartment, and Reyson had decked his big, sexy body out like he was going clubbing.

"Felix, you are underdressed," Reyson said, snapping his fingers.

I nearly wet myself. Reyson did exactly what I'd been threatening to do to Felix but wasn't actually going to do it because I valued my junk. Felix was *sparkling* with glitter and had glow sticks in his dreds. He looked fabulous. I knew he would. There was not a being on this entire planet that couldn't be enhanced with a little glitter.

Felix was not amused.

"What the shit is in my hair? Reyson, I literally don't care if you can blink me out of existence. I'm going to murder you!"

Reyson just chuckled. I was about to explode because I couldn't believe Reyson had gone there. But I wouldn't say a fucking thing because this was my idea, and Felix struck me as a spiteful little shit who would take it out on my dick because Reyson made him pretty.

Ripley darted forward and kissed the pissed-off right off his face.

"It's just one night, and you *do* look sexy."

Felix just grunted.

"I'll keep everything but the glow sticks. My hair is important. I've not cut it in my entire life. So *never* mess with my hair again."

"Apologies then, cat," Reyson said.

The glow sticks were gone in an instant. If he had said something about his hair before, I would have dropped it. I enjoyed ribbing him, but not over things that mattered. I liked Felix because he could take a fucking joke and just threw your nonsense right back at you. Felix pulled Ripley into his side.

"Now that I'm covered in glitter against my will let's get this party started."

CHAPTER 10
RIPLEY

This was exactly what I needed. I usually had a healthy social life outside of the library. I missed going out with Ravyn or just by myself. I enjoyed hanging out with the guys. No, I loved it. It just felt like so much shit had happened since Hettie showed up and said she needed help to raise her dead Uncle Seth. None of us had time to just relax.

Yeah, every time we won something, things turned around, and we lost too. We rescued Talvath, then lost Bram. As far as we all could tell, this was a win. Dorian had lost his witch. I knew he had a backup, but probably no one with as near the influence as Silvaria. If he did, they might have gotten busted at the raid on the bank.

I'll bet that douche fuck wasn't expecting that.

Reyson managed to get a functioning strobe light on the ceiling of my living room. I guessed that was all Balthazar. We ate like kings, and now we were dancing. I tried to get Ravyn and Killian over here. *No one* partied better than my twin sister. She was usually my wing woman and creep detector when I was trolling for dick.

71

She profusely apologized and promised a raincheck. Ravyn had a lot to do to prepare the museum for the dig in Norway. The Cult of the Aether Sisters was one of the most dangerous covens of witches in our history. The entire supernatural community to put them down.

They trapped them in their fortress and set it on fire. Valentine brought a team of people out there to dig around the burnt-out remains of the fortress most sane people didn't go near because none of those witches had been given the rites. If people wanted them dead when they were alive, you had to be pretty stupid to want to deal with their ghosts.

Valentine was pretty fucking stupid if he would cheat on my sister.

Still, he found a hatch buried in the rubble that led to a basement of sorts. It was full of skeletons and relics. If a dangerous coven had objects in their secret underground lair, there was a good chance they were volatile. Ravyn had an entire room at the museum specifically to deal with that kind of thing. She was buried in research mode at the moment.

I got it. I wanted her here, but I didn't want her hurt when she started working with those relics. She sounded more excited about the dangerous shit headed her way than Valentine coming back, even if she dyed her hair, so I was okay with her not being here so I could get some booze into her and set her straight.

Right now, I was enjoying being in a bump and grind fest with four hot men. Reyson danced exactly how you'd expect an ancient god who hadn't been on Earth in a long time to dance. It was wild and savage. Honestly, he was better than some of the people who waltzed up to me at clubs when the music was pumping, and I was getting my groove on.

We all started mimicking him. It was freeing. I could picture us all on a mountain in front of a fire under the stars dancing to worship Reyson. I knew he'd never ask for that, but I could see it in my mind.

Everyone danced closer to me until I couldn't keep track of who I was touching or kissing. My body was on fire. Yeah, we were taking five minutes from the demon apocalypse to have a party, but could we take ten to have a little orgy? Dorian was technically boarding a plane right now.

"Guys, would you be opposed to taking this party to my bedroom?"

Gabriel just chuckled.

"Look down, Ripley. We're all on board."

I let my gaze travel downwards. They were all dressed in leather for this party, and those trousers were doing little to hide four massive erections. They wanted to play. My horny lizard brain was going into overdrive with the possibilities. Did I have the right toys for this? My collection was pretty big.

Fuck it. I had a god here. He could produce what I didn't have.

I ripped my tank top off and slung it over my shoulder. I sauntered towards my bedroom and tossed a glance over my shoulder.

"Step into my office."

CHAPTER II
FELIX

F inally, I hadn't had a good orgy since I died. I knew
it was only a matter of time when Ripley started
building her coven. Fucking Dorian Gray. This
would have happened before now if it weren't for him.
Wanker. It was happening now, and I intended to show my
witch a good time.

Ripley liked sexy underthings. She was wearing a red
lacy bra today. We all crowded into her bedroom, and I just
took her in. She was so fucking beautiful. I ripped the
ridiculous leather vest with spikes Reyson had put me in off
and took a step towards her.

A very naked Balthazar came barreling out of nowhere
and tackled Ripley. How had he managed to get out of that
outfit so fast? It was more complicated than mine. I'd given
up trying to figure out that vampire. Ripley and Balthazar
crashed onto the bed, laughing. Ripley looked over his
shoulder and beckoned us over.

We didn't need to be asked twice. We fell into bed. I was
only interested in kissing Ripley. I totally didn't mind when
Reyson and Balthazar wanted to take a break from that to

kiss each other because it meant I was only fighting Gabriel for her lips.

I didn't want to fight Gabriel, though. I was pretty sure Reyson already had plans for Ripley and Balthazar. I desperately wanted to share Ripley with Gabriel. He was a brother warlock, and between the two of us, we could teach each other things from our grimoires and only get stronger.

I nibbled on Ripley's ear.

"How'd you like to be shared by two warlocks?" I purred.

Gabriel let out a little growl. Ripley arched her back and pulled my hair.

"Lilith, please. I absolutely would."

I peered over Ripley to Reyson and Balthazar.

"Take five. This is the Gabriel and Felix show, and I intend to make use of every inch of this massive bed."

Reyson got out of bed and pulled Balthazar to his chest.

"I enjoy live theatre, cat. If you're putting on a show, make it entertaining."

Balthazar bit Reyson's nipple and smirked at us.

"Something tells me even though women wore pantaloons back in Felix's day and the human church would burn you for getting kinky, the cat is a total *freak* in bed."

I threw a pillow at his erection. The human church was a major problem back then, but even the humans were filthy behind closed doors. Kink wasn't invented in this century. Even Reyson could tell him that.

Ripley pulled me into a kiss.

"Come get freaky with me, Felix. Gabriel, you know where I keep my toys."

So, did I. I didn't peep like a creep when she was using them, but it wasn't like it was a secret when she got a new one. She posted unboxing videos to social media when a new one came in. Thank Lilith the supernatural community wasn't prudes because instead of firing her, some of the board members liked her videos.

"Grab the vibrating butt plug with the fluffy tail," I called to Gabriel.

"Ooh, excellent idea," Ripley said. "I haven't used that one yet."

Gabriel popped up from her toy drawer, waving the butt plug, her Hitachi wand, and some lube like he had just found treasure. He made a good choice. I knew that was her preferred toy because she talked about it like it was her best friend. Honestly, she could have saved a page getting ripped out of her grimoire if she just played with ol' faithful instead of Dorian that night.

Dorian was always going to target her for raising Reyson because she was a powerful witch. He needed Reyson, not a revenant, and Ripley was trained to get him what he wanted. He didn't have to fuck her. There were plenty of reasons I wanted to beat the pretty off Dorian Gray, but that was a big one.

"How did you know that's my favorite?" Ripley asked.

Gabriel tossed me the Hitachi wand and climbed into bed with us.

"Every woman is different, and I love learning how to please them, but if they've tried a Hitachi wand or a flogger, it's generally their favorite."

We didn't have rechargeable sex toys back in my day, but that was totally true about floggers if they were open-minded enough to try a little spanking. And Ripley totally was.

"A flogger is hanging in my closet door."

Gabriel's pupils got so big, his eyes practically turned

black. He jumped out of bed again and opened her closet. Ripley didn't just let anyone break out her floggers. I didn't watch when she was having sex, but I heard all about it. She didn't invite many men back here, but she had itches that needed to be scratched sometimes. I was glad I could finally scratch them.

Ripley crawled on all fours and waved her ass at Gabriel. He didn't need any further invitation. She gave me a smoldering look.

"Get your cock over here, Felix."

I slid in front of her and rested my back on the pillows. Ripley took my cock deep down the back of her throat, and I groaned. Gabriel got up to his business behind her. Ripley was moaning as he fingered her ass and worked the butt plug in. As soon as it was situated, he fired it up so that it started vibrating.

Ripley started moaning all over my cock. I was in sheer bliss. Especially when he started smacking the flogger down her back and thighs, and she took it out on my cock. I tangled my hair in her curls and moaned. Ripley gave my cock a hard suck and dragged her lips all the way to the tip before popping it out of her mouth.

"I want you both inside me now."

We hadn't worked out the logistics of this threesome. It just happened naturally. Ripley climbed up my body and gripped my cock. I groaned as she slid down me. I felt the bed shift as Gabriel moved.

"The fluffy tail is sexy as fuck. I hate to remove it, but I really want to claim your ass."

Ripley started grinding against my cock and tossed a look over her shoulder.

"Then, get over here and fuck me, Gabriel."

"Shit," Gabriel growled.

Gabriel took his time until he was fully seated inside her. Shit. She was just so tight and wet. We took it slow, but she was egging us on to go faster and harder. Ripley had never been breakable. She wasn't afraid to start fistfights with the boys before she got her magic, so I knew she could handle Gabriel and me.

We gave her exactly what she wanted, and she gave it back. She was a little feral. She was biting and scratching. I wasn't the least bit mad about it because I liked a little pain with my pleasure, and it meant we were making her feel good.

"Shit!" Ripley howled, raking her nails down my chest.

I wouldn't be able to last much longer. Ripley was hot and wet around my cock, and with Gabriel also inside her, things were snug, and I could feel him too. I finally let go when I felt her clamp down on my cock, and she savagely bit my neck.

Gabriel let out a tremendous roar, and we all collapsed on a heap in the middle of the bed. I wanted more of this. I hadn't been a part of a coven since I died, and this was a great one. This one centered on Ripley, and we were all fine with that. We were here to protect her and add to her skills.

I knew we'd all be here for every battle, but I also wanted more of *this*. Not the orgies, just an entire night of spoiling her and making her laugh. If it led to the bedroom, I was here for that too. Now that I had opposable thumbs, I intended to spoil her rotten.

We just needed to hope turning Dorian Gray over to Hell was going to stop them from coming here and killing us all.

CHAPTER 12

REYSON

I was playing with Balthazar's hair while we watched the show, but Felix was the one purring in the aftermath. I was glad I left that little addition when I gave him his body back. He was angry about the alterations to his cock, but I knew what I was doing with that too. Ripley *clearly* loved it, and I intended to marry Ripley, not Felix. So I was happy to give him his body back because it meant a lot to her. I left the purr because it was amusing to me, and I made his cock a little more cat like in case she wanted to play with it.

I let them snuggle and enjoy the aftermath because I was getting my own with Balthazar. He tended to be an impatient vampire except for when it counted, and that's what I loved about him. He was happy to let them have their moment, no matter how long it seemed to last.

Gabriel finally sat up and stretched.

"I think we've hogged Ripley enough. It's Reyson and Balthazar's turn."

That was one reason I liked Gabriel. He was fierce in battle, but despite mistreatment by his peers, he was always generous with us. If I was a mere mortal and spent my life getting shat on by everyone and met someone like Ripley who didn't care about that, I certainly wouldn't be open to sharing her. I was okay with sharing my wife because all the possibilities said I was supposed to. Gabriel didn't have that, but he still made Felix get out of bed so Balthazar and I could get in.

I was fairly certain Balthazar wanted a repeat of our last tryst, and I'd happily give him that whenever he wanted, but not tonight. Aside from finding a werewolf or a willing Bram to satisfy my shifter curiosity, I'd had many of my sexual needs met since I came back. Sex with Ripley was more than I could have fantasized about. I wanted to play with Balthazar and Ripley together too, but I had other uses for him tonight. I had an itch to scratch.

What was the phrase he used?

"I desire to be in a sandwich with a librarian and a vampire," I announced.

"I'm so here for that," Ripley said.

Balthazar just sat there with his mouth open. I was fairly certain I was not the first man to ask Balthazar to fuck him in the ass. He was probably quite good at it, which was why I asked him.

"I think you broke him," Felix said.

"I'm assuming you've done that before?" I asked.

"Well, yeah, but the most important person I ever did that with was a politician's son who was so far in the closet, he offered me hush money to never tell a soul he was a bottom. You're a fucking *god.*"

Was that it? I had to remember I was the only one they had met. So what were they teaching these mortals about us now that he thought I was above asking him?

"Some of the newer gods are prudes. I *would not* want to

spend time with them. The old gods and many that came after fully explored all the pleasures our vessels could offer us. This isn't new to this century, and people certainly weren't offering bribes to keep it a secret they liked that kind of thing. Some of us have shape-shifted into different genders to see what it feels like. Loki once had sex as a horse and saved his sister from having to marry a giant. I need to check in on him. He was always a lot of fun, and he's definitely not hanging out in the Aether."

I decided I was going to do that once this nonsense with Hell was over. I knew there were plenty of gods still on this planet mingling, even if they weren't currently being worshiped. I had no interest in reconnecting with some of them, but I always liked Loki and his family. If I knew Loki, he was probably richer than a king now and working a job where he could cause a lot of mischief.

"What if I do it wrong?" Balthazar said, wringing his hands. "I've never had butt sex this important before."

Ripley tackled him and flung him on his back. She straddled his waist and looked down at him.

"You forget, I've had sex with you before. Reyson had sex with you while you were fucking me. We know how you fuck, dude. Reyson wouldn't have asked unless he wasn't sure you were going to make his prostate sing. Fuck closeted politician's sons. You've leveled up in your bisexual vampire quest. Now, nut up and put your dick in Reyson's ass."

I'd given plenty of pep talks in my day. If I were traveling on business, I'd sometimes give them to warriors who were hopelessly outnumbered because I needed them to rise up, overthrow a regime, and bring some much needed chaos to an area. Not all chaos was bad. Sometimes, it ushered in a golden era.

Ripley's pep talk was certainly different from any of mine, but it was definitely effective. Balthazar was back in the game. He grabbed her and yanked her to his chest so he could kiss her.

"Sorry, sometimes I get a little neurotic. I'm over it. This is going to be the best butt sex ever."

I could be ungraceful and playful sometimes when I needed to be. This was definitely that time. I belly-flopped on the bed and pulled both of them to me. Yes, I was a god, and yes, I helped create the universe, but I didn't consider myself more important than anyone in this room. If I did, I knew that would be the end of Ripley's growing feelings for me. Besides, none of us gods were infallible, even if some of us liked to pretend we were.

I nuzzled Ripley's neck and ran my fingers through Balthazar's hair.

"I think I would like to experience modern sex toys. Not the kind with tails, though Ripley was extremely sexy sporting one. They made them out of all sorts of things back in my day. I was fond of the ones carved out of rose quartz the witches made, but I'm very curious about the ones you have now."

Ripley bit Balthazar's ear and pinched my nipple.

"You all have an open invitation to my toy collection. The butt stuff is in a box next to the restraints."

I loved she was so open. I just knew if I ever met the woman, I was going to make my wife, she was going to be sexually free like Ripley. She had a wide array of toys, and she wasn't asking me to deny anything about myself. Yes, she was asking me to share her with other men, but we asked her to let us share with each other. I knew *plenty* of goddesses who would have tried to castrate me for asking to sample a werewolf.

Balthazar was an affectionate vampire, and I loved that about it. As soon as he had what he needed from the drawer, he took a running start and jumped on top of us. We had toys, and Balthazar was ready to proceed. I desperately *needed* to taste my witch.

I knew Ripley would have fought back magically or physically if someone laid hands on her when she didn't want them to, but she laughed when I grabbed her and flipped her on her back. I laughed too when Balthazar brought his hand down on my ass. Only a vampire would be cheeky enough to spank a god.

I tossed my long hair over my shoulder to give him a smirk. He was biting his lip and looked nervous.

"Shit. Sorry. It was right there and just so firm and perky. I got caught up in the moment."

Sometimes, I forgot how young these people were compared to me and how little time they had to experiment with literally everything.

"Balthazar, I'm older than the universe. I've experimented with spanking people and having them spank me. You are not the first to lay your hand on my ass. Do what comes naturally. I won't get angry with you for a kink."

"Excellent," Balthazar said.

His fangs popped out, and he spanked me again. I chuckled and turned back to Ripley. What I wanted was right there. I dove in and tasted her honey. Ripley tasted divine, and she was just so responsive. She immediately started yanking my hair with one hand and pressing my face closer with the other. I wasn't even mad.

I let out a little growl when I felt Balthazar's tongue. That was also a favorite, but I didn't just demand everyone do it because not everyone was into eating ass. Balthazar was divine at it.

This was exactly what we needed to distract ourselves. I was pleasuring my witch, and I let out a little groan when I felt his fingers replace his tongue. The toy was next. I nearly lost it when it started vibrating. Why hadn't I thought of that? I could make stone vibrate, but I never thought of it before. Vibrating sex toys were right up there with Oreos and Frappuccinos with things I wanted to build an effigy to like they used to make of me.

I waited until Ripley came on my tongue before I said anything. I wanted her fully satisfied, and honestly, I just enjoyed hearing her screaming my name in pleasure. People used to pray to me, but it was always ill-wishing terrible things on people. I *much* preferred Ripley's sex noises to any prayer I ever got.

"I'm ready to proceed," I announced.

Ripley yanked me up to kiss me, and I felt Balthazar spank me again. Now that I had given him permission, he was certainly handsy. I wasn't complaining because I always enjoyed it when someone was bold enough to go there with me. Unfortunately, not many people were, even when I asked.

"Get that massive god cock inside me right this minute," Ripley growled.

I loved it when she got bossy. She'd never been afraid of me, even from day one. That was why she was going to make such a good wife for me. I needed to be challenged, or I'd get bored. So I happily gave her exactly what she wanted. I'd lived several places in this world, but this felt like home. It felt amazing being inside her.

I felt Balthazar move behind me. He tended to be a frenetic person who liked to play rough with Ripley and me, but not when it counted. He knew exactly what he was doing and took a care not to hurt me, though he had spent ample time preparing me.

Balthazar's hips met my ass, and I let out a contented sigh. I'd been with Ripley, and I'd watched her have sex before. She wasn't one of those women that wanted you to look deep in her eyes and say sweet things while you made love. Ripley wanted raw passion and the bruises from where your hands gripped her hips afterwards.

So, did I. I wanted to give Ripley exactly what she wanted, and I wanted Balthazar to fuck me with every inch of his vampire speed and strength.

"Balthazar, there are certain perks to having a vampire in your bed, and I want you to give them to me. I also expect you to bite me."

I felt the need to say it. I didn't want him holding back or being anything less than who he was when he was with me. Ripley grabbed my hair and gave it a yank.

"Reyson, there are certain perks to having a god in your bed, and I expect *you* to give them to me. Of course, I also wouldn't mind if you bit me either."

I nipped at her nose. Finally, I quoted a movie she had me watch she told me she loved.

"As you wish."

We started slow but built things up to a pace we were all happy with. Ripley did all the little things I enjoyed, but most people were too afraid to do with me. She bit, scratched, and pulled my hair just right. I was going to have Balthazar's fingerprints bruised into my hips because he was just perfect.

I felt Ripley flutter around my cock. Balthazar flung himself over my back and sunk his fangs into my shoulder. Nosferatu did a wonderful thing making their bites painful or pleasurable. Of course, they could use their fangs to defend themselves, but more people were willing to let them feed on them when their venom was an instant orgasm if done right.

I already would have come hard between Ripley and Balthazar, but his venom just made it even more intense. I threw back my head and roared as I came.

We collapsed on a heap in the bed. Felix blew out the candles, and he and Gabriel joined us in bed. This was our reprieve, and we desperately needed this.

Tomorrow, we'd be back at work trying to round up Dorian Gray for Hell.

CHAPTER 13
BRAM

I had barely slept since we got back to Hell. Talvath wasn't either. There were these coffee beans culti-vated in an area of Hell that only someone like Talvath could afford. They had something similar on Earth, but it was a little different here in Hell. These massive cats that only existed here ate the beans and shat them out, where someone's job was to collect them.

People drank poop coffee on Earth because of the taste. They drank it in Hell because something about the Hell cat's digestive system upped the caffeine content, and you started seeing noises. I tried it once and thought I was dying. My heart was pounding in my ears, and I was sweat-ing, even though Talvath liked his estate kept chilly.

Talvath drank that shit by the pot. He could get a little uppity when he was trying to right a wrong, but this was a massive wrong, and he was hitting the shit coffee really hard. We really needed help, but now he didn't trust anyone in Hell, and he didn't want to go back to Earth with me to get it there because those sigils were out there now.

He'd been through a lot. I saw the state he was in when

91

I woke up at the library. What he *needed* to be doing right now was taking ten minutes to rest and deal with what he went through. He could do that if he let me bring everyone from the library here. We rarely did that here in Hell, but we could make exceptions when some asshole betrayed everyone here.

I'd been running between Talvath and Anod for what seemed like hours. Talvath wasn't a hacker. He was a demon boomer who got mad at his laptop all the time if anything got updated. He was one of the smartest people I knew when it came to laws, history, and lore, but sometimes, he clicked on things he wasn't supposed to, and I had to get the big gay orgy off his screen because he couldn't figure it out.

I knew my way around a computer and smartphone, but up to a point. I didn't get into things I shouldn't because not even Talvath could protect me if I got caught. Balthazar could. I was pretty sure he could figure out our servers here with no problem.

"Bram, the men having sex is back. Come fix it," Talvath said.

I sighed. It was always gay porn. Talvath wasn't a prude, and he didn't care I was bisexual, but I never thought of him as a sexual person. I didn't even know he dated before he bought me. There'd never been a single woman in this house that I could remember. I just didn't know how he always ended up getting his laptop stuck on a gay gang bang.

"You aren't a hacker, Talvath. Neither am I. One of the guys at the library is. If I brought him back here, he could help."

"It's just not done, Bram. I know they are your friends, but you'd be putting them in danger—especially since they have a god with them. Have you forgotten why we live totally separate from Earth?"

"I haven't forgotten. I also told them the truth about Hell and our deals. They had a right to know since they were risking their lives helping me find and rescue you. Reyson was furious about what happened to Lilith. It's such a major part of our history, but the witches and warlocks feel like Lilith has abandoned them. She created them too, but she's here with us, and there was a time they were being massacred. Reyson said none of the other gods knew what was going on, or they would have stepped in. They still don't know. That was the first Reyson was hearing about it. I get all that was ages ago, but I think when this mess with Dorian Gray is over, he intends to find that god and kick his ass."

"You know that, Bram, and now you've told me, but everyone else in Hell has a healthy mistrust of any god but Lilith because of what happened in the past. And I don't really buy your Reyson, and the other gods had no idea what was happening."

Did I actually know more about a subject Talvath dedicated his life to studying than he did? All because I met a god who was obsessed with my dick? If this situation weren't so fucked up, I'd start laughing.

"I need you to keep this between us. When I talked to the people at the library, they offered a blood oath to keep what I was telling them a secret. Reyson revealed a good bit about gods too. They aren't all-knowing, even though some of them pretend to be. They make mistakes. They are spat from the Aether with a purpose, and they all have different powers. Reyson can see possibilities, but he can't outright see the future. None of the gods would have known what was going on with Lilith unless she asked for their help, and she didn't."

"Fascinating. I'd love the chance to sit down and interview an open god like that. Especially one of the original ones. It doesn't change how things are perceived here in Hell. Someone is already after me. I'd have more if I brought outsiders and a god here. You'd be in danger too."

"Talvath, you know I love you, but you're miserable at computer stuff. If your research involves a library and dusty books, you're in your element, but every time you use your laptop to try to find something, I always have to get porn off your screen. We need help."

"I don't disagree with you, but we can't go back to the Library of the Profane. If Dorian tricked the librarian there into raising a god, and that's where he's living, Dorian will head there next. Reyson can handle a pesky human. We need to be worrying about the real problem—someone betrayed all of us. I've put in a request to see Lilith."

I really hoped Anod came through with a vision soon. The witches and warlocks at the library seemed disappointed in her she had retired to Hell and left them to fend for themselves. I knew how they felt. Lilith also created hellhounds. We lived in the same realm as her, and she hadn't tried to help us this entire time.

No, we couldn't rely on Lilith. She had ample opportunity to do so if she was interested in being a god instead of living it up in her fortress with her angel lover. I really needed Anod to have a vision to get Talvath to break all his rules about bringing outsiders here.

CHAPTER 14
BALTHAZAR

This was it. We were snatching Dorian Gray in the morning. We had our beautiful orgy, and the next day, we went back to watching until his plane landed. I sent a message to Kaine to see if Silvaria broke. She hadn't, but they were trying to crack the passcode on her phone. I offered to come in and do it for her phone and everyone they busted at the bank, but he said they had to do this by the book because they were all high profile.

I was up all night with Felix drinking coffee and watching Dorian's apartment. We had a bit of an antagonistic relationship, but I counted him as a good friend. Everyone was sleeping while I streamed the cameras in Dorian's apartment to the flat screen. We were pigging out and watching.

"Do people really do cocaine off a stripper's arse? I thought that just happened in the movies Ripley liked to watch."

I was going to have so much fun corrupting this cat.

"I've done it before, but it's not as fun as they make it out to be. Especially if she's wearing body glitter. That one is. Dorian has glitter all up in his nose right now. Pretty much the only way to get it out is to set yourself on fire."

"What is it with you and glitter, eh?"

"It makes me feel pretty. This world can be an ugly place. So if something makes you feel pretty, you should grab it."

"I'll toast to that," he said, holding up his teacup.

I clanked my coffee cup with his, and we went back to watching. Dorian had all his rich friends there, but I could tell a lot of them were missing because Kaine had arrested them. It looked like there was expensive wine, caviar, and plenty of cocaine, but this was the kind of party I hated—too many pretentious people.

"Ripley wanted to put a stripper pole like that in the living room. She thought she'd take some classes to get into shape. It never panned out. We should talk her into it," Felix said.

"Dude, I am *boss* at pole dancing. I also know silks and hoops. I could teach her."

Felix cocked an eyebrow at me.

"Is there anything you *don't* know how to do?"

"Oh, yeah. Totally, but since I'm my own boss and I'm the vampire Robin Hood, I just take classes if I want to learn something. I've taken plenty of classes and been shitty at something at the end, but me and the stripping arts just clicked."

"You are so much more secure in your masculinity than I am, Balthazar. Men just didn't do that the last time I was alive."

"Yes, they did. They did everything I do and what you see now in this century. They just couldn't do it in public because other people got butt ass offended about it, even though it was none of their business."

"I'll drink to that. I'm glad things are different now. Dorian is kicking his guests out."

"It's about fucking time. The sun is almost up. Those people are higher than the Queen of England, and they made a mess," I said.

"You *did not* just insult the queen in front of me, vampire!"

I started giggling. He was just so fun to poke at. He'd probably think up something to throw at me soon to get back at me.

"High people are just so *messy*. They didn't even use coasters, and that coffee table is an antique."

"I don't think Dorian cares how much that coffee table costs or what goes on it. The stripper was draped across it while people were snorting cocaine off of her," Felix said.

"Do you see the craftsmanship on that coffee table? Using it to hold up strippers and not making people use coasters is *way* more offensive than any insult about the queen."

"Shut up. No, it's not. Though if you're in there before his cleaning crew, I wouldn't touch anything in there. It's probably sticky. Sweaty people were fucking everywhere."

"I was kind of hoping Dorian was going to partake so we could have rated his performance," I said, refilling my coffee. "I can't imagine someone being alive as long as he has and still not be able to locate the clitoris."

"Gross, Balthazar. He's covered in bronzer. I don't want to see if that's a full body thing."

"I'm a little curious. I have no-no places I don't wear glitter, but I'm not nearly as vain as Dorian Gray."

"Some people are staying behind. Look."

I squinted at the screen and blew up that camera, so it took up the entire screen. I could get the camera feed, but not the sound. The people that stayed behind were shady as fuck and didn't look like his usual crowd. I didn't see them partaking in the cocaine and orgy festivities, and pretty much everyone was snorting or fucking. These guys had been lurking in the background watching.

If I were at an orgy where drugs were involved, and some creepers were hiding behind shit and watching, it would have been an instant boner killer. The old rich were a weird bunch. I was new rich from stealing shit, and I knew how to watch my back. I knew someone could swoop in and take it away at any point, even if it was all kept in an offshore bank account. Shit, if I were that stripper on the coffee table, I would have robbed those fuckers blind.

"Those have to be bodyguards," I said. "I'll bet they are demon touched. He's not going to be taking any chances after he's gotten this far."

"Especially since his very human arse just wanted to be forever pretty. I can't get over the sheer stupidity of that. If you're a human and knowing about us doesn't freak you out, why that? The witch summoned the demon for him, and Talvath was willing to cut a deal with him. He could have asked for magical powers. Instead, all he wanted was to be pretty and keep the party going for as long as possible."

"I don't think demons run two for one specials, Felix. It was either magical powers and a brief life or immortality and a longer amount of time to figure out how to screw Hell out of the deal. Of course, we already know Dorian is good at manipulating supernaturals."

"He's still a vain plonker who is shitty in bed, and I hope all of you rough him up when you go grab him."

"We will," Reyson said, joining us on the sectional.

It was pretty early in the morning, and everyone would

wake soon. Unfortunately, Dorian hadn't gone to bed yet. He was still talking to his henchmen.

"If those men don't leave, you might have to fight off some demon touched bodyguards," Felix said.

"That's expected and child's play for me. So just stay behind me until I get rid of them."

That was so fucking sexy. I was a scrappy little bastard who could handle myself in a fight just fine, but I'd happily hide behind the big sexy god and let him protect me from evil things. I didn't always get to play the damsel in distress, but I always wanted to.

After that, I'd really like to break Dorian Gray's nose.

CHAPTER 15

GABRIEL

I couldn't do a damned thing about what people thought about my family, but I could bring some karma down on Dorian Gray. We still didn't have a demon to hand him off to once we grabbed him, but that gave me a little time alone with him to let him know how much I didn't like him.

Felix and Balthazar stayed up all night watching the camera. They honestly could have slept. Nothing really happened until the rest of us woke up, and now they were both hopped up on caffeine. Felix was just a little jumpy, and we were leaving him here with Ripley. Balthazar was about to douse himself in glitter, sprout wings, and fly out of here. We really didn't need a jumpy vampire on our team.

I realized I had made an error in my judgment. Balthazar had done this kind of thing before, and he wasn't remotely impaired. He was still paying attention to the cameras when we weren't and getting ready to leave.

"Possible problem, my dudes. They all just disappeared into Dorian's bedroom closet. That can only be a closet door. We all know Dorian is shit in bed, but he has a reputation with the ladies. Dorian Gray is not even remotely in the closet with other men. This is bad, right?"

"If Dorian Gray is making sex tapes and hiding relics on his ceiling fan, he's probably keeping the shit he doesn't want people to see in his walk-in closet," Ripley said. "If one of those men asked for the ability to portal from a demon, they wouldn't go in the closet to do it. Everyone from the party is gone. He doesn't know we are watching his cameras. I'm sure he's aware he's got an agent tailing him now. He thinks he's safe in his penthouse."

"Well, they aren't coming out, so they are probably up to something nasty," Balthazar said.

"It's time to go," Reyson said. "Grab onto me and stay behind me until I can deal with the fiends in the closet."

Witches and warlocks had been trying to figure out how to create magical doors to step anywhere in the world. No one had ever managed it. So I thought it was pretty damned cool I would get to experience it with Reyson until I actually did it.

I didn't remember being in the Aether in a previous life like Reyson and Felix, but I think we briefly went there. My body went freezing cold, and blackness and a million stars surrounded me. It was over instantly, and I was in Dorian's bedroom, but I needed five minutes to get my bearings. Fucking Balthazar wasn't even fazed. He was bouncing behind Reyson, ready to get this show on the road.

Reyson stalked over to the closet and kicked the door in. The walk-in closet was massive... and empty. So, where the fuck did they go? Balthazar stomped into the closet and looked around.

"That's not possible. I was watching the camera feed the entire time. They never came out!"

Reyson kicked a costume dummy with a tacky jeweled

tuxedo hanging from it so hard across the closet, it shattered a wall-to-ceiling mirror in the back that took up the entire wall. Lilith bless Reyson and his little god tantrums because there was our answer. There was a hidden door behind the mirror.

Dorian had certainly done his homework protecting that door. It was made of thick steel and had a fingerprint scanner to open it. He'd tried to ward against every supernatural creature in existence, and some of this shit didn't even work.

The aconite would cause a rash to a shifter but wouldn't be fatal unless it was ingested. It wouldn't keep an ambitious shifter out. I was sure the demons had ways to get around the sigils. The protection sigil and salt on the ground in front of the door wouldn't keep an angry spirit out. They could make a draft stronger and disturb the salt. A powerful witch or warlock could burn the sigils off meant for us.

"Garlic?" Balthazar shrieked. "He knows about the supernatural enough to get them to do his bidding, and he thinks hanging garlic from the door is going to keep a vampire out? I'm offended on behalf of all vampires. When we eat food instead of blood, we want *all* the flavors. I don't know a single vampire that doesn't triple the garlic in any recipe they cook. I ate a whole jar of garlic stuffed olives once without even realizing it until it was empty. I should bite him and make it hurt."

I wasn't even a vampire, and I was a little offended by the garlic. That had never been a thing and was a subject of mockery that humans even thought it worked. Vampires were decadent creatures by nature. Every single one I had ever met was just as particular about their regular food as they were the blood they drank. But we didn't really have time to get offended by the fact that Dorian Gray was an idiot.

I waved my hand and burnt everything off the door, including the garlic.

"Don't think about the evil garlic. We need to be figuring out how to get through that door. It's not going to unlock without Dorian's fingerprint, and I doubt all the sigils are the only protection on the door. Blood locks aren't the only security systems witches offer. If you *really* want to make sure someone doesn't steal your shit, you can get a safe made with enchanted steel and the blood lock. They made the vaults in the bank where they arrested everyone with it, and I'm guessing this door is too."

"Enough of this nonsense. Every time I run the possibilities when I have us splitting up, it gives me a bad feeling. I need to get back to my witch, and an enchanted door isn't going to stop me."

I expected Reyson to try kicking it or punching the damned thing. If anyone was going to be able to get through thick, enchanted steel, it was going to be a god. Instead, Reyson just hollered at it. He roared at the damned door so hard, all Dorian's clothes fell on the floor, and I think my brain rattled around in my skull a bit.

It was worthy of a banshee shriek when they were using it as a weapon. Even a banshee wouldn't have done a thing to that door using their voice, even though they could kill with it.

Holy fuck. The door disintegrated into steel shavings because Reyson was mad at it. Remind me never to piss him off. He didn't flex his god chops often. Sometimes, it was easy to forget he helped create the universe.

When Reyson wasn't conjuring modern junk food or things to impress Ripley, he was fucking *terrifying*.

Balthazar was the king of not being able to read the room. He let out a little shriek and smacked Reyson on the ass. He seemed to do that a lot now that he had Reyson's permission.

"That was sexy as fuck. Let's go snatch the human who thinks fucking *garlic* will stop a vampire and get back to the library. I dislike bad vibes that have any of us in danger."

If I had done that to Reyson, he probably would have done me like he did that door. Balthazar just had this way of being completely inappropriate. Ripley and Reyson ate it up, and I would admit to being amused at his boldness. Reyson was furious, and I certainly wouldn't have gone there with him at this moment.

Reyson just grunted.

"Get behind me. This ends now."

CHAPTER 16
RIPLEY

I believed Reyson when he said something bad would happen if we split, but I thought I'd be safe in the library with Felix. We both knew how to fight, and the Library of the Profane had its own magical security system. I knew some of the spirits were corrupt, but there was still plenty on our side.

Even without Reyson barging in with possibilities and telling me I needed to claim them, I would have noticed the library giving out that many all-access library cards in that short amount of time. Every one of them had different skills that came in handy for the battles we won so far.

If a fucking god said not to split the dream team up, you should always listen. But, unfortunately, we kind of didn't have a choice with my job, and it shouldn't really take long for the guys to kill the men in Dorian's closet and zap him back here.

Except something wasn't right. Every day, when I opened the library, regulars were waiting to be let in. Some people had retired from their jobs and spent the day at the library, keeping their brains active by researching anything they wanted.

I knew every last one of them. They were waiting for me to unlock the door no matter what the weather was. Unfortunately, none of them were sitting on the benches outside the library when I unlocked the front doors, and I was getting ominous vibes from the cloudy sky.

I didn't like it.

Felix had a chair pulled up to my desk and cocked an eyebrow at me when no one followed me in. He'd been patrolling this library in feline form since I got my library card when I was a student at the academy. He was a constant at the library since I got hired.

The regulars knew he was my familiar, but they'd always stop to scratch his head, and they'd sometimes bring him cat treats. Of course, Felix couldn't thank them in anything but head butts and purrs before, but he liked them just as much as I did.

"Something is fucked up, Ripley. I can understand one of them being sick enough not to be here, but not all of them."

"Stay alert, Felix. They come even when they aren't feeling well. The only time they stay away is if they are contagious. Reyson had a bad feeling about this, and I don't think he felt much better about you staying behind. He knows I can handle myself in a fight and that I learned a good bit of that from you, but something clearly isn't right."

"I know, Ripley. Reyson and the others should be back by now. Gabriel can kill a revenant, and Balthazar has his vampire speed and strength. Reyson can probably just think Dorian's henchmen dead. It should have been over by now."

"Should I text Balthazar? He always has his phone on him."

"I wouldn't. If they aren't back yet, it means something went wrong, and they don't need to be distracted. They can handle anyone in that closet. We're all taking Reyson's warning seriously, especially Reyson. They will get back here as soon as they are able."

"It's not just the regulars, Felix. No one else has come in either, and that's unusual. The Academy of the Profane has a library since not all the students are approved for library cards here, and some don't bother, but those who do have library cards are in here researching for class. There's always some harried academy student in here by now who waited until the last minute to write their research paper."

"That's because you and Ravyn graduated, and they can't try to bribe you into writing it for them."

"We could have made bank if we didn't have ethics and a healthy fear of getting kicked out."

"Did you see anything when you unlocked the front doors?"

"I just looked at the benches and saw they were empty. The sky looks creepy today. It didn't look like a storm, it looked like a really fucking bad omen. Shit, that's probably why none of the witches are here. I didn't want to be out in that either."

"Well, I'm going to do a lap around the building. A bad omen would get more people in here for tarot card readings and researching what was coming."

"I get why you need to, but I don't want you out there, Felix."

"Ripley, I'm not going out there like *this*. I can still change into a cat. You literally asked me to spy on Ravyn's boyfriend when you were at the academy. I didn't get caught then. I can sneak out and see if there's something keeping people away."

"If you die out there, I'm going to be so mad at you. Reyson might not be able to bring you back."

"I'm not going to die, Ripley. I need to take a look because there's a reason no one is coming in. We can't risk someone we *don't* want coming in here. Reyson had a bad feeling, and he's not back yet. I don't like it."

I grabbed Felix and pulled him into a bear hug. Whatever might be outside the library that was keeping people from coming inside, it wasn't actually in here with us. The library was a safe place. Whatever was keeping Reyson and the others, I knew they could handle it. Most of the retired regulars had been badasses during their day. It would have taken a *lot* to run them off. They loved this place. They would have run in to defend it if someone was threatening the library.

"I'll be right back."

"Don't you dare say that to me, Felix. Everyone says that in horror movies when they go investigate something and end up gutted by the serial killer outside. I'm too horny to be the final girl, Felix. I need all of you alive so we can have more orgies."

"I'm not dying when I just got my body back, and we've only had one threesome, Ripley."

"You'd better swear on that."

"I swear, Ripley. Stay inside."

Felix shrunk until a cat crawled out of his clothes. I didn't have to open the front doors to let him out and let anything out there know he was roaming—every witch or warlock who was given a familiar went everywhere with them, even the library. Familiars couldn't exactly use the toilet, and they weren't making me scoop litter boxes for the entire witching community as part of my librarian duties.

Cats weren't the only animals who were familiars. They came in almost every form. There were plenty of dogs and birds too. There was a pet door at the side of the library where they could go outside. When he was stuck as a cat, Felix had a litter box, but he found the whole pooping in a box thing offensive, especially if it wasn't completely pristine. He much preferred pooping in the extensive gardens in the Library of the Profane. I'm sure the grounds crew had opinions about that.

Felix snuck out the pet door like he always did. Our bond worked over a distance, and I heard from him almost instantly.

"This is terrible, Ripley. If Reyson and the others had used the front doors, they would have seen it and stayed."

"What the fuck did they do to my library?"

"There's a dead shifter out here. He's been mutilated. They used his blood and entrails to paint sigils against every supernatural creature on the bricks. They moved one of the marble busts and stuck his head on it. They stuffed aconite in his mouth."

"Felix, get your ass back in here now."

Just then, I heard the jingle of bells that the front door was opening. It wasn't Felix. Felix was super anal about being naked in the library. I now knew every inch of his body without clothes, but he wouldn't have walked through the front door naked with a dead body out there.

I called my magic to my fingertips and went running. I didn't know who was here, but I was not in the mood for this shit. Someone was about to learn the hard way not to leave dead bodies on the grounds of my library. Who was going to clean that blood and entrails off the walls? First, I was taking care of this shit, and then I was contacting Kaine.

I didn't see anyone in the lobby. Dorian was just standing behind the closed front door. How the shit did he get here, and where were Reyson and the guys? I might not be able to kill Dorian without his painting, but I could zap his ass so hard he regretted ever setting foot in my library.

Dorian just smirked at me. He opened the door a crack and threw something on the floor. Dorian gave me this silly little wave, pulled a gas mask from his back pocket, and put it on.

Motherfucker. I knew how to fight the supernatural. All of us relied on our gifts for everything. Dorian used human gas on me, and it worked almost instantly. I fell to the floor, choking.

The last thing I saw before I blacked out was Dorian Gray's expensive wing-tipped shoes in front of my face.

CHAPTER 17
REYSON

Something wasn't right. I had a terrible feeling in the pit of my gut, and I didn't like it. Was this what fear felt like? I could handle myself and everyone in this room. That wasn't what was bothering me. My witch was away from me, and I didn't know what was happening there. There had already been too many surprises so far.

Gabriel and I both called a light to our hand to light the way down the dark passage behind Dorian's mirror. There was a staircase leading down to who knows what. Wherever Dorian and his henchmen were, they weren't in this passageway. I couldn't sense them.

"It reeks of demon in here," Balthazar said. "Whichever demon betrayed Talvath is with him or someone working with them. I can't hear their heartbeats, so they aren't with us."

The staircase led to another door with a fingerprint scanner. I kicked it in and ended up breaking another mirror. I thought Gabriel was going to faint with all the mirrors I had smashed, but I wasn't a warlock like him. I'd been alive long before that superstition got started, and I'd been around plenty of broken mirrors. Maybe the bad luck thing didn't affect me because I wasn't mortal.

Either way, I'd smash every mirror Dorian Gray used to admire his reflection if it meant destroying him and getting back to my witch. I stepped through the broken glass and looked around.

We were in the apartment just below Dorian's, and this one wasn't decorated like a pompous ass lived there. It barely had any furniture at all except a bed and a couch. This wasn't someone's residence. Someone used it to sleep when they were in the area.

"This whole place reeks of bad demon smell. Bram and Talvath *did not* smell this bad. Dorian's demon contact lives here."

"Well, they aren't here now, and I doubt they will get their security deposit back," Gabriel said. "Those hardwood floors are probably original to this building and have been meticulously kept up. Rent in this place isn't cheap, and those floors are probably a selling point. They defaced the shit out of them painting those demonic symbols."

"We need to get to the library *now*. Demons and Hell-hounds can realm travel. They can come and go from Hell to Earth, where Lilith has barred the rest of her siblings from visiting. It would make sense they have a sigil to travel anywhere once they are here too. I had a bad feeling about splitting up. We should have moved in on him *much* sooner. Dorian thinks he needs a god to get out of this mess. He's probably gone straight to the library."

"Shit," Balthazar hissed. "There was *nothing* on any of his devices about secret passages and contacting his demon friends to come to his cocaine orgies."

"This isn't your fault, Balthazar. You aren't going to find something that isn't there. Grab onto me. If they haven't gone to the library, I'm not sure where else they would have gone."

As soon as their hands were on me, I made sure we all made it back to the library as fast as possible. Ripley wasn't at her desk and Felix was missing. In fact, the library was completely empty, and that was unusual. My eyes started watering as soon as I got my bearings.

"There's only one heartbeat in here, and it smells like the gas canisters human cops like to use when they get a bug up their ass to bust a supernatural rave."

My nails dug into my palm. This was my fault. I *knew* splitting up was a bad idea. Our plan should have been flawless, but I was old enough to know better. We all knew Dorian Gray managed to get demonic help at the expense of everyone in Hell. This one vain human had caused so much trouble, and now someone I cared about was missing from this library.

"The heartbeat is in the lobby," Balthazar said.

We all went running. There was a strange odor in the lobby, and my eyes and nose wouldn't stop running. I saw Felix's black cat at the back of the lobby lying there with white foam coming out of his mouth. Ripley was gone. I'd lost my witch. I'd deal with that later. I wasn't losing Felix too.

I scooped him up and carried him back to Ripley's desk, where the air was a little more pleasant. Whatever had happened here had been fast. Ripley had proudly given us a tour of the entire library when we got our library cards and an invitation to stay with her.

Felix had changed and gone outside for something. He'd barely made it through the pet door before he was disabled. It was fast. If Ripley had been in trouble, Felix would have changed back and fought to protect her. He didn't even get that chance.

I laid my hands over Felix and tried to heal whatever damage that weapon had done to him. I had serious questions about the weapons human law enforcement used to break up parties.

Felix started mutating as his body tried to make the change. He was still disoriented, and it took him a few minutes.

"What took you so long, and how did you lose him? Someone graffitied the building with a dead shifter to keep people away, then Dorian snuck in and gassed the place. He took Ripley."

We needed to reevaluate everything we thought we knew, and we needed to find Dorian. He went out of his way to have Ripley raise me. He'd been promising everyone a god could get them out of their deals.

What in fuck did he want with my witch?

CHAPTER 18
FELIX

We were all a right sight. Every last one of us thought this was our fault, but none of us were mind readers and could predict Dorian's every movement. Fuck, I was blaming myself super hard. Dorian must have been lurking around the library, and I didn't see him because I was focused on the dead shifter parts all over the wall.

When I was on the other side of the building, he made his move to get back in through the front door. I realized as soon as my head was through. I didn't know what that gas did to humans or why it was even legal to use, but my eyes started burning, and I could barely breathe. I fought as hard as I could to shift into a human again and blast him with any magic that would disable him, but I couldn't manage it.

I could see Ripley on the floor and Dorian moving towards her in a gas mask, but I blacked out before I could shift and help her.

The Library of the Profane was now an active crime scene. Balthazar called Kaine as soon as I told them about the mutilated shifter outside. Kaine had agents on that and was interviewing me about Ripley's abduction. After he found out why our group separated, he was furious.

"Seriously? I told you not to blow my investigation, Balthazar!"

"You wouldn't have found out about the secret passage in his apartment or that it leads to a second apartment with his demon ass buddy without us!"

"And that's why none of you are currently in handcuffs and a cell. I have agents at his penthouse. You made a massive mess, but he didn't bring your librarian back there."

"Get the shit out of my way right now! Ripley was my sister. If you don't move, I'll curse you so hard, you'll regret ever seeing my face!"

I had called Ravyn from Ripley's desk phone to let her know they had attacked the library. Ravyn didn't run the museum by herself like Ripley did. She ran most of it, but other employees were there to help her since they locked her away with dangerous objects a lot. I was glad she was here.

"Let her through, Kaine. That's Ripley's twin."

All Kaine did was let out a little growl and throw some stink eye in that direction, and everyone parted to let her through. Killian was on her heels, and she looked stressed out.

"How did this happen? My sister can fight off any threat to this library without breaking a sweat."

"Dorian used some kind of gas human police use. We were both out in almost an instant. We couldn't do anything to fight it because it was irritating our eyes and lungs before it got us."

"Dorian Gray has human help too? How many people are in on this, exactly?"

"Not exactly," Kaine said. "There are websites specifically for humans to purchase those kinds of things. They are usually hidden from search engines but well known among certain groups. They believe they will have to go to war with the government, and then there's going to be another civil war. So they stockpile food and any weapons they can get their hands on. It wouldn't be hard for Dorian to find and purchase a gas like that online."

"No, he didn't. I've been through his computer. He wasn't even Googling those kinds of sites."

"Balthazar, that's not just a human conspiracy theory. Plenty of supernaturals have bought into it too. We've raided a few of them with weapons just like this. That's the whole reason I know about it. We're having to put protocols in place at the bureau because of it."

Ravyn threw up her hands and shrieked.

"What the actual fuck is the world coming to when people aren't relying on their supernatural gifts? I hope you have a plan for getting my sister back."

"We had nothing to connect Dorian to that warehouse before legally, but murdering a shifter and kidnapping a well-respected librarian puts him on our radar. We can make a legal case that Dorian is technically supernatural since he made a deal with a demon for immortality so that he can't use the fact that he's human to get off on the charges. We've tapped his cell phone, and Balthazar is watching his online activity. There's been nothing so far."

"We need to be figuring out why he took Ripley when he's been promising everyone Reyson and how exactly he knew we were splitting up," I said.

"That fucker!" Balthazar yelled.

He zipped off upstairs using his vampire speed, and I could hear things crashing upstairs in Ripley's apartment.

He'd better clean that up before we got Ripley back. Ripley wasn't the only one who didn't like living in a messy place.

Balthazar zipped back down and slammed something down on Ripley's desk.

"Dorian has a secret cell phone I wasn't able to find in his records. It's how he was communicating with his demon friend and how he was watching this. I started thinking about that whole night with Ripley where he was shit in bed. He wasn't trying because he didn't need Ripley in some sexual spell. I don't care how pretty you are. No one is going to stick around if you are bad at sex.

"I was also thinking about the page he stole from her grimoire. He couldn't have made that potion with no magic. He stole the page as a diversion and planted this camera in the living room. Dorian knew damned well Ripley was going to figure out Reyson was a god and which god. She takes her librarian duties seriously and would have made sure he stayed in the library. That fucker has been watching us this entire time. He's not just making creepy sex tapes in his penthouse."

That utter plonker. I was creeped out. Most women didn't secretly record men in the bedroom and use those tapes to exploit them, but that's exactly how I felt right now. Ripley's apartment had been my home since she got this job. She brought men back sometimes, and I was okay with that when I was a cat. I had no interest in watching.

Dorian wasn't just listening to all our plans. He saw plenty of intimate moments between all of us. I liked Reyson. I had a ton of fun introducing him to modern junk food and *Doctor Who*. Gabriel and Ripley were both helping me reconstruct my lost grimoire when we weren't figuring out this Dorian mess. I had fun with Balthazar staying up all night giving a running commentary on Dorian's cocaine party.

Was he watching all that like some creepy pervert?

"So, Dorian Gray is a creeper. Big shocker. Why did he snatch my sister?"

None of us knew. He needed a god, not an insanely powerful librarian.

"We'll have to treat this like a hostage situation," Kaine said. "Ripley is pretty high profile in the supernatural community because of her job at the library. She's also a powerful witch. You don't snatch someone like that unless you have demands."

"He can take his demands and shove them up his ass. I've beaten the shit out of men in bars for disrespecting my sister. She's got some pretty powerful boyfriends now. I might not be able to kill him without his painting but give me ten minutes, and he'll tell me where it is because he wishes for death."

We all wanted ten minutes alone with Dorian Gray. Reyson would end him for this, and I had a feeling he was going to get creative. We needed to regroup and come up with a better plan. We still had Hell to deal with.

"I have agents digging into every property Dorian owns, but he's wealthy enough to have a few under shell corporations and not his name. Balthazar, I'm not even remotely saying my agents aren't capable of finding those, but you have ways of finding them faster. Get on that. We'll find Ripley."

"We need to change our game plan when it comes to Hell," I said. "Dorian needs to die for this. After what he did to Talvath, I don't think they care how as long as he's dead, and I think they can appreciate Reyson doing it for hurting his witch. Dorian has the traitor with him. Let's kill Dorian and give them the traitor."

"I like this plan. I want to watch," Ravyn said.

"I'll dig into his investment properties."

"None of that is needed," Reyson said. "I tried to use astral projection to find them, and I can't."

"What does that mean?" Killian demanded, wrapping an arm around Ravyn.

"I think they are in Hell. It's the one place in the cosmos I can't go because Lilith put it into the spell when she created that realm."

Shit. Ripley always had her phone in her pocket. It wasn't in the lobby. I looked before Kaine, and his agents showed up and started processing evidence.

Our only way of getting to Ripley was through Bram, who hadn't seemed to have checked his phone yet, and now the only person who had Bram's number had been kidnapped.

CHAPTER 19
RIPLEY

M y eyes and lungs were burning. My entire mouth tasted like I drank a home perm. When I cracked my eyes open, I had no idea where Dorian had taken me. They propped me up against a cage with my hands behind my back and duct tape over my mouth. Dorian was making damned sure I couldn't use magic against him, but he clearly didn't know everything about magic.

My battle magic teacher at the academy was a former agent with the Paranormal Investigation Bureau. He was a hard ass and just as famous as Kaine was. He prepared us to fight our way out of any situation, even one like this.

I heard a noise behind me and tried to turn around.

"Before you think of using your magic on me, know you can't kill me, and you're safer in here than out there. You're in Hell, Ripley Bell, and they don't take kindly to outsiders here. They don't know we're in this little estate, but not all Hellhounds are like your Bram. They'll rip you apart before you can even ask for help. They know their place and are proper guard dogs."

Oh, fuck no. If I could see him, I was going to make his entire body break out into boils. Kidnapping me and bringing me to Hell aside, that was just a shitty thing to say.

"I have no desire to hurt you, Ripley. It's in my best interest not to. If I remove your gag, can we have a civilized conversation?"

I nodded. I could wait with the boils. I learned a good bit from the movies Felix enjoyed watching. If the evil villain wanted to talk, keep them talking. They always launched into some sort of maniacal monologue that revealed their plans and was the key to beating them. Dorian was a vain motherfucker. I'll bet he'd already written and rehearsed his villain monologue in front of a mirror. He probably filmed it and intended on posting it to social media when he was sure he'd won.

Dorian opened my cage and stepped inside. He didn't just take the duct tape off my face. He untied my hands too. He was deranged enough to think whatever he was about to tell me, and the fact that I was in Hell meant I wouldn't fight back. He locked the cage and pulled a chair up.

"I'd love to move you somewhere more comfortable, but I need you to cooperate with me, Ripley. You're vital to my plans."

"I thought Reyson was vital to your plans. So what can a witch do to get you out of your fucking deal?"

"We need Reyson to get us out of our deals. You're vital to controlling Reyson."

Shit. All this time, we were worried Dorian had something magical up his sleeve that wouldn't work on Reyson. But, just like the gas at the library, Dorian took a very human approach to this. There wasn't any magic in this world to force a god to do what you wanted. Dorian knew that when he was making those promises. So, he kidnapped someone Reyson cared about.

"Oh, man, did you fuck up, Dorian Gray. Reyson doesn't need your painting to kill you. He's possessive of the family we've built since you tricked me into raising him. He's going to be *pissed* you kidnapped me and stuck me in a cage."

"Not if he just hears me out. He can save a ton of lives by helping us."

"Why should he? No one *made* any of you summon and demon and ask for anything. No one forced you into manipulating a witch into doing it for you. Honestly, the supernatural community should have made your corpse disappear as soon as you made it known you knew about us. You're a shit lay. If I were that witch, I would have killed you myself."

"You're missing the point, Ripley. It's demons that are the real villains here. Men are flawed. You can't put that kind of temptation in front of us and expect us not to take it."

"You sound like every rapist who ever ended up in court and didn't feel sorry about it. It's not our clothes or what we drank that night, and just because the demons are offering doesn't mean you *have* to take them up on it. You made your deal. You had a good run, and you had an entire book about you. Pay up, buttercup. No one likes cheaters, whether it involves your dick or payment."

"I really do hate this decade," Dorian groaned. "Things were so much easier before women's rights and feminism."

"You're batting really low on me, not cursing your dick, and there's no witch here to remove it."

"I've had *zero* complaints in that department. Maybe you're just frigid."

"Okay, asshole, I would have given you half a bonus point for rubbing my left labia lip for two minutes because you were at least in the vicinity of my clit and made an attempt. You're old enough to have figured out how vaginas work by now, Dorian. They even do it in porn."

"Shut up, Ripley. I said I didn't want to hurt you, but you are trying my patience. I had hoped you'd at least be a little sympathetic for your fellow supernaturals on Earth."

"What's your end goal here, champ? Even if Reyson somehow agrees to kill Talvath and get you out of your deal, how do you intend to stay safe from Reyson? You can't exactly hole up in Hell. They are going to have big opinions on what you did to get out of your deal. Many people hate you right now across two realms, and you didn't exactly ask for magical powers with your deal."

"You let me worry about that. You've been useful to me without knowing it, and now I need you to earn your keep. I grabbed your cellphone when it fell out of your pocket. My demon compatriot used your fingerprint when you were passed out to unlock it and download an app that will allow you to make phone calls between realms.

"I need you to call your boyfriend and tell him where you are. Tell him you are unharmed and will remain that way as long as you both cooperate. Talk him out of doing anything stupid. Soothe his rage at losing. Once he's onboard, everything else will be done by text message. I'll get him the exact ritual to summon Talvath and force him to Earth. Reyson doesn't *have* to kill him. He just needs to get him to tear up my contract."

"You don't care who you fuck over, do you? You knew Silvaria was going to go down for that warehouse eventually, but you still had her keep your demon there, knowing she put her name on it. I don't know for sure, but I'm guessing the demon that is helping you don't have a problem with all demons, just Talvath."

"You know nothing. Make the call, and maybe I'll let you out of your cage."

"I want total privacy for this phone call. I want you out of here, and I know you're a creeper who likes to hide cameras everywhere. So if there's a camera in here, I want it off."

"You've lost, Ripley. Reyson can't come here and save you. None of your men can. You can't escape either because you're an outsider here. The sooner you admit it, the faster we can end this."

I shrugged and batted my eyelashes innocently. Dorian didn't know every little thing about me. One of my men was already here. Bram hadn't answered my text, and when I tried calling, it was like one of us didn't have service. Apparently, I needed a demonic app to call people in Hell.

Bram had better answer his fucking phone because I was making two phone calls as soon as Dorian got his ass out of here.

"I just want some privacy while I talk to my boyfriend. If I'm trying to convince him not to murder you and you're in the room, he'll think I'm under duress. He's really protective and all. He's *much* older than you, but he's totally a feminist. If he thinks I'm using your words and not mine, he'll get murdery. I know him better than you do."

"Fine! There are no cameras in here. I wanted them, but my demon friend draws the line at hidden cameras inside his house. He'll change his mind really fast if you do something stupid."

Dorian's demon friend had an odd set of principles. He was willing to damn his entire realm giving out those sigils, he was fine with Dorian raising a god to kill his friends, and he had no problem assaulting my library and kidnapping me.

I guess even Dorian's fucked up demon friend thought it was creepy to hide cameras and spy on people.

As soon as I was alone, I drew in a deep breath. I knew she had fucked off to Hell with her angel lover, but if there was *any* time for Lilith to answer a witch's prayer, it was now. Her little safe space was in trouble. So I fired off a little prayer to Lilith and hit Bram's number in my contacts.

It rang once, then twice.

"Hello?" Bram said.

I'd never been more grateful to have a man answer my call in my entire life.

CHAPTER 20

BRAM

Talvath managed to get an audience with Lilith and her fallen angel friends. It must be nice to be important. I was still a little bitter I'd nearly died trying to save him, found an entire group of friends that had the skills to help him figure this out, and he chose a retired god who hadn't wanted to do a damned thing in the realm she created instead of the god who had been actively helping this entire time.

I was also pretty furious that I had more first hand knowledge of Dorian Gray and this plot than Talvath did because I was there when Balthazar and Reyson found information in real-time, but I had to wait outside while Talvath told them what I told him. I was one of Lilith's creations too. She could at least look me in the eye and hear me out if she wouldn't do anything to help the Hellhounds.

I was pacing and furious when my cellphone rang. It shocked me when I looked down at saw it was Ripley. She wanted to program her number in my phone, so I gave her mine. I'd wanted to text or call her this entire time, but it would have been impossible without modifying her phone to communicate between realms.

She needed this app written by a team of demons that I was trying to figure out how to get on her phone before Talvath woke up and yanked me back to Hell. There was no way possible Ripley could call me unless she was in Hell, and there was no way possible for her to be here.

"Bram? Thank Lilith. Dorian gassed the library and kidnapped me to Hell. I'm at the house of your traitor. I haven't seen his face, just Dorian's. Apparently, Dorian's whole promise for controlling Reyson wasn't magical. It was kidnapping me. Dorian said Hell doesn't like outsiders, and if I escape, I'll be killed. This isn't good, Bram. Reyson is going to tear the cosmos apart to get to Hell. He's creative, and he's decided we're getting married. He'll find a way, and a war is going to break out here."

Shit. We just did not need the God of Chaos trying to blow our front door down. Dorian had been very careful so far, but I was almost certain he'd made his first error. I had a plan, and it involved pissing off a god and a few fallen angels. I literally didn't care how offended they got. This had gone on far enough. First, they hurt Talvath, and now he took Ripley. Dorian Gray didn't care who he hurt as long as he got out of his deal.

"Sit tight, Ripley. Do everything Dorian asks, even if you are just faking it. He's right about one thing—if you leave that house, you're in danger. No one will give you time to explain or care that you are also one of Lilith's creations. They are going to think you broke in and try to fight. I have a plan. If it works, we'll have Reyson and Lilith on our side."

"How do you plan on doing that?"

"Talvath is an important demon. He's in there with

Lilith now. They are going to have to deal with listening to a Hellhound whether or not they like it."

"That's badass. Tell them they need to let you come back to the library. You can't just announce that your cock is pierced to a god, a librarian, and a bisexual vampire and fuck off to Hell for the rest of your life. Plus, we all just dig you, and you're family now."

That gave me the swell of courage I needed to do what needed to be done. For Ripley, for all of Hell, and for the Hellhounds too.

"Hang tight, Ripley. Help is coming, and Dorian is going down."

"Stay safe, Bram. I have to call Reyson now. Dorian thinks I just called him. He knows more than he should, but he doesn't seem to get we all have a bond with you."

"You too."

I hung up my phone and stuck it in my back pocket. Ripley and the others had been fighting for me since they met me. They wanted my freedom, and they risked their lives to save both me and Talvath.

I squared my shoulders and marched straight to the ornate doors they were all behind. I could have knocked. I probably should have. If Talvath outranked me, then Lilith and the fallen angels certainly did. I already knew how that was going to go down. They would send the least important person in the room to answer the door, and they would try to dismiss me.

I was honestly tired of being dismissed and ignored in all of this.

I lifted my steel-toed combat boot and kicked the fucking door in. Let them ignore me now. There were two massive angels with their wings out and their swords drawn. Talvath jumped to his feet and stepped between us.

"Wait! Bram saved my life. I'd still be in that shipping container if it weren't for him. He has vital information, and he should have been in here giving it this entire time. He wouldn't have made that entrance unless it was important."

An absolutely beautiful red-headed woman peered around one of the angel wings and stared me up and down.

"Sit, please. I never said a Hellhound couldn't be in my presence. I'm quite fond of them. If there's any intel on this mess, I'm guessing he got it first hand. Can I get you something to drink?"

That was certainly new. Lilith sounded like she had a lot of respect for us, considering she hadn't done a damned thing to help us. I couldn't think about that right now.

"Dorian Gray is in Hell with the traitor, and he's kidnapped the woman I'm pretty sure I'm falling in love with. The God of Chaos is also in love with her, and Dorian thinks if he kidnapped her somewhere Reyson can't go, he'll do his bidding. I've spent time around Reyson. He'll make a cosmic mess getting his witch back, and me and all the other men who love her will help him. She also has a very powerful twin sister who doesn't fuck around."

Lilith looked seriously amused at all of this. She had this ethereal smirk on her face.

"I'm guessing you have a plan to bring Dorian Gray and the traitor to justice and save your witch with as few casualties as possible."

I did, and they weren't going to like it. I wasn't even sure if Lilith would go for it since she barred other gods from visiting her realm.

"Yeah, I do. There's an entire team with unique skills surrounding the witch Dorian kidnapped. Reyson can see possibilities. He can let us know if a plan is a bad idea.

Second, her familiar has his body back and is a powerful warlock who can change into a cat and sneak into places. Third, one of Lucifer's descendants is with them, and he knows how to kill revenants. Finally, there's a vampire who can hack anything on the planet.

"I say I go get them and bring them here. Balthazar can track her using her cell phone. We'll have the location of Ripley, Dorian, and the traitor. I think everyone wants to kill Dorian Gray at this point, so we'll have to figure that part out later. The traitor needs to be taken alive to make sure they are working alone. While we're taking out Dorian and the demon, Felix can sneak through the house as his cat until he locates Ripley and frees her. Honestly, Ripley and her twin sister are pretty good with curses and are probably going to want to play with Dorian before someone kills him."

"And they should. Dorian Gray has come for two of my creations now and put my Hellhounds in danger trying to defend them. I agree with this plan."

"You're going to allow another god here?" one angel said.

"I put that precaution in place because of one god— your creator. I couldn't keep one out without keeping all of them out. I had no problems with the others, Samael."

"Reyson seemed pissed about what happened. I think he intends to find that god and kick his ass," I said.

"Then, let him come," the other angel said. "He can help."

"You're just bored because we're retired, and you're looking for a fight, Lucifer," Samael said.

"We're *all* bored. Lilith is a god, and we're angels. We're not meant to sit back and let people do things we don't agree with."

"Lucifer is right," Lilith said. "This is a little wake-up call we need to be more involved. Things are going to change here."

"You can start with the Hellhounds," Talvath said. "As you can see, Bram is articulate, well-read, and we wouldn't have any of this information without him. He risked his life to save mine."

Lilith tossed her hair over her shoulder.

"That's the first thing on my agenda. I haven't been to Earth in a very long time. So I think I'll take a vacation there to bring these people back here to help with this mess."

I was glad Lilith was fired up and ready to get involved, but now that I'd met my second god, they sure were weird.

CHAPTER 21
GABRIEL

We seriously underestimated Dorian Gray, and we were standing on the site of a massacre committed by humans that should have told us they were perfectly capable of hurting us, even without magical gifts. He had ample time to put this plan into motion. We were good, but none of us were mind readers, and now he had Ripley.

We were all pacing and pissed off. Killian was the only one who could kind of soothe Ravyn. Between Ravyn and Reyson, they were ready to destroy the entire cosmos to get Ripley back and kill Dorian Gray. I knew exactly how they felt because I did too.

Balthazar's phone started ringing out of the blue. I didn't peg him for having Dolly Parton's *Jolene* as his ringtone, but oddly, it fit. Of course, I hoped he didn't intend on answering that. There were other things we needed to be worrying about.

"Shit! It's Ripley! Hello? Bitch, you'd better be okay. If he even broke a fingernail, we're going to get creative."

"Put it on speaker, or you'll get another curse on your dick," Ravyn growled.

"Calm your tits. I was. Ripley, you're on speaker."

I was pretty amazed at the things that came out of Balthazar's mouth and that he didn't end up cursed more often. He totally didn't deserve the one he had when he ended up at the library, but at no point in the history of witches had telling one to calm their tits when a situation was this bad ever ended in anything good.

"Tell me you're okay, my witch."

"That gas was no joke, but it's getting better. Listen up because I don't know how long I have. I asked Dorian for total privacy while I made this call, but he doesn't strike me as patient. I couldn't contact Bram before because my phone wasn't modified to communicate between realms. So Dorian had to get his demon friend to do that so I could give Reyson his ransom demands.

"I got in touch with Bram, and he's going to find a way to get you all in Hell. Dorian's entire plan for controlling Reyson wasn't magical. He knew I would keep him in the library, and he was hoping feelings would develop. Unfortunately, it always involved kidnapping me."

"He planted a camera in your living room, Ripley. The page he stole out of your grimoire was just a distraction," Felix said.

"I'm going to murder him. I know Bram has a plan, and he's going to bring you in, but I can still zap his ass and throw Dorian and his demon in the cage they have me in until you all get here. Everyone is saying it's a spectacularly bad idea for me to leave this house."

"Okay, no one puts my twin sister in a cage unless it's a kink thing."

There was a pop of light, and suddenly, there was a

beautiful red-haired woman and two massive men with her. She and Reyson shared and glance and a nod like they knew each other.

"You'll do nothing of the sort. You're going to cooperate and tell Dorian that Reyson is willing to do everything he asks as long as you are unharmed. Don't risk your life."

"I'm sorry, who the fuck are you, and why are you telling me what to do?"

I had a feeling I knew. The woman had silver eyes, just like Reyson. I'd never seen a single person with eyes that color until Reyson. She just appeared the same way I'd seen Reyson do.

"I believe you prayed to me shortly before your Hell-hound lover kicked the door to my office in to announce someone had kidnapped you," Lilith said with this serene smirk on her face.

"Yeah, well, there are several people in my library who want a chance to climb that pierced, tattooed flag pole but haven't gotten the chance because Bram is holding back because he knows he has to go back and be someone's property when this is over. He's not my lover yet because he's a slave in your realm," Ripley snapped.

Only Ripley would tell off the fucking god who came here to help from a cage in Hell when she should have been worried about getting out of there. What if Lilith was a petty god and fucked back off to Hell instead of bringing us back to get our witch? I doubted she needed us.

There was this uncomfortable silence, then one of the men with Lilith got right up in my personal space and started sniffing me. I wanted to shove him back with a little magic, but I didn't know if he was Lilith's bodyguard or lover, and I really didn't want to piss her off, so I let him.

I drew the line when he licked my cheek. I drew magic

to my fingertips, but he shocked me and yanked me into an enormous bear hug. Orion was around my neck and let out a hiss because he was getting smashed.

"This one is the Morningstar," he called to Lilith. "This one is my blood."

Of all the messed-up family reunions I thought would happen if Lucifer ever came back to Earth, getting licked and hugged certainly wasn't on my radar. He looked genuinely happy to see me.

"I could have told you that without you licking him, Lucifer. It might have been ages since you sired his ancestor, but he looks just like you," the other man said.

"That's enough, Samael," Lilith said. "Lucifer never wanted to leave his offspring. Let him have his reunion. Ripley, it might shock you to know, but Talvath has been campaigning to change things for Hellhounds for decades. He would have let Bram stay if it had made him happy. I have use of Bram right now, and then you can have him back. I'm coming out of retirement, and things are going to change. Bram leading this operation is going to do that for the Hellhounds."

I was just starting to understand most of what Reyson did or said. I didn't get Lilith at all. She'd been ignoring us witches and warlocks for centuries. She hadn't seemed to care about what happened to Hellhounds before. Why now? I was glad because she was our only chance to get into Hell and not get attacked by the residents there.

Felix felt the exact same way.

"I'm not going to question your motivation for getting off your ass now when the love of my life is in danger, but we need an actual plan."

"Ripley is going to hang tight and feed Dorian lies about

Reyson's cooperation. Bram spoke highly of all of you. I have different gifts than Reyson. All gods do. Reyson and I will brainstorm together. I've heard the vampire in your group can get into anything with an internet connection. He'll have the resources to track Ripley's cellphone.

"Once we have a location, Samael and Lucifer will scout the location from the skies to see if our traitor is working alone or has demons protecting their estate. Once we know what we are dealing with, we'll attack. The familiar will change back into his feline form and sneak through the manor to find Ripley.

"There are still some details to figure out, but that's what Bram has come up with. Lucifer and Samael were warriors before they fell. They agree it's a good one. No one will question any of you being in Hell if you are with us."

Lilith was responsible for the creation of plenty of people in this room. Even though I knew she was in Hell, not really listening, I still prayed to her by default when I needed to. I'd been doing that a lot lately with this Dorian mess.

Still, she wasn't really one of us. Could we even trust her? We all looked to Reyson.

"If you help get my witch back, I'll help fix your sun. No tricks, Lilith. Do we have a deal?"

"It was I who created the witches and taught them how to make a blood oath. Would you like to spill our blood and seal it that way?"

Reyson just grunted.

"Ripley, tell Dorian what he needs to hear about my cooperation. Then, if he allows you to call again, make sure you're alone so we can keep you up to date."

"We'll have to speak in code. He wants everything else

done by text message, and I'm sure he will want to read them. The only reason I got privacy for these phone calls was that I told him Reyson would definitely kill him for manipulation me."

Reyson just snorted.

"I would have killed him for being an inadequate lover to you. There's no scenario in this situation where Dorian lives through this."

"You'll have to be crafty," Lilith said. "I created witches and warlocks to be exactly that. Manipulate that bastard through your text message, so he doesn't see us coming. Let him think he's won. Let the traitor think they are getting what they wanted, betraying all of Hell. It's going to make it that much sweeter when they realize all that planning and all the people they threw under the bus to get there still wasn't enough, and they lost."

Kaine was still sitting with us because his people were still gathering evidence, and he thought Dorian would eventually call with demands.

"Hell is not even remotely in my jurisdiction, and I've got a teenager at home with two broken feet whose magic just awakened early, but if you need a dragon, you've got one. But, unfortunately, the kid that broke Beyla's feet has disappeared, so I can't eat him. It would be nice to take out some of that rage on Dorian Gray and this traitor."

Oh, fuck. I got Reyson and Lilith being mad about this. I knew why the rest of us were mad. Dorian Gray didn't lay a finger on Beyla, but Kaine was tired of his shit, anyway. He was about to unleash his dragon on him.

Lilith broke into this devious smile. She'd been fairly relaxed like she was on vacation this entire time. But she looked downright dangerous right now. I was probably more scared of her than I was of Reyson, and I'd seen him in action.

Dorian Gray was about to find out the hard way what happened when you fucked around with one of Lilith's creations.

CHAPTER 22

RIPLEY

Holy shit. Lilith not only answered my prayer, but she also showed up at my fucking library. And I was stuck in this cage and couldn't give her a proper tour. I was pissed, to say the least. I didn't know why she was coming out of retirement now, but I wasn't looking a gift horse in the mouth. She was bringing my guys to Hell, and she was promising to help the Hellhounds.

Dorian had little patience. I was saying my goodbyes when he came barging in, glaring at me.

"That took a long time, Ripley. You'd better not be up to something."

I plastered an innocent look on my face and rubbed my fingers together where he couldn't see. I knew several ways to cast magic without being obvious about it, and Dorian Gray now had a raging case of treatment resistant crabs. Those buggers weren't going away without magic. Don't fuck with witches.

"You gassed my library and kidnapped me to manipulate a god, Dorian. How long do you think it takes to calm a

155

man down when you kidnap his future wife? You wanted the God of Chaos. You're going to have to give me longer than ten minutes to deal with his moods."

I tried not to smile as Dorian's feet started doing a little dance as my magical crabs went to work. Suck it, asshole. I'd get much more creative later. I know Lilith and Reyson said to cooperate with Dorian and let him think he had won, but he needed me alive and unharmed for this plan to work.

"And what did he say?"

"I have to pee, Dorian. I had a lot of coffee before you gassed me, and I've been in this cage since I woke up. I still have bodily functions, and I have to eat to stay alive. Did you even take that into account when you snatched me?"

"I'm not uncivilized, Ripley. There's a bathroom just beyond that door. I'll let you use it as soon as you tell me what I need to know, and I'll have food brought in."

"Reyson is mad, but he knows he doesn't have a choice. So he'll do what you ask."

"Are you going to be a good little witch when I let you out? I tried to get some of the magic dampening bracelets like they use in the supernatural prisons to keep you docile, but it proved too difficult for my source to sneak a pair out."

Score one for the prison system. Supernatural prisons were never for profit like the human prisons were, but they had some of the same problems. The fact that someone who worked in one was willing to sneak something that took away magic from the inmates for an immortal human for some cash told me exactly how they treated the inmates. I was guessing the fact that they skimped on costs for a lot of things for the prisoner's care, they kept damned good track of the inventory they paid for in case someone wanted to steal.

"What exactly do you think I'm going to do, Dorian? I'm in an unfamiliar realm where people don't like outsiders, and I can't exactly kill you without your painting."

"No, you can't, but it still hurts when people try."

I filed that away in my spank bank for later.

"Can I pee now, Dorian?"

He was blocking the door to my cage. I could have easily blasted him out of the way. I wanted to. This fucker was going to give me a bladder infection if he made me hold it any longer.

"I just don't trust you. You're mouthy and not like the usual witches I work with. I'm going to need some assurances. Akul! I need assistance."

A grumpy looking demon came stomping in with a female Hellhound who looked seriously beaten down. He was an older demon that appeared to be Talvath's age. Akul was clearly wealthy. He was dressed to the nines. His makeup was expertly applied, though not as good as Balthazar's. Akul was covered in jewels.

He didn't give his Hellhound the same care. He dressed her in rags, and it looked like he provided her with the bare minimum to clean herself. I felt my rage growing. Akul was now on my list of people I wanted to kill. But, he was also one of Lilith's creations, and I had a feeling he'd know if I used a little magic on him, so I kept it to myself.

"What is it, Dorian? I told you that you could keep your pet witch here, but I expect you to handle it."

"I couldn't get the bracelets to suppress her magic. Ripley is one of those modern witches who just can't do what she's told without having her own opinion about it. I don't trust women like that, and neither should you. Can you get one of your Hellhounds to babysit her? You have plenty."

"Seriously? Do you know how much Hellhounds cost and how long it takes to break them? They all have duties. I can't spare one to babysit your witch."

"I'll pay you enough to buy two new Hellhounds if she kills one. The god has agreed to do what I ask as long as she remains unharmed. Do you want Talvath and your hit list taken care of or not? The only way that doesn't blow back on you is if you do it my way. There's no way for anyone to tie you to this."

Akul just grunted.

"Fine. May, bring your mat in here and watch this witch. Try not to hurt her unless absolutely necessary. And get her something to eat. I don't need her bitching to her boyfriend that we didn't feed her."

This demon was *stupid*. Not just because he gave Dorian the means to destroy everyone in Hell just to kill a few people. He believed Dorian when he said no one could tie him to this. I had a face and a name, and I had big opinions about this whole thing. I'd fuck Akul over in a heartbeat because of how he treated his Hellhound.

"May, the witch has to use the facilities. Let her use them and get her back in her cage. Bring your mat in here. You have my permission to nap when she sleeps, but otherwise, I don't want your eyes off her. Happy, Dorian?"

"Yes. I'd like to take a shower now."

It wasn't ball sweat causing those itchies. I waited until Dorian and Akul left and turned to the Hellhound. May was so different from Bram. That had everything to do with Talvath. Bram had this swagger about him. He smiled easily as if something was funny. May was just beaten down.

She shuffled towards my cage door to lead me to the bathroom, and that was when I realized she'd literally just been beaten. I could see the bruises and whip marks on her shoulders where her shirt didn't cover. I felt my rage rising.

I did my business and went back to my cage. I didn't want to give Akul any more reason to beat her now that he'd assigned her my babysitter.

"Do you have a preference for food, miss?"

"Ripley, please. Anything is fine, but do you think you could bring me some comfrey and aloe and something to grind them up with?"

"The master will be mad if you do magic, and I'm not supposed to hurt you."

"Yes, but your master hurt *you*. I was going to make a healing poultice for your back. It's not right. You're a living being. You shouldn't be purchased as a pet, but even where I come from, if someone mistreats their pets, someone takes them away, and sometimes, it's a felony."

"It's not like that here. It hasn't been like that since I've been alive. If he finds out you tried to make my punishment less painful, he'll beat the other twelve Hellhounds he owns and make me watch. He does that sometimes if beating us again will keep us from working."

"Things are going to change, May. I don't think I need to tell you that your master has started something he probably can't finish."

"Things won't change, miss. We hear things in this house. There are a lot of demons who would see us free. Even the ones that don't find the breeding farms inhumane. Many demons make a lot of money with those. Akul is one of them. He doesn't just own stock in several of them. He owns six females and six males. We don't just have duties around the house. He's made himself richer, sending us there to make more Hellhounds for demons for the work they don't want to do.

"A lot of demons are like that. They view the people who want to change things as a threat to their livelihood. We know what Akul has done, but he has allies. They don't know this plot he's hatched, but they'd keep his secret if he told them."

"Can you keep a secret, May?"

"We keep a lot of secrets in this house, miss."

"What if I told you Lilith is now involved, and it's just a matter of time before my people figure out where I am? I know Akul expects all of you to shift and defend him, but all of you owe him nothing. Every single person coming for me wants things to change for the Hellhounds, and some of them have the power to do that. So all I'm asking is that when they come, you don't fight."

"I can't promise that, and I don't dare tell the others. Oscar is Akul's favorite. He's treated better than the rest of us. He reports everything back to Akul. Most of our beatings are because of Oscar. He would find out your friends are coming and warn Akul. Some of us may back down if Lilith is there, but Oscar won't."

"Snitches get stitches. I'm quite attached to a Hellhound, and I hope to keep him as my lover when this is over. Maybe if they see Bram, everyone but Oscar will back down."

May gasped and looked scandalized.

"Hellhounds are only allowed to mate when the female is fertile, and there will be pups. *No one* in Hell wants to take one of us for a lover just because."

I laughed because it totally wasn't just me that wanted to keep Bram.

"There's an entire group of us back at my library. Bram is family now. We all want him back with us, and I'm not the only one interested in having him as a lover."

May gave me a sad smile.

"It seems nice where you live. I'll get you something to eat. But be careful if Oscar comes in here. He's deranged and enjoys hurting people."

I tried to even the score when my rescue party got here and save a few Hellhounds. I gathered a ton of intel, but Dorian took my phone. I couldn't get it to my guys unless we had another private phone call. I was sure Dorian intended to read all the text messages he wanted me to send.

I got speaking in code, but we didn't have time to establish that. Fuck, I hadn't even given all the guys my safe word yet. I was pretty sure if I could name drop Akul, Talvath would know where I was. I could let them know Akul had allies that would protect him.

I was in a cage being guarded by a Hellhound, but I still had a few cards to play. I was going to get another private phone call whether Dorian liked it or not.

CHAPTER 23
REYSON

I knew *of* Lilith, but I'd never met her before. We all felt it when the Cosmos spat out another god. There used to be just a few of us, but as our creations multiplied, so did the gods. Some of the younger gods, I counted as friends, but some of them, I didn't know at all.

Lilith was pretty famous and a mystery to a lot of us. I had a million questions for her I'd love to ask once I had my witch back. But, I knew she didn't *have* to come to the library and bring us back with her. She certainly didn't ask for help before. Lilith was probably perfectly capable of finding Ripley and dealing with her traitor without us.

Lilith had every reason to distrust the other gods after what happened to her, but here we were in her lush manor. Bram and Talvath were sitting on a chaise waiting for us. I was just so happy to see that Hellhound. I yanked him to his feet and kissed him.

I wasn't stupid. I knew the entire reason we were here was that Bram risked everything to stand up to Lilith. She could have felt the way demons felt about Hellhounds and killed him on the spot.

Bram was an excellent kisser, and his tongue had a bar of metal through it. Lilith cleared her throat.

"I see several of you are fond of Bram."

"Some of us have no desire to kiss him, but he's still family," Felix said.

"Yes, well, Hell has use of him right now, and so do I. We have people here in Hell who are proficient at getting into electronics, but at this point, we don't know who we can trust. I hate it, but it is what it is. So what does your hacker need to locate the librarian?"

Balthazar just shrugged. I couldn't begin to understand how he did the things he did from those devices. I hadn't gotten one yet, and I hadn't been sure I wanted one before. If I had one of those cellphones, Ripley could have called me when she needed me. Felix didn't have one either. Gabriel and Balthazar were the only people back at the library with one of those devices, and Gabriel usually had his in his back pocket.

"I can do it from my phone, but I'll need whatever was done to Ripley's phone to give her service down here."

"Give me your phone," Lucifer said. "Samael is pretty, but he's hopeless with electronics."

"Shut up, Lucifer. I'm an angel married to a god. We don't *need* cell phones to communicate. You just like the camera feature."

"Hey, I'm *famous* on Earth now. Humans are terrified of me. They think all their fuck ups are my fault. They think I'm running Hell. They created angels to be beautiful. I'm allowed to be vain, Samael."

"Not totally. You abandoned your family to live with your name," Gabriel snapped.

Lucifer looked up from Balthazar's phone. Gabriel had a lot of anger towards his ancestors, and I couldn't say I blamed him. However, I think most of his anger was towards the one that made a mess after he made that deal and not Lucifer, but only one of them was currently in the room.

Lucifer looked like he understood why this conversation had to happen, but the entire thing was painful.

"You don't understand what it was like for us. Most all the other gods wanted their creations to go out and populate the world. It's not like that for angels. We're all male, and total obedience is required. We aren't allowed to question anything, just blindly follow orders. When we were sent for Lilith and her creations, we were told to be as cruel as possible. Some of us were.

"Samael didn't think it was right. He was the first to question our orders, and they punished him for it. It drove him straight to Lilith, and he wanted to help her. We have ranks. Samael was underneath me, so I was sent to bring him back.

"I had every intention to, but I saw how happy he was. Samael had something they had denied us. He was in love. We'd only ever been allowed to love our creator, but loving Lilith just lit him up. So I didn't bring him back. I defected too.

"They considered my betrayal greater than Samael's because of my rank. Samael would have been punished for making a mistake if I had brought him back. They thought I knew better and did it anyway. Hence me being responsible for the fall of man.

"I fell in love with one of Lilith's original witches. We had a beautiful family. But, by then, Lilith had created Hell and moved her other creations there with Samael. I *wanted* to stay with my family, but I had the angels and a petty god after me. In addition, they spread the story among humans that all the evils in the world were because of me.

"I wanted to bring my family here with me. Believe me, I did. I begged my wife, but she was a stubborn witch. Lilith had left, and so had the rest of her creations. Staying with my children was her way of sticking it to the angels and my creator. She kept her given name and moved away with her coven, but she passed information down so that the Morningstar name was brought back, which it did, or you wouldn't be so angry with me."

Gabriel just grunted. That whole situation had me angry, but for different reasons than Gabriel. I never felt the need to put my mark on the world with my own creation, but I knew most of the gods that did. None of them wanted total obedience. They didn't want to babysit their creations or micromanage them.

We were a bit lazy in that regard.

We also didn't police who they fell in love with. It took a special kind of ego to forbid your creations to have sex, so they didn't love anyone or anything above you. Why *wouldn't* anyone want their creations to multiply? Fuck, I think many of my siblings created who they did hoping for world domination.

"Dorian must have taken her phone and turned it off," Balthazar announced. "I won't be able to get a location until it's back on. She said everything will be text messages from now on, so it'll probably be Dorian we're messaging with."

"You underestimate Ripley," Felix said. "She'll be playing every angle. She's gathering intel. Dorian might intend to keep her phone and send all the messages himself, but she's going to get her phone back and call us. I don't need to be able to see the future to say that for certain."

I didn't want to rely on electronic devices and wait for Dorian to turn it on. Not when I was well, *me.*

"This realm keeps gods out unless you've invited them. Are there any other surprises here? I'm not sure it's possible to neutralize a god's power, but I'm also not sure how you created an entire realm to keep us out."

Lilith just gave me a cheeky wink.

"A girl has to keep some of her secrets, big guy. I wouldn't create an entire realm without a little insurance policy. Yes, I made sure no one who intended to harm my creations could get in, but I wouldn't create a realm that took away *my* magic in case my creations decided to hurt *me.* Your magic works just fine here."

I didn't know what Lilith's gifts were, but I knew she was perfectly capable of locating one of her creations without Dorian Gray turning a cellphone on so Balthazar could find her. I also knew if her magic was strong enough to create Hell and keep me out, she didn't really need any of us to deal with this problem.

"You're up to something," I said. "You aren't a trickster either, so it's probably not hijinks that all work out in the end."

"No, I'm certainly not a trickster, but you're in love with one of my creations, and I just watched you kiss another. Yes, I could find your witch and apprehend this traitor without you, but I'm playing the long game here. I have goals in mind for Hell, and I need your help with those. Now, can you get over your ego so we can proceed?"

"I'll show you mine if you'll show me yours. I can astral project. I can find my witch now that I'm here."

"And if you hold my hand and pool your magic with

mine while you do that, you can actually speak with her while you're there. Why do you think it's always my witches they call when the spirits aren't cooperating?"

"That's a neat trick," I admitted.

"I get you two need to flex your big god dicks and wave them around in a show of dominance, but Ripley's phone is back on, and I have a message that is clearly from Dorian."

"I *do not* wave my dick around," Lilith snapped.

"Dude, you were totally waving it around in Reyson's face. I got pre-cum in my eye. I'm just an innocent victim in all the dick waving," Balthazar said.

I adored that vampire. He just said whatever he was thinking and didn't care who he was saying it to. Not even I knew exactly what Lilith was capable of or how she would react to it.

"What does the message say?" Lilith demanded.

"It's a photo of a bunch of symbols and what Reyson needs to say to summon Talvath and kill him. It says to stay tuned because he has some hit list of demons he wants Reyson to kill."

"That's the traitor's doing," Talvath said. "Someone has a problem with me and several other demons, and they want their hands clean of the murders. They want Dorian and Reyson to take the blame for it."

"Did you find her?" Felix demanded.

Balthazar held up his phone. There was a map with a flashing dot on it. Talvath perched his glasses on the end of his nose and squinted.

"That's an exclusive area of Hell. It's a gated community that the worst demons tend to congregate in. People tend to live there because no one gets past security unless they want them to, and they don't have to deal with things they don't like. The houses are pretty far apart. Is there a way to zoom in?"

"This is as close as I can get in two minutes. I need a bit more time. You might want to do that astral projection thing while I work and find out what you can. We work better as a team."

I held out my hand to Lilith.

"Let's go contact my witch."

CHAPTER 24
RIPLEY

It was different when Reyson cooked entire feasts and served it to all of us. He did that because he enjoyed it, and if Reyson ever felt like not cooking, we were all capable of feeding ourselves. I ate because I was hungry, but I loathed the idea of May cooking for me and serving me because she didn't have any choice in the matter. I knew plenty of people had maids and in-home chefs, but they paid them and didn't beat them for no reason. That wasn't May.

After she brought me my food, she dragged a thin mat into the room my cage was in. It looked like it barely provided padding from the floor, and she had no pillow or blanket. I was furious. I had been angry about it before when I listened to Bram, but now that I saw it, I was furious.

I was trying to find the right thing to say to May. Unfortunately, I didn't live here. I couldn't barge in and tell her it was going to be better now when it had been bad for Hellhounds for longer than she'd been alive. That was just cruel. Supernaturals did the same thing humans did when it came to their gods. If shit was blowing up in your face and you had hit rock bottom, it was always some god's plan for you. I always thought that was a shit thing to say to someone. Lilith and Reyson technically *did* have a plan, but it wouldn't improve her situation right this minute.

I saw May visibly tense, and this sense of malice came over the room. I turned around, and I couldn't believe who I was seeing.

"Bram?"

No, not Bram. This Hellhound had the same face and build, but he definitely wasn't *my* Hellhound. I knew that even without seeing he didn't have the same piercings and tattoos Bram did. This Hellhound had an evil glint in his eyes, and I didn't like the way his aura made me feel. Definitely closely related to Bram and gave serious credence to the nurture versus nature theory.

"Oscar, witch. If it were up to me, I'd just rip you apart and be done with it. Akul shouldn't have put May in here to babysit you. May should have had the insolence beaten out of her by now, but she still wants to fight when the others are getting beaten. She's probably whispering nonsense in your ear, but you aren't living through this. Dorian was foolish enough to drop Akul's name in front of you. He's not going to leave you alive to whisper it to anyone. Don't get attached, May. This one will not save you."

Oscar stalked out. What an absolutely garbage individual. He had to be related to Bram, but they were nothing alike. That one little henchman monologue answered a ton of questions for me about this plot. Akul definitely wouldn't have wanted me to see his face or hear his name unless he was intending on betraying Dorian too.

I had a feeling they both had plans to fuck each other over. Dorian didn't say how he intended to live through

Reyson's wrath when this was over, but I was pretty sure he thought he could hide in Hell until Reyson calmed down. Dorian wasn't safe here either, and I was sure he intended to go back to Earth, eventually.

It wouldn't just be Reyson after him. Demons would hunt him even if he knew those sigils. Dorian would trade Akul's name for his life. He was like this sentient cockroach who just *would not* die, even if you blasted it with magic, hosed it down with hairspray to get it a little high, and smashed it with your shoe.

Man, it would be so much fun to fuck them both over when my crew showed up.

I suddenly felt a very comforting presence in the room. I could smell patchouli and clove, and there was only one person I knew that smelled like that. Reyson was with me. I smiled to myself. Of course, he was here. He was making sure I was unharmed, and he wouldn't wait for Balthazar to do his thing, even though Balthazar got results deathly fast.

I broke into goosebumps, and I felt Reyson even stronger. There was also a prickly presence with him that was just as strong that I'd never sensed around him before.

"Ripley, I'm in Hell. Lilith is here and helping me communicate with you while I astral project. I will kill him for caging you."

"Save the rage for later, big guy. We're here for intel."

I was guessing that was Lilith, and she was right. Reyson got a little wordy when he wanted to kill someone. Honestly, most hexes and curses took less time. I couldn't break out of here, even if I wanted to. I was outnumbered, and Oscar was a psycho. Even if the other Hellhounds on this estate wanted things to be different like May did, they couldn't help me. They'd be beaten, and they had nowhere else to go.

"The traitor's name is Akul. There are twelve Hellhounds here. One of them is completely evil, and I'm certain he's related to Bram. Akul makes a lot of money breeding Hellhounds and forces his to do so whenever they are able. May told me she thinks he wants Talvath and anyone who wants to shut his golden goose down dead. I'm pretty sure Akul intends to kill me and pretend like he's the hero that stopped Dorian Gray when this is over."

"I'll kill them both right now!" Reyson growled.

"You can't do anything like this. Not even our powers combined can do that. We need to get back and figure out a plan. Talvath will know Akul. Ripley only has limited information. You'll have to leave your witch."

"I can drop a little chaos on both of them like this. Ripley, will you be okay if we leave you?"

I heard Lilith laugh in my head.

"She's a witch. She can handle herself just fine until the cavalry arrives."

She wasn't wrong. I could probably fight my way out in a pinch as long as all twelve Hellhounds didn't gang up on me. Oscar might have threatened me, and Akul might have plans, but they couldn't do anything yet. They needed me alive because they thought Reyson was cooperating.

They pissed off a lot of people and made promises to a good bit more. They couldn't afford any mistakes, so I was safe long enough for us to pull this off.

"Go, Reyson, but come back soon. I'd really like to put the magical smack down on Dorian and Akul."

I heard Lilith laugh again.

"I'm sure you've already done something to Dorian Gray, Ripley."

"Magical crabs are nothing compared to what I have planned."

"Hang tight, my witch. I knew you wouldn't disappoint with intel. We'll be back."

"Try not to hurt the Hellhounds when you get here. Akul abuses them pretty badly. The one I think is related to Bram is pretty bad, and you'll probably have to fight him, but the others are just victims."

"We'll try, Ripley. There's a very good chance Bram and this other Hellhound are closely related. So we might not have to fight him either. He could easily turn on Akul when he sees how differently Bram has lived his life," Lilith said.

I felt them leave me, and a sense of unease settled over me. It wouldn't be that easy. Even with all the supernatural power on our team and two gods, something was going to go wrong. I saw the look in Oscar's eyes and the damage to May's back. Oscar wouldn't have an epiphany when he saw Bram.

He was going to shift and try to tear him apart. Someone had better let me out of this fucking cage before that happened.

CHAPTER 25
BRAM

I'd never been under so much pressure in my entire life. It felt like if I unclenched, I was going to shart out my stomach and die in front of two gods. I kicked in Lilith's door because I panicked when I found out Ripley was in Hell. I knew I had to act quickly because Dorian and our traitor were in the same place. If I was freaking out, then everyone at the library definitely was, too, and I knew shit got broken when the God of Chaos was upset.

I just wanted Lilith to let me bring them all back to Hell so we could figure this out. Hellhounds had been great generals and strategists in the past, but I was pretty far removed from that. I wasn't just trying to free someone I cared about and capture the demon who hurt Talvath. I was now the poster boy for every Hellhound here, and if I fucked this up, nothing would change for us.

It was way too much pressure.

Lilith and Reyson finally came out of their trance and got straight down to business.

"Do you know an Akul?" Lilith asked.

"I think your brother is there, Bram," Reyson said.

What the actual fuck?

"Akul has his fingers in politics," Talvath said. "Lobbying politicians isn't allowed in Hell like it is in some places on Earth. It's so illegal they will kick you out of office and bar you from ever running again. Even corrupt politicians won't risk it.

"There's long been a movement to change things for the Hellhounds. It's pretty heated on both sides of the argument. Akul is an extremist who benefits greatly from the way things are now. If things changed, he would lose his major source of income and actually have to pay people to run his estate.

"It's been put forth to be put into a bill several times. There was enough support for it numerous times. Every single time, at the last minute, the writer of the bill would withdraw it with no comment. We've long suspected blackmail was involved. Now that all *this* is happening, it wouldn't shock me."

"That's quite a lot of shit instead of just admitting you shouldn't own people as property," Felix snapped.

"I agree, and I'm trying to avoid a civil war here like what happened on Earth over this exact same matter," Lilith said. "There was a horrible one in the past that led to the enslavement of the Hellhounds in the first place. This has long gone past trying to prevent an uprising again. People like free labor and the profits from owning them. It's time that stops."

"Then why haven't you done something about it?" Felix demanded.

He wouldn't let this drop, and I knew why because I had talked to him about it. I couldn't say I didn't want that answer either. We all did. None of this would happen right now if Lilith had stepped in sooner.

"Hell isn't a monarchy, and I'm not the queen. I didn't make a few creations, demand total obedience, and forbid them from falling in love like Samael and Lucifer. I *wanted* them to be clever and think for themselves. I wanted them to find love and happiness. The entire point of their being was to be self-sufficient.

"In the beginning, there were a few of us. We all wrote laws and figured out what we wanted this realm to be like together. They multiplied and eventually didn't need me anymore. I can't manipulate anyone and force them to do my bidding. No god can, even if they like to pretend they can.

"Even saying I was in support of freeing the Hellhounds probably wouldn't be enough. You see how far Akul is willing to take this. Putting those sigils in the hands of a mortal puts this entire realm in danger. He's willing to kill off everyone who disagrees with him. That's the one thing I'm unwilling to do, and that's what would have needed to happen if I had stepped in before this mess happened."

"I need to say something about this plot," Talvath said, clearing his throat. "That is Bram's brother with Akul. Bram's mother had two pups. I wanted to keep them together. It's cruel that none of the Hellhounds know their family. Everything was in the works to have both of them come and live with me, but the Akul got involved.

"It was no secret I thought the Hellhounds should be free, and I'd never had one before. However, Akul and his followers knew it would be bad for their cause if someone like Bram was presented and showed that Hellhounds were perfectly civilized beings with feelings that didn't deserve what was being done to them.

"Akul swooped in and purchased Bram's brother from underneath me. I'm guessing Bram and his brother look just alike, but Bram's brother was raised differently than Bram. I have no doubt if they ever put those laws forth to be voted on and I asked Bram to testify on behalf of Hell-hounds, Akul would have produced his brother to discredit Bram."

I had a brother? I didn't know my parents. They hadn't even been in love. They were forced together when she was fertile, and we were taken away shortly after she gave birth. I could have known my brother. Talvath tried to keep us together. Talvath was great and played with me when I was younger, but sometimes, I wanted to rough house when I was shifted. I held back because I didn't want to hurt him.

I could have had a playmate and my blood with me if it weren't for fucking Akul. He hadn't just hurt Talvath and kidnapped Ripley. He took my brother and hurt him even worse.

I would have been perfectly happy to be grilled by any government official if I had been asked if it meant things were better for Hellhounds. I knew exactly what Akul would have done if he had my brother and needed to discredit me. My brother had been raised to be cruel and volatile.

And I was going to have to fight him to get to Akul, Dorian, and Ripley.

It wasn't fair. I wanted this to be over.

"When do we move?" I asked.

"We need to figure out how to get past the gates in that neighborhood," Talvath said.

"Oh, Ripley said there are twelve Hellhounds there, and she'd like us to try not to hurt them," Reyson said. "I know where she is now and can get us there."

"I can help with transportation too," Lilith said.

"What about alarm systems?" Balthazar asked. "I don't

know about everyone else, but I don't particularly want to fight my way through twelve Hellhounds I'm not supposed to hurt to get to Dorian and Akul. Isn't that just going to give them time to flee back to Earth? I have questions."

"Akul won't have any serious alarm system. The neighborhood he lives in doesn't allow anyone who isn't invited through the gates, and he's fine with using his Hellhounds as shields. Getting to Dorian and Akul before they flee to Earth will be a problem," Talvath said.

Lilith and Reyson both broke into evil grins.

"We didn't just check in on Ripley. We explored that entire manor. I know where their rooms are. I'll take a team to Dorian's room, and Lilith will take hers to Akul's. Ripley is being held just down the hall. Felix will shift and sneak down the hall to free her. There's a female Hellhound watching her, but she tries to help the other Hellhounds there. She won't stop you."

Felix didn't even flinch and agreed to it. Female Hellhounds were bigger than the males when they were shifted and fierce fighters. I personally wouldn't have wanted to risk going up against one unless I had to.

"When do we move?" Felix asked.

"There's no better time than the present," Lilith said.

Here we go.

CHAPTER 26
RIPLEY

I knew they were coming. Probably pretty soon. Dorian still had my phone, so I couldn't exactly check-in. I was *super* glad I never responded to horny men who wanted nudes. If I didn't trust someone I liked not to share that shit if they got butt hurt about something I did, I certainly didn't trust Dorian Gray with the photo storage on my phone if it was full of nudes. Vain selfies, yes. My tits? No. I had *some* limits.

Dorian and Akul had left me alone. I didn't know what was going to happen first. Dorian was talking to Balthazar because Reyson didn't have a phone. If *anyone* was going to get Dorian Gray hot and bothered enough to come in here and give me my phone back, it was going to be my sexy vampire.

Unless he was being the picture of cooperation because they were about to storm the castle, defeat the dragon, and rescue the princess. I was on board with that, too, because this fucking cage wasn't even remotely comfortable. I was semi-okay with my ass being in it at the moment because I was pretty sure if I wasn't, this was some kind of punishment for the Hellhounds here. Felix got super dramatic if I had to put him in the kennel to take him to the vet.

I got it now.

I saw May visibly tense in the corner and got that same sense of malice in the room. It was either Oscar or Akul again. They felt similarly.

I had so many questions about Oscar. I knew enough about being a twin to recognize one when I saw him. I hadn't actually spoken to Talvath, but Bram spoke highly of him. If Akul could purchase twelve Hellhounds, I was certain Talvath could have kept these twins together. If he were a decent demon like Bram always said, I would have thought he would do it.

I was missing something, and I hated that.

I'd figure that out when Oscar wasn't leaning against the door sneering at me. I knew Bram was dangerous. I'd seen him shifted in action. I knew if he lost control, he could attack me and rip my throat out. I was never worried about that with Bram. Bram made me feel totally safe, and he snuggled like a total beast.

Ravyn and I had a lot in common. We even had the same taste in men. We also grew up together and were always inseparable. Oscar was nothing like Bram. I couldn't imagine Bram looking at anyone the way Oscar was looking at me.

"I can't kill you yet, but I am a little curious what it's like to fuck a witch. There has to be a reason they didn't invite your kind when Lilith made Hell. I'll bet you're too much temptation for the men who live here," Oscar growled, rubbing his crotch.

I threw up my hands. I was *done* with the men in this house, and I was not getting raped by a Hellhound today. They created me with all the tools I needed to defend myself against that. I called magic to my fingertips and let it crackle.

"I'd suggest you go jerk off in a cold shower and think twice about that, dude."

"Run along, May. Be grateful it's not you tonight. I have a witch to entertain me."

Okay, yeah, fuck waiting for the dream team to come save me. I didn't want to rob Bram of his brother, but his brother was kind of a rapist turd. I didn't just owe him because he thought he had every right to me just for existing. I owed him payback for May and every female Hellhound here.

I guess May was done with it too. Before I could get enough magic in my hands to throw at him, she shifted. May was tiny in her human form, but her Hellhound was absolutely massive. I saw Bram when he was shifted, and May was even bigger.

She jumped between Oscar and my cage and bared her teeth.

"You can't deal with another beating right now, May. Just leave. We can easily replace you. Akul *needs* me. It's why I'm treated better than the rest of you. He'll punish you for challenging me, but he'll kill you if you attack."

Something wasn't adding up. Oscar didn't strike me as the type to talk things out. I had a feeling he was important here because of his resemblance to Bram. Oscar had no problem raping May and getting her beaten, but now that she was challenging him, it was like he didn't want to fight her.

May didn't give him a choice. She was more done with the men in this house than I was. She lunged at Oscar's throat. Oscar's Hellhound exploded, and I got why he tried his words first. Oscar's Hellhound was the same size as Bram's but nowhere near the size of May's.

They collided, and Oscar ended up on his back. I'd chip in with a little magical assist if needed, but May was kicking his rapey ass just fine. The noise brought everyone in the house into this room. Akul kicked the door in, and I could see Dorian and the Hellhounds peering over his shoulder.

"What is the meaning of this? May, stop this at once!"

"She's doing you a favor," I yelled. "Your Hellhound decided it was a good idea to come in here and try to rape me. He'd be dead right now if it were me fighting him, and Reyson is going to have big opinions about him trying."

"Seriously, Akul? We need her unharmed," Dorian whined. "That includes rape threats from your pets."

Akul flung some sort of magic at the fighting Hellhounds, and they were blasted apart. I really hoped Akul would side with May on this instead of Oscar just because he had a penis.

"Oscar! What made you think you had my permission to lay a finger on my prisoner? How many times do I have to tell you that if you have needs, use one of the Hellhounds here?"

Oscar shifted back and looked stunned as he rose to his feet.

"I want May punished. She tried to attack me," Oscar whined.

What a little bitch.

"In this case, May was right. You could have fucked everything up, Oscar. I *should* punish you in this case, but you know I won't. Go to your room and don't come back in here if the witch is too much temptation."

Before Oscar could stomp his pouty naked ass off to his

room like a petulant child, there was a crash down the hall. Oscar went on high alert.

"There are strangers in this house!" he snarled.

Showtime.

The entire estate started shaking. Akul and Dorian were trying to run out of the room, but no one could stand on their feet. The roof was suddenly ripped off, and a massive dragon was perched on the house frame. I guess Kaine didn't want to miss this.

"To the portal room! Now!" Akul yelled.

They were planning on fleeing to Earth, but they couldn't do that just anywhere. Before they could even get two steps, Kaine swooped forward and plucked Akul out of the room with his claws. He just kind of yeeted the demon in the air.

Ravyn and I used to really like human cartoons that came on late at night. Akul made the exact same noise as cartoon villains made when their elaborate boobytrap backfired, and they got catapulted into the distance. It was really beautiful.

An angel with massive white wings caught Akul like he was playing dodgeball with the demon and flew off with him. Kaine's massive golden eyes winked at me, and he followed. Something told me that dragon was having *a lot* of fun breaking shit in Hell with zero rules.

Dorian was stuck now. He couldn't portal out of here without a demon, but he wasn't going down without a fight. He looked to his only ally in the room—Oscar.

"Grab the witch. If you get us both out of here, I'll set you up nice and wealthy on Earth. Then, you can have as many witches as you like."

Oh, fuck no. I didn't use magic on him before because it was May's fight. I'd zap him so hard, all his body hair fell off, and he looked like one of those Sphinx cats, but as a Hellhound. Man, that would be fucked up.

Everyone in the doorway fell as a blur zipped into the room. When it stopped, Balthazar was standing there holding Felix. He set Felix down and smacked him on the ass.

"Go get our witch. I'll handle the human."

Oscar jumped in front of Dorian, then Bram stepped into the room.

"My brother is mine," Bram growled.

CHAPTER 27
FELIX

I couldn't astral project like Reyson or find Ripley with her cell phone like Balthazar could. But, I was still her familiar, even if I had my body back. I could still sense her, even if she were far away. She was stressed and uncomfortable. Ripley was still dealing with some of the side effects from the gas, but she knew we were coming.

We had this neat little plan to grab Dorian and Akul, get Ripley to safety, and not harm any Hellhounds there. We were about to leave when it hit me like a punch in the gut. They tied me to Ripley through magic, and I could feel what she was channeling right now. This wasn't mischief magic. She wasn't taking the piss and amusing herself at Dorian's expense with little hexes.

"We need to change the plan. Ripley is using battle magic, which means she's in trouble. She's stubborn and can be hot-headed, but not when it counts. She knows we are coming, and she knows she's outnumbered. So Ripley wouldn't be fighting unless she was in trouble."

"Grab onto me," Reyson snarled. "We're leaving."

"New plan," Lilith announced. "I wanted to do this with

as little mess as possible. Get in, get out. We're going to make a big one. Kaine, I want you to shift and take to the air with Samael and Lucifer. If Akul has friends in that neighborhood, a dragon and two angels should flush them out. Again, please try not to kill the Hellhounds there. Disable them, but don't kill them."

I needed to get into the room Ripley was in as quickly as possible, and going in as a cat was out of the question. I looked to Balthazar.

"Can you get me in the same room with her as fast as possible?"

Balthazar gave me a curt nod, and everyone agreed they would be right behind him. Reyson and Lilith would be hunting down Akul and Dorian if they weren't in the same room so they could grab them before they escaped.

Kaine cracked his neck and gave Lilith a dangerous smile.

"To be clear, you're giving me permission to unleash the full wrath of my dragon on this estate?"

"Yes. Just try not to set the entire neighborhood on fire. Some of those people might not be involved in this, and the trees in that area are as old as this realm."

Kaine looked like a toddler who had just been given an entire cake to demolish. He had kind of been this grumpy fuck about the rules when it came to this entire investigation. I knew he wouldn't have hesitated to throw all our asses in jail if someone caught us breaking one.

I guess it wasn't surprising he looked giddy about catching the bad guys with no rules in another realm when he bent them all the time working with Balthazar.

Lucifer and Samael came to stand next to Kaine.

"Can we get a little door?" Samael said.

Lilith waved her hand, and a door appeared that

seemed to open into the sky. Damn. Witches and warlocks had been trying to figure out how to do that for *ages*. Lilith didn't give us that ability when she made us. We didn't have sigils to travel like demons did, either. I could be mad at that later.

Lucifer grabbed Kaine and threw him through the door. He barely fell before this massive dragon burst into the sky, and he beat his wings.

"That's so badass," Lucifer said, jumping in after him.

Samael went through, and the door shut.

"Ripley isn't using battle magic anymore, but the fact that she was in the first place is bad."

Lilith waved her hand again, and another door appeared leading to a hallway.

"I know cats don't like being held like babies, even though they are perfectly the size of little babies, so you might want to hop on my back if you want a vampire ride, Felix."

I let out a little grunt and hopped on Balthazar's back. Everyone else snuck through as quietly as possible. We didn't want to tip off the Hellhounds because we didn't particularly want to fight them.

Fucking Balthazar gave me a little bounce and threw back his head to scream "Yippee-ki-yay, motherfucker!" before charging through the door.

If those twelve Hellhounds hadn't scented intruders yet, they certainly heard that. They'd just better get the fuck out of our way so I could get to Ripley.

CHAPTER 28
BRAM

This whole plan was going to shit. Reyson and Lilith had gone down the hall so that Lilith could destroy Akul's portal sigils before he could get there, but they didn't need to worry about that. Everyone was crowded around one door, and I could scent Ripley in there with a human and a demon.

Between Balthazar, Felix, and me, we could have handled them, but Kaine decided to be a little extra and rip the entire roof off before we could even set foot in the room. At least Akul was taken care of. I heard Dorian give a verbal offer to a Hellhound in the room. Balthazar and Felix zipped into the room, and I stepped inside.

There was a naked Hellhound with my face that looked like he'd already gotten his ass kicked before I got here, looking like he was totally on board with taking Dorian Gray up on his offer. Why did it have to be my brother? I really didn't want to fight him, and every other Hellhound in the room looked like they might want to be grateful at this turn of events.

"My brother is mine."

Balthazar used his vampire speed to get to Ripley's cage. There was a naked female Hellhound who moved to help him. I was willing to bet money she was the one who whooped my brother's butt. You had to be a special kind of stupid to fight a female Hellhound, even one that had been beaten down and abused.

Felix flung magic at Dorian. He flew across the room, slammed against the wall, and stuck there like they coated it in double-sided tape. The other Hellhounds looked utterly confused, but they didn't want to fight us. My brother was the only one who thought he could take all of us.

"Bram, I've been dying to meet you. Akul promised me we'd face off one day. You're a disgrace to Hellhounds. You've been domesticated and lost touch with who you are. I'm going to enjoy killing you."

What kind of brainwashed horse shit was that? We weren't feral wolves that needed someone to pluck us from our homes and breed the wildness out of us, so we made good pets or hunting companions. They had created hellhounds at the same time as demons. We had never needed anyone to tell us how to behave or train us not to poop in the house like the animals here that were suitable for keeping as pets.

I never even knew about my brother, but Akul told him all about me. All lies. I was going to rip that demon apart. My brother was willing to fight me to the death, and I had no desire to kill him. He was just confused.

"It's not supposed to be like this for any of us. So stand down, brother."

The Hellhounds in the doorway started pressing forward until they all stood at my back. How odd. They didn't know us. We attacked their home, but it looked like they all really wanted to fight my brother. What in actual fuck went on in this house?

"You can't reason with Oscar," one of the males said. "Akul singled him out for a purpose when he purchased him. Oscar has been raised to be like every negative stereotype about Hellhounds because that's what Akul needed him to be. He's a rapist and is cruel for no reason. Oscar gets off on having us beaten. We couldn't do anything about it because he's Akul's favorite. Akul didn't even punish him and just sent him to his room when he tried to rape this witch."

"If you don't want to kill him, the rest of us do," Felix called. "Reyson will wipe him from existence for just thinking about it."

"You tried to rape my librarian?" I growled at Oscar.

"If I had known you were fond of her, I would have gotten May out of here before she shifted to fight me and fucked her twice."

I was done. I could understand Oscar's situation a little, but it really seemed like he *enjoyed* being like this. Was this even my fight? He might know me, but I just found out he existed. He hadn't hurt me the way he hurt the people in this room. Oscar came at Ripley, and for that alone, I could have killed him, but the Hellhounds in this room needed it more than me.

"Akul is gone. He won't be coming back. Things should be changing for us in Hell. We can—"

I wasn't talking to Oscar. I was pretty sure he wouldn't hear me. I was speaking to every Hellhound in this room. Oscar still thought he could win. He shifted and lunged at my neck. I braced myself and called my Hellhound, but something flung Oscar across the room. A furious Reyson stalked in.

"Did I hear you correctly that you thought you could lay hands on my witch?"

Oscar just snarled at him.

"Rapey Hellhounds aside, Ripley's cage has a blood lock on it," Felix said.

"I'll bleed to get her out," Ravyn said. "We can wonder twin this like the one at the warehouse."

"Um, hello?" the naked female Hellhound said. "There's no need. Akul usually keeps us in this cage with his own lock on the door. When Dorian brought his prisoner, he used his own lock. I've seen him open it."

"What's your name?" Reyson asked.

"May," she squeaked.

Reyson moved forward slowly with his hands up.

"I saw you in here watching over my witch. I know some of those injuries are from Akul, but I'm guessing the fresh ones are from defending my witch from this asshole. May I heal your wounds? You have my eternal thanks."

We were all grateful to May. I had no doubt Ripley could have fought Oscar off magically. She probably would have killed him. Akul wasn't even remotely a stable demon. He wouldn't have reacted well to Ripley killing Oscar. May put her life in danger to save Ripley.

I wasn't a leader, but she looked straight to me for an answer. Did she want my permission?

"It's okay, May. You didn't deserve anything Akul did to you. It's not painful. He can make you better."

It was so fucked up. There were two gods in this room, and all the Hellhounds were looking to me for answers. May gasped as Reyson healed her injuries. Lilith snapped into action.

"Use Dorian to unlock the cage. He might as well be good for something. If anyone else is hurt, I'd be happy to heal you. Akul has been arrested, and this place is no longer hospitable. You're welcome to stay with me while we sort out this mess. You can come and go as you please, and I don't expect you to do any work."

May seemed to be the spokesperson for the Hellhounds. She bowed her head.

"Please, it's not that easy. Akul's wife is worse than he is. She's having her daily visit with her friends, but she'll be back."

There was a crash downstairs and a lot of shouting. Akul's wife was here right this minute, and it sounded like she brought all the housewives from the evil part of the demon suburbs.

We were fucked.

CHAPTER 29
RIPLEY

N o one told me Akul had a wife. Someone married that thing? With all the rights women had now, there was absolutely no excuse to settle for a shit man in this day and age. Was Hell ass-backward, and she needed him to have a bank account and a house? I had questions.

I was also stuck in this cage unless Dorian bled on this lock before all those people downstairs made it up here and started attacking. I had big opinions about being in a giant cage in the first place, but I had bigger ones about being stuck there when a massive fight was going on. Something told me these bitches weren't even going to back down when they realized Lilith was the reason Akul got yeeted out of the house by a dragon and carried off by a fallen angel.

"Kill anything that doesn't belong here!" someone yelled. "Tell your Hellhounds to do the same."

"Not to be a pest, but can someone get Dorian's blood over here before they get up the stairs?" I said.

Ravyn snapped her fingers, and Dorian unstuck from the wall. He floated in the air over to my cage.

"Get over here and bleed, you little bitch," Ravyn said.

"You can't make me," Dorian pouted.

"Read the room, asshole. You aren't even getting a participation trophy for this. You kidnapped my twin, and I'll take as much blood as I want. You *should* be worried about what the men fucking her are going to do to you."

Oh, man. Ravyn just *was not* fucking around. She magically slit Dorian's throat all over the lock. The lock popped open, and my cage door opened. Dorian fell to the floor, choking on his blood. I stepped over him but gave him a kick to the gut on the way out.

"Quit whining. We don't have your painting. It's not like that was fatal, and you had it coming."

"When that heals, I'm dying to know where it is because I decoded all your magical decoys."

"It's around his neck," Talvath said. "It's always been a portrait locket. Can someone get him out of here? May is right. Akul's wife, Vegran, is terrible, and all her awful friends are on their way upstairs. Vegran was probably not only fully aware of this plan but supported it. She'll pick up right where Akul left it to bargain for his freedom."

That bitch was brunching while I was in a cage in her house.

Lilith waved her hand, and a magical door appeared. That was a neat trick. It sure would have been nice if she had given it to witches. I would have poofed myself straight out of the fucking cage. Bram picked Dorian up and threw him through the door. Talvath followed, and the door closed behind him. Everyone was yeeting villains today.

I waved my hand and conjured May some clothes. Real clothes, not those shapeless sacks Akul and his wife gave her. I was sure she would shred them when she shifted if she wanted to get a little revenge on the wife, but I gave zero shits.

It was pretty amazing. Every Hellhound in the room except Oscar looked to Bram for instruction, even with Lilith and Reyson here. Reyson still had Oscar plastered against the wall, but he had shifted back. I had a feeling Reyson intended on killing Oscar very slowly, but now his damned mouth was free, and I hated everything that came out of it.

"Vegran is going to slaughter all of you. She's a proper demon wife. An asset to her husband in every way. She supports him in *everything*. She'll free him."

"Can someone shut him up?" Lilith. "Literally none of that was my intention when I create female demons. She's not a proper demon wife. She's just an asshole who invited her neighbors to her execution."

"I wanted to play with this one. He thought he had the right to touch my witch without her permission."

Lilith rolled her eyes.

"We don't have time for that, Reyson. I created the female Hellhounds to be bigger and stronger than the males. May already kicked his ass and was probably stopped from killing him by Akul. What do you think bored, rich housewives do in Hell when they tend to be evil bitches? They pool their evil bitch collective and write all kinds of dangerous new sigils. Why do you think they haven't come up the stairs yet? Demon magic is all in the sigils. They aren't searching just yet. They are painting them all over the walls. They can't hurt us, but they can hurt everyone in here, including your witch."

Well, that was some shit. I *did not* watch my sister slit Dorian Gray's throat to get me out of this cage to get blown up by the Real Housewives of Hell. I didn't even like any version of that show back on Earth.

"Just get rid of him, Reyson. May would have killed him, but Akul broke the fight up."

"I have a better use for him," Reyson growled.

Reyson put his hand on Oscar's forehead, but his brain didn't start leaking out of his ears like every other time he did this. Oscar tumbled off the wall, and Reyson kicked his ass straight out the door. What was he up to?

"What are you doing?" Bram hissed. "He hurt every single Hellhound here, and he tried to hurt Ripley. Akul would have used him to make sure we are slaves for the rest of my life."

"I was thinking of Ripley's television. We all need eyes on downstairs. So I turned Oscar into Netflix! I'm hoping he goes down there and tells them Lilith is involved, and it gives them enough pause for us to get down there, destroy the sigils, and round them up."

"They won't," May said. "They will draw even more dangerous sigils. They are both depraved. They think nothing can stop them, not even gods. Vegran probably cooked up a sigil she thought would work just in case."

"We need to get down there, *now*," Lilith said. "Those sigils won't do a damned thing to us, but they can kill everyone here."

Reyson grabbed Lilith and disappeared on us. I got that both of them were indestructible, but everyone here had been affected by this, and the people downstairs had Hellhounds with them that were probably treated just as badly as the ones here.

"Let's go kill some housewives!" I yelled.

Bram turned to the Hellhounds.

"No one will be angry if you don't join the fight, but

there are others down there in the same situation you are. We don't want to hurt them. We want to bring them to Lilith or Talvath's until we can change things for Hellhounds for good. I know you fear Vegran. They *want* us scared of them.

"The whole reason things are like this is that *they* used to fear *us*. They degraded us and beat us until we thought we were less powerful than they were. If we can turn their Hellhounds to our side and have two gods on our team, we *can* beat them."

The Hellhounds were good and rallied. They were hooting and hollering and ready to fight for their freedom. I knew they'd be shifting anyway, but I snapped my fingers and gave them all some badass battle leathers. Entrances were important for magical fights.

"Let's end this!" I yelled.

CHAPTER 30
REYSON

I didn't care who these women were or how important they thought they were. They weren't hurting anyone in this house. Lilith and I appeared in the middle of the living room. These savages were painting sigils on the walls from the blood of their Hellhounds. They were all standing there half-naked with their heads bowed as the demon women dipped their fingers in the cuts they made on their chest.

The sigils were elaborate, and they hadn't finished most of them. All the women had a good bit of them tattooed on their skin. This was wrong. I'd been all over the universe, bringing chaos. I'd seen terrible things over my long lifetime, but this was pretty bad.

I'd fought Hellhounds before. Before all this nonsense. They were fierce fighters. They could have easily fought off these women before they sliced their bodies up. I was done with this. I wasn't okay with slavery back in my day either. I waved my hand and all the sigils burned off the walls.

The women turned to glare at us. Lilith and I didn't have to announce who we were. They had probably never met her before, but they would have known that we could easily kill them from the power we were giving off. They all looked towards a pinched-faced woman that had to be Vegran.

"You didn't tell us Lilith was involved!" one of the women snapped.

"A minor inconvenience. Hellhounds, attack!"

"Wait!" Lilith said, holding up her hand.

Now was really not the time to talk. My witch and my friends were upstairs. We needed to get to the killing.

"Hellhounds, I'm not just here because Akul betrayed everyone here. I'm here for *you*. Things need to change, and I want to help you, not hurt you."

"This is stupid. If you don't attack right this minute, I'll have the flesh peeled from all of your backs," Vegran sneered.

Lilith waved her hand, and Vegran's entire mouth disappeared. Her eyes widened, and her hand flew to her face like she could somehow bring it back. The Hellhounds were hesitating. I knew they probably hadn't been taught to read or write like Bram had, but they were definitely smarter than the demon women in the room.

Lilith said demon magic came from sigils, and they all had them tattooed on their flesh. They took offense at what Lilith did to Vegran and flung magic at her. It didn't do a damned thing to her, but it burned a hole in her top. Lilith tossed her red hair over her shoulder.

"That was just rude. This was one of my favorite shirts. Samael loves me in this top."

At that point, most sane people would back down and beg for forgiveness, but that wasn't anyone in this room. The Hellhounds fell to the floor and covered their heads, and all the demons started flinging magic at us. It was ruining my clothes, but it was barely a tickle on my flesh. All the furniture and plaster in the room were taking more damage than Lilith and me.

That was when I felt her. I could pick out my witch in the middle of a room full of demons flinging magic everywhere. She joined the fight. I'd be honored to fight any battle beside her, but these demons were willing to attack their creator. They didn't care what I would do to them if they hurt my witch.

I just really needed her to stay out of this and let Lilith and I handle this.

"Oh, fuck no. You *do not* throw shit at my god," Ripley snarled.

Ripley flung magic at the demons. It hit one of them right in the chest. Her body went rigid, and her flesh turned black. She fell over dead, and now all eyes were on my witch. It warmed my heart that she killed to defend me, but these demons were seriously unfocused.

I thought they came to avenge Akul, but they seemed to operate on some kind of hive mind. They didn't attack us until Lilith shut Vegran up. They saw they couldn't hurt us, but now that Ripley had killed one of them, it was like Lilith and I didn't exist. They were solely focused on my witch now.

They were evil demons, but they certainly weren't very smart or organized. Felix yanked Ripley out of the way, and everyone standing behind her dove out of the line of fire when every single demon flung something at my witch.

I was about to end this nonsense, but Bram and all eleven Hellhounds shifted, with Bram taking point. I noticed their magic kept bouncing off of Bram, and I remembered he was covered in tattoos. If demon magic came from sigils and could be tattooed on and Talvath intended Bram to free the Hellhounds, I was betting Talvath wrote some sigils for Bram to make him immune from assassination attacks.

Lilith seemed to hold back and letting this play out. She made those demons. She could easily blink and unmake them, but she wasn't. I was holding back because this was her realm and her creations, but I was about to blast these demons across Hell because Bram was mine too. Lilith put her hand on my arm when I raised it.

"Wait for it."

Wait for what? We were past the point of waiting here. The Hellhounds on the floor who ducked when magic started flying realized Bram was immune to their magic and led eleven Hellhounds. He was taking the brunt of the magic for them and just kept going.

The demon women were now focused on Bram and the Hellhounds charging towards them. They weren't even paying attention to the ones on the floor, but the Hellhounds were certainly watching Bram. They got to their hands and knees and shifted.

I got it now, but I didn't like Lilith using Bram like that. It wasn't enough to just swoop in and free the Hellhounds. Not when they'd been beaten down for so long. They needed to be given their power back. They needed to know they were just as powerful as demons because that was how Lilith created them.

And the complacent demons who abused them needed a little fear in their life. Vegran and her friends weren't afraid of Lilith and me, but they were certainly shrieking in terror when they got mobbed by Hellhounds.

That was certainly... graphic. I understood the Hellhounds had a lot of pent-up rage, but a flying decapitated head nearly struck me in the face and got bits on my shirt.

The shirt was already destroyed, but I really hated getting blood on me.

I felt a small hand slip into mine. I didn't have to look to know it was Ripley. I could pick Bram out of all the Hellhounds. They were all built similarly, but they had distinctive faces. Bram let out a growl and took off running. Did we miss one?

Oh, yeah. I released his rapey brother, and he hadn't been in the room. I had killed no one yet, and I owed that Hellhound. Maybe Bram wanted to kill him? Oscar wasn't my brother. Maybe Bram wouldn't mind if I helped and only killed him a little.

I kissed Ripley on the forehead.

"Oscar is still out there."

We could hear the growls and snarls of a Hellhound fight in the next room. There was a yelp and then silence. That had better have been Oscar that died. Bram was mine. I kissed him and marked him so. It would devastate Ripley. We would all feel that loss.

Gabriel had introduced me to action movies. I was quite fond of the genre. Most of the walls had holes blasted through them. There was smoke everywhere from plaster debris and little fires burning everywhere. I could see a hulking shadow coming through the door.

Bram was covered in blood and ash, but that was a movie star entrance right there. He stalked through the smoke like the victor he was. He marched straight up to Ripley and pulled her into a kiss. I started clapping. Everyone at the library kept telling me not to clap at the TV because it wasn't like live theatre, and they couldn't hear me.

This deserved a clap. Bram was pretty badass, and every Hellhound here deserved it. They didn't need us gods. They did this by themselves. We were basically just here for support. This was all Bram.

Lilith joined me, and so did everyone from the library. Ripley would have clapped too, but she had her tongue down Bram's throat. All those Hellhounds who rallied behind Bram seemed a little scandalized he was kissing a witch. Lilith caught on to that quickly.

"Demons and Hellhounds used to marry each other," she said. "You were never meant to only mate when the females are fertile and never see that person again. I created you to find love with whoever you wanted, even witches. Honestly, you're compatible with any creature on Earth.

"This place isn't habitable, and if you don't live here, I don't really want you going back home somewhere these women's husbands will abuse you for their mistakes. I have plenty of room at my place for you to stay while I get things changed for good.

"I only ask one thing in return. You won't be asked to wait on me hand and foot. You won't be asked to do anything at all at my house. I have paid demon servants who will take care of your needs. All I ask is that you speak the truth when asked. If called upon to tell your story, be honest about how you were treated, what you witnessed in your homes, and what happened here today."

The Hellhounds were all nodding and murmuring in agreement. Ripley looked at Ravyn. They'd always been able to communicate wordlessly. They snapped their fingers, and everyone had clothes on. Much better clothes than the ones they had come here in. I waved my hand and cleaned the blood and dirt off of them. I noticed Ripley left Bram naked because she was probably enjoying the view just as much as I was.

"We should leave before this place collapses," Lilith

said, creating another door. "We need to interrogate Dorian and Akul so I can find out exactly who has those sigils now."

We all stepped through. I wanted a shower and some time alone with my people, but I hoped Lilith would let me in on the interrogation. Dorian had been a massive pain in my ass, and I had a lot of opinions on Akul and his wife.

They wanted the God of Chaos. They thought they could manipulate me by stealing my witch. It was time they found out who they really raised.

CHAPTER 31
RIPLEY

I barely had the chance to process I'd gone to battle with Lilith herself, and now I was in her big cushy castle because there was just too much to do. Reyson, Lilith, Bram, and Talvath were tag-teaming Dorian and Akul to find out exactly how deep this plot went and who had those sigils now. Of course, Reyson could have just plucked that information out of their heads, but Lilith and Talvath wanted their brains intact for now.

Bram was mostly working Akul to piss him off. Honestly, I was surprised Akul hadn't spontaneously combusted from that. Akul literally betrayed Hell, raised a god, and intended on killing a bunch of demons to continue to profit from Hellhound slavery. He purchased Bram's twin brother from underneath Talvath and turned Oscar into a monster.

I honestly wanted to be in the room while Akul had a little man baby bitch fit because Bram beat him, but there were all these Hellhounds here that needed our help. They were dazed, confused, and honestly thought they didn't deserve to be here. They really needed Bram. Ravyn and I were both pretty shitty at feelings.

The Hellhounds had showered, and Lilith's servants were bringing food in. My parents weren't wealthy. We never had servants. We didn't even have a dishwasher for a little while. Ravyn and I begged for our parents to get one, and they told us they gave birth to twin dishwashers. They thought that was much funnier than we did.

If I was uncomfortable having people bring in a seven-course meal on ornate silver platters and breaking out the good China, then these Hellhounds definitely were. I didn't even own fancy plates I only brought out for company. It just seemed weird to spend money on something I wouldn't use.

"Ripley, are we supposed to eat this?" May asked. "We've cooked things like this before, but we can't eat it."

I furrowed my brow. I'd seen Bram eat Oreos dipped in a Frosty. I was certain they could eat a roast.

"What have they been feeding you?"

Just then, this absolutely *stunning* dog walked in. It was smaller than a Hellhound, and I was pretty sure it was just a dog. But, it was still pretty big with sleek muscles and an inky black coat. It had big ears that stood straight up. She trotted straight up to May and booped her knee. May scratched her ear.

"This is a Dolrun. It's a breed of dog in Hell. They are loyal, fierce pets. They make us shift and eat the same thing they do."

Okay, I got they needed Akul for information, but I really wanted to march in there, and pistol whip him with his own dick.

"May, Bram spent a lot of time at my library on Earth. I watched him eat whatever he wanted without getting sick.

He even ate chocolate. I never once saw Bram eat dog food. If he were in here, he'd take a bite and show you."

The Hellhounds started moving closer to me. That food smelled amazing, and I was starving. They had to be hungry, too, and be able to smell it. I kind of wanted to fetch Bram. Ravyn was sitting next to me, totally bewildered by this entire thing. I wasn't expecting Balthazar to give me an assist.

"I'm not a shifter, but I am a vampire. Have you heard of us? I have to drink blood to survive. I can eat all this and not get sick too. Bram baked us all a lovely cake for Felix's birthday, and I watched him eat four pieces. I've also seen him eat Taco Bell and not explode. If he can eat five Dorito tacos without farting us out of the room, you can totally eat anything you want that isn't dog food."

Solomon was one of Akul's Hellhounds. I got vibes off him he was into May. He puffed up his chest and looked directly at her. Yeah, totally into May.

"I'll try it first. If Bram can do it, so can we."

"We can," Duke said. "I'll do it too."

Ravyn elbowed me in the ribs. Oh, man. Duke was into May too. All the male Hellhounds started chiming in that they would eat first. If they weren't looking at May, they were looking at one of the other female Hellhounds. Balthazar rested his head on my shoulder and sighed.

"I love happy endings."

"It's not over yet," Felix said. "Between Kaine and the others, I'm sure they'll get information out of the prisoners. We might have to fight again. What do you think Lucifer is doing with Gabriel?"

Everyone who wasn't here in this room was working over Akul and Dorian except Gabriel and Lucifer. Lucifer talked Gabriel into leaving because he wanted to show him something. Gabriel didn't particularly want to leave, but I got the feeling whatever Lucifer wanted to show him was important, so we all talked him into going.

"Hey! This is amazing. You should try it, May," Solomon said.

"I can feed you if you want," Duke said.

Ravyn elbowed me again. She was going to leave a mark at this rate. I was hoping May had this little Hellhound harem when this was over because I really liked her and wanted her to be happy. Both of the guys seemed unsure about how to flirt with her, and it was adorable. Everyone seemed unsure about this new freedom, but I guess watching Bram kiss me and Lilith telling them it was okay had lit a fire under them for secret crushes they might have harbored.

Pretty soon, we were all eating, and the food was delicious. It would have been good even if I had spent my entire life eating dog kibble. That was fucked up, by the way. I felt like I needed to say something, but they didn't teach classes on the feels at the academy, and even if they had, I wouldn't have taken one. Public speaking always made me feel like I was going to vomit up my internal organs.

Felix stood up like he had something to say. Yeah, Felix could handle inspirational speeches. Most of the time, he was a dick when he was giving me one, but if it wasn't my fault that time, he gave damned good pep talks. Ravyn and I just would have ruined it as soon as we opened our mouths.

"Hellhounds, I want to say something. I'm a warlock. I was created by Lilith too. I died and was brought back as another one of her creations. I came back as Ripley's familiar. The other god you met was able to give me my body back. I used to pray to Lilith, but I never put much stock in the gods before because my prayers were never really answered.

"I'm guessing all of you feel the same way considering everything we've seen since we got here. But I've gotten to know Reyson, and he gave me a second chance at life. I get what Lilith said about why she hadn't stepped in on your behalf before. Akul and his wife did a lot of nasty shit when their way of life was threatened. So many demons and many innocent Hellhounds would have died if this whole unfortunate situation hadn't kicked the door open for Lilith to get involved.

"I *know* she's going to pull this off. This is going to be a new age for Hellhounds. Don't be scared to try new things like food. Don't be afraid to say you don't *like* something. You don't have to love everything you try, but it shouldn't stop you from having experiences. Life is way too short to keep doing something you dislike. Not when you will have options now. Fall in love. Eat whatever you want. Overthrow the patriarchy just because if you like. But *live*."

Duke beamed at Felix.

"You sound like May. At night, when we were in the basement on our mats, she'd tell us things were going to be different one day. If Oscar heard her, he'd get her beaten, but she never backed down or changed her story. She was usually his target."

We all knew what that meant when it came to Oscar. She let it happen, so it didn't happen to one of the other female Hellhounds. She didn't fight back, even though she could have easily killed Oscar because Akul would have punished all the other Hellhounds in front of her before he killed her.

May was probably one of the bravest people I knew. I

was so glad all her dreams about things being better one day were about to come true.

I just seriously hoped someone wasn't about to beat it out of Akul that he was working with more demons because I really didn't feel like dealing with their wives again.

CHAPTER 32
GABRIEL

Lucifer was just weird. Enough time had passed that no one really associated my family or me with all the stories about him. Even the supernatural community believed he was ruling over the demons in Hell and handled the deals that were being cut. Fuck, even I kind of believed that.

In a way, I guess I kind of blamed him for the deal my ancestor made that seemed to dictate my entire life five hundred years later. I knew now he wasn't running anything in Hell. He was kind of the third wheel for Lilith and Samael. Lucifer honestly seemed a little lonely and happy to meet me.

I hesitated when he wanted me to leave with him. Some of that had to do with lingering resentment, but a lot of it had to do with us being needed. Kaine probably should have handled the interrogation for both of them since no one was letting Reyson melt their brains for the answers, but they were all trying.

I knew that wasn't my forte, even if there were spells in my grimoire that could have assisted with that. But, no, all those Hellhounds just looked utterly lost. They looked like they were trying to have hope but didn't want to have too much. It was like they thought not even Lilith and Reyson could change their fate.

Ripley said something to me when I hesitated that made me say yes. Lucifer had been looking at me with puppy dog eyes every time we were in the same room. He might be this ancient angel with an epic backstory, but he might actually need this moment with me more than the Hellhounds needed me right now. So I agreed to leave with him.

His estate was right next door to Lilith's. We walked over in silence, and he didn't say much when he let me inside. I looked around. There was *stunning* artwork all over the walls and beautiful sculptures everywhere. I could appreciate it as a painter. I strolled around his sitting room, taking them in.

"Who is she?" I asked.

They were all the same woman. She was lovely and whoever painted her did so with loving detail.

"My witch wife. The one who broke my heart and stayed behind with my children to stick it to my creator. I got why she did it. She was always stubborn and before her time when it came to causes. I've always wanted to go back. I wanted to see if what she always wanted came true. I didn't want to put anyone in danger if it was. My creator is petty and famous for grudges.

"I've spent all this time here painting her and my children and wondering if my legacy lived on. I wasn't expecting you to end up in Hell, but Lilith always says everything happens for a reason. I can't help but think fate involved you in this so we could meet. You look like me. I know you don't owe me anything, and you have every reason to despise me, but I was hoping you could tell me about my family."

Yeah, I could do that. And if Lucifer was an artist, we had something in common.

"I paint too. I learned how to do magical painting in high school. We found a lot of Dorian's decoy paintings, and I could decode them. I didn't know it was around his neck this entire time."

Lucifer beamed at me.

"I'd love to see your work."

I could do that too. I opened my phone and flipped to the gallery of my artwork. I offered Lucifer my phone, and he just had this look of wonder on his face as he flipped through the photos.

"This is amazing. Are these magical?"

"Most of them. Some of them are just sketches because I was in the mood to draw."

"I see how that lovely witch looks at you. Hold on to that one. If you can get her to sit for you, paint her. Capturing her beauty in a painting is like bonding."

Was I getting advice about women from Lucifer himself? It honestly wasn't bad. I had no intention of ever letting her go.

"My grandmother was a Morningstar. She kept her name and gave it to her children. She was the one who taught me how to paint. She said many people in our family history were artists."

"That makes me happy. Have there been any angels in the bunch?"

He looked like that idea absolutely terrified him. My grandmother was big on family history, and she used to tell it to me all the time. For as far back as she knew, the angels hadn't bothered us.

"Not as far as I know. At least, not as far back as my grandmother's stories went. We've all been witches and warlocks. My family hasn't been big on mixing with other species, but a few took lovers that way. There are Morningstar shifters and vampires now. There might be more, but you have a fairly large legacy on Earth."

Lucifer smiled sadly because I could tell he really wanted to meet them but didn't want to put them in danger. I was glad I did this. He was nice, and I could tell he was lonely. He hadn't introduced me to a new wife. I guess the witch he had left behind had been it for him.

"If you put that app Ripley and Balthazar have on their phones, we could keep in touch when we go back to Earth. If Bram gets to come with us, he could bring us back here for visits. I'm sure he'll want to come back to talk to Talvath. We could all have dinner."

"You'd do that?"

"Well, yeah. I'm not a monster, and you're my family. You weren't the one that made the deal, and you didn't make him. All you did was leave for your own safety. You tried to do what was right for your family. I know that. I'd love to keep in touch."

That was the truth. I needed this just as much as Lucifer did.

"Can I be honest with you about something, Gabriel? I *know* Talvath and Lilith will want Bram to go back with you, especially since everyone there loves him. It's the next stage in his journey. I think Bram knows that too, deep down. He might not want to leave, though. There's quite a lot of work to be done with the Hellhounds still. It's not enough just to free them. There's housing, jobs, and education. Bram is probably one of the few Hellhounds here who can read and write.

"I know what all of you want. I know what Lilith and Talvath want. I love happy endings and want one here. But, in the end, the final decision is Bram's. He could do a lot of good if he stayed here for a little while helping out. The Hellhounds are looking to him for answers. I'm not trying to be mean, and I think he deserves love and happiness. But, unfortunately, his life may end up like mine where he has to leave those he loves behind."

I shook my head. He didn't know Ripley, and this wasn't an era without cellphones and apps like when he had to leave. Ripley and Reyson had both claimed Bram.

"Ripley and Reyson aren't going to stop Bram if he wants to stay here and help, but you don't know them like I do. They can and will make a long-distance relationship work until Bram can come back to the library. Ripley is dedicated to her library, but she'll find a way to help Bram. I can't picture Reyson getting and keeping any type of job. He takes his snack seriously, but he's also very caring, considering he's the God of Chaos.

"Even if Bram chooses the library, I wouldn't be shocked if you find Reyson wanting to come back and help. Shit, Felix doesn't even have a social security number, and the records for his birth and death might not exist anymore. He'll probably unvelcro himself from Ripley's side to help. Balthazar can probably write an app to help. *I'll* help."

"You're a pretty great warlock, Gabriel, and I like the people you made into your new family. I know it means nothing, but I'm proud of you."

I grabbed Lucifer and pulled him into a hug because it *did* mean something to me. My grandmother was the only person in my family who had ever said that to me. My parents just wanted me to accept the way things were and keep my head down. They didn't want me to fight to change things. My parents wanted me to take a boring job with humans like they did.

What I did for work bothered them, even if I was doing exactly what they created me to do with magic handed down from my family through the ages. Lucifer rebelled and broke the rules. He wasn't an obedient little angel accepting the status quo.

I didn't come here for a pat on the back or because I thought it would change a damned thing for me. I came because it was the right thing to do. *That* was what Lucifer was proud of, but I knew if I told him I was trying to fight back against a community that would shun me in whatever ways I could, I knew not only would he be proud of that too, he'd probably want to help.

Ripley was right. She usually was. I needed this just as much as Lucifer did.

CHAPTER 33
REYSON

Dorian Gray was an irritating little monkey. Rich people back in my day liked to keep them as pets as a sign of their status, but they always tried to domesticate the wrong type of monkey. Some of the bigger apes were wonderful and had ways to communicate. However, some of the smaller monkeys could have been created by a trickster god because as soon as you took them out of the jungle and invited them into your home, they started flinging feces and pulling hair. Dorian Gray was definitely one of the poop slinging monkeys.

Kaine was running in between the rooms we had Dorian and Akul in. Talvath, Lilith, and Bram were handling Akul, which left me with Dorian. Honestly, this could have been solved in five minutes if they had let me, but they wanted them alive for some reason. The *only* reason I was holding back after I found my witch in a cage was that this wasn't my realm and Bram's future and the future of every Hellhound here rested on whatever the fuck Lilith's long game plan was.

I knew Dorian's portrait that gave him immortality was

around his neck now, but I hadn't removed it. Mainly so I could take out some rage on his face without killing him.

"It's over, Dorian. This plot of yours failed. Tell me what I need to know. Who did you give those sigils to?"

Dorian smiled through all the blood on his teeth.

"You think I didn't take into account that if Akul was willing to betray his people that he was also going to stab me in the back? I still have an ace up my sleeve."

If this smug little asshole thought he had *anything* that would manipulate Lilith or me into letting him go, he had another thought coming. We crashed his little party when he tried that the first time. I was *done* with Dorian Gray and his ego.

"This is how things are going to go, Dorian. Perhaps your mommy spoiled you and told you that you could do anything you wanted because you were destined for greatness. Perhaps all those people who celebrated you for making that deal and told you how pretty you were made you think you could piss off two gods and still get what you want. Unfortunately, there is no card you could possibly play here.

"You'll notice I left your portrait around your neck, so I don't kill you. Lilith wants you alive. I have this neat little trick and a theory. You see, I can just put my hand on your head and find out *everything* I need to know. It has an unfortunate side effect of totally liquifying your brain. Now, this is just a theory, but I think necklace will keep you alive through all of that. You'll feel everything. I would imagine regrowing an entire brain while your body heals would be *agonizing.* Still glad you raised the God of Chaos, Dorian? Still think it was a good idea to kidnap my witch and put her in a cage? You have nothing. You can tell me, or I can take it as painfully as possible."

He was still smirking. I was a fucking god. I helped create the entire universe. I *earned* my massive ego. What did Dorian Gray actually do that he thought I wasn't totally serious about any of that? I had a feeling Lilith wanted him alive because she had something much worse planned for him than what I was thinking. I hoped we could collaborate on that because I had some good ideas.

"Hear me out and pass this on to Lilith."

I would let him finish, but I was probably going to melt his brain anyway because he kept pissing me off.

"I had been getting witches to summon demons other than Talvath trying to find one to get me out of my deal. Then, I met Silvaria. She had also made a deal for prestige and power. We worked nonstop until we found one who put us in contact with Akul. Akul and I came up with this together, and Silvaria wouldn't stop bitching that I cut her out of it.

"We didn't just raise you to kill demons and break contracts. You were our insurance policy against Lilith in case she investigated all the demons dying and got close to Akul.

"Akul had a condition that I didn't give those sigils out to anyone. I was already fairly certain he intended to betray me when this was over, but I didn't want to give him cause. I needed Silvaria and her connections to the supernatural community to make the promises Akul wanted me to make for his hit list.

"She can be insufferably needy and whiny. I wasn't about to use any of my properties to hide Talvath. Even one buried under shell corporations could be traced back to me. The only way she would let us use her warehouse was if we shared the sigils with her.

"I made her do a blood oath not to share them with

anyone, but I took out my own insurance policy. I have all those sigils on a cloud server. If I'm not returned to Earth unharmed, one of my associates will release them to everyone I contacted who made a deal. They'll just torture them until they find out how to kill them and get out of their deals."

I was done with this nonsense. I might be new to this century and things like the internet, but I knew what the cloud was. I also knew it was an online thing that required those complicated passwords like the social media site Balthazar tried to set up for me. I also knew that even if Dorian Gray managed to pick a password those infernal sites actually accepted, Balthazar had ways of figuring it out.

I walked over and punched that smug look off Dorian's face. I felt some of his teeth break and cut my hand, but I didn't care. Dorian's head snapped back, and he slumped in his seat. I was still going to melt his brain later, but according to everyone, he was all over social media, which meant his cell phone was always close.

Dorian was dressed in this ridiculous suit that was now tattered and bloody since I'd been beating on him and blasting him with magic because he took my witch. His cell phone was in the front pocket in some kind of battle armor that saved it from my attacks.

Just then, Kaine came in.

"Anything? Akul is still being a petulant child because Bram ate his wife."

"Dorian's ego is good for something. He thought he could blackmail his way out of this. He seems to have forgotten there's not a cloud server in existence that is safe from Balthazar. Can you watch him while I get Balthazar his phone? I punched him pretty hard. He won't wake up until he heals. I have information for Lilith."

"Didn't he have a camera planted in Ripley's apartment? So he knew damned well Balthazar was a gifted hacker, and he still kept that on a cloud server? I would have gone with paper copies in a safe deposit box after seeing that boy in action."

"Dorian Gray has a bigger ego than some of the gods I know with much bigger resumes. He legitimately believed revealing a cloud server was going to get Lilith to let him walk out of here, and Balthazar would never find it."

"Get the phone to Balthazar and go tell Lilith what he revealed. All Akul is doing is flinging profanities at Bram for his wife."

I shrugged. She had it coming. I wouldn't be mad if Bram ate Akul either. I don't think anyone would. But we needed to find out who connected Dorian and Akul in the first place.

I could always test that theory about Dorian's necklace protecting him from a little brain melting. Nothing would give me more satisfaction.

CHAPTER 34
BRAM

I wasn't sure why I was asked to be here. I also wasn't sure why they wouldn't let me leave. Lilith tried getting into Akul's head by informing him that me and an army of Hellhounds ripped his wife, her friends, and his prized Hellhound apart. I got what she was doing. She was trying to break him, but it wasn't working.

Talvath didn't exactly raise me in the arts of interrogating criminals. He taught me to speak for myself and have my own opinions. My opinion on this was that it would go much smoother with me out of the room. Honestly, no one should have been in the room except Kaine. Kaine did this for a living, and he made his point when he ripped the roof of Akul's house and flung him into the sky.

"Who is involved in this plot, Akul?" Talvath snapped.

"I should have given Dorian the tools to kill you when you were captured," Akul spat. "That was my intention all along, but the pretty boy didn't want to get his hands dirty, and he didn't think he could spin this to people on Earth if they actually had to fight for their lives."

I let out a little growl. I really just wanted to rip his head off like I had done his wife. Talvath was the epitome of cool. He looked like he was utterly bored, but I knew better. He was pissed and holding it in. That was the best way to piss off Akul.

"It was pretty stupid to partner up with a vain human, Akul. I'm just curious how you found him. I've made deals with countless people, but he's the only human. You could have picked a more powerful being who actually asked for greater magic instead of wanting to be pretty for as long as possible. Honestly, I'm a little shocked at the stupidity behind all this."

"Fuck you!"

"Bram didn't kill your wife, Akul. You did. You were the one with this massive assassination plot. We would have tried to talk her down when she came to defend you, but all your Hellhounds said she was pretty awful and probably in on it. She attacked Lilith, you know."

"Lilith attacked me first! In my own home!"

Lilith just let out a merry laugh.

"You attacked my creations long before we descended upon your home. You were going to kill demons so you could continue to abuse Hellhounds, and you had a witch in a cage."

"Fuck you too!"

We weren't getting anywhere. Akul was a belligerent little asshole who didn't think he did anything wrong. We needed something more extreme. Like, god extreme, but Lilith just seemed to want to taunt him.

The door kicked open, and Reyson strolled in. Kaine came in shortly after. Reyson cut his eyes to Kaine.

"I thought you were watching Dorian?"

"Felix wanted ten minutes alone with him when I

brought Dorian's phone to Balthazar. I think he's angrier about this than any of you. You might all be into Ripley, but he's known her longer. I think Ravyn is also dying to get her hands on him, but she's trying to help the Hellhounds right now. Let me handle this."

That was where I needed to be right now. I needed to be with all those traumatized Hellhounds that came back with us. I wasn't a soldier, and I wasn't a cop. I got Lilith was playing some sort of long game here, but at the same time, what about those Hellhounds?

"I should be with them," I said.

Reyson pulled me to his side and wrapped his arm around my waist.

"Give it ten minutes, okay?"

That seemed to set Akul off more than anything. Two guys snuggling is that pissed him off? Seriously? Then, I remember. All he thought my dick was good for was making pups for him to profit off of. Maybe I was a petty little asshole and *could* be of use here.

I pulled Reyson into a kiss. He crushed me to his chest and his tongue tangled with mine. He could certainly kiss. He knew why I was kissing him and put on this big show. I was big, but Reyson was massive. He practically bent me backwards he was kissing me so hard. We just kept going as Akul totally lost it.

He started fighting the bonds that tied him to his chair and shrieking in rage. Akul was angrier about me kissing Reyson than he was I murdered his wife. Reyson pulled away and nipped at my earlobe.

"I have plans for you later, and so does Ripley," he purred, setting me on my feet.

Lilith waved her hand, and Akul got this massive shock and went still.

"Hush. There's nothing wrong with a little bisexuality. You aren't allowed to get offended by that in my presence. Kaine? You had an idea."

"Yes, I did."

Kaine's eyes turned gold, and his pupils went to slits. His skin broke out into hardened scales, and he blew smoke out of his nose. Finally, Kaine got right in Akul's face.

"Your boy broke. He always intended to betray you. He put the sigils you gave him on a cloud server. I'm sure you thought you were going to kill him when this was over, but he had a backup plan. He spilled all kinds of details to Reyson."

Seriously? That could be detrimental to all of Hell. Reyson knew that, but he didn't seem worried. He knew something I didn't. He let go of me and went to join Kaine.

"I know you were connected to Silvaria and Dorian through another demon. They summoned several before they got one who connected them to you. Who was that demon?" Reyson growled.

"Give me a minute," Kaine said, marching out of the room.

What now? I already knew Akul wouldn't talk. I might not be a cop, a god, or a high-level demon, but I knew that. The only thing keeping him alive was the information he had. And he was being pretty fucking arrogant like he thought someone was coming to rescue him.

Akul settled into his chair and smiled at Reyson. I hadn't gone to some fancy demon university like he had, but I wasn't even remotely that stupid. Reyson's fist snapped out and connected with his nose.

"Don't smirk at me!" he roared.

Every painting on the wall shook. Akul slumped in his chair and was knocked the fuck out. Lilith didn't seem remotely worried, and I didn't know why. Akul had been sitting there pretty smug while we all fired questions at him. I could have easily torn him apart. Talvath knew enough magic to kill him. Lilith made him. She could easily unmake him. He was acting like this was just an inconvenience.

"He's been stalling this entire time," I said. "He thinks someone is coming to save him."

"That's why Samael isn't here," Lilith said. "The destruction to Akul's estate is pretty obvious, as are the dead bodies we left behind. He's called a meeting of everyone in that neighborhood. My honey is a trained soldier and was created to hone in on deception. He's also quite good at creating it, though he'd never do that with me. If Akul wasn't working alone, Samael is finding that out now, and they won't be breaking things in my house."

Kaine came back in with Balthazar trailing behind him as Akul was stirring. Kaine smacked Balthazar on the back so hard, he nearly face planted right into Lilith.

"The data on the cloud is gone. I can't believe he was dumb enough to keep it online, *knowing* Balthazar can hack anything. Even if it were on the cloud, I would have gone with hard copies in a safe deposit box if I was going to try to drop it like a bomb to try to blackmail two gods."

Balthazar smirked at us. Honestly, he had every reason to go on a bragging spree right now because those sigils just *could not* fall into the wrong hands.

"I couldn't read his messages before because they weren't being backed up to the cloud, but I have them now. Dorian wasn't just messaging with Akul. Vegran was part of this too. Those were the only messages with details only someone in the know could have. The messages with Silvaria have a lot, but Dorian left things out. The person with access to his cloud server is named Hank, but there's nothing there anymore."

"And I was banking on that when I had one of my agents pull Silvaria from her cell for further questioning," Kaine boomed. "Dorian Gray has plenty of properties. If you weren't planning on throwing someone under the bus, the logical thing would be to rent something at that yard under a fake name and pay with cash. The people who own it probably give zero fucks about that as long as they get their money. So I put her in front of my best sirens to inform her of that and ramp up her emotions."

"Did it work?" Talvath asked.

"It's still an ongoing conversation, but my agent let it slip about the hidden cameras in Ripley's apartment and that Dorian would have known she was going to be arrested. She's happy to spill her guts, even without the threat I had in my pocket of us telling Lilith. Anyway, the demon that hooked up Silvaria and Dorian with Akul and Vegran is named Salgrak. She said he was really young and offered to put feelers out for the right price. Between Silvaria and Dorian, he made a killing. I'm guessing he took money from Akul too."

"He's not in Dorian's phone," Balthazar said. "He might just be a greedy fuck who didn't think they were going to take it this far."

"I know he is," Talvath said. "Not everyone is cut out for being in the deals and soul collection business. The first few years after you get hired are pretty brutal. It's commission only. Not everyone is willing to make deals, and even if they are, it's not a guarantee you're the one getting summoned. The ones who want to stick it out until it becomes a well-paying job resort to all kinds of things. Most normal demons just work harder and get a second job, but we have all types here."

"Fixing your sun is going to take care of a lot of long-term problems and prevent something like this from happening again, but it's going to put a lot of demons out of work," Reyson said.

"Good," Talvath said. "The soul collection business was only beneficial to Hell because it kept our sun alive. It didn't bring any money into our economy, and the job has always drawn two types of people. I took this job, and many other people did it for the good of the realm. Many other people took it because giving people their darkest desires for their souls was a power trip for them. Personally, I'd rather it be fixed. I'd rather move into a new position educating the Hellhounds that will be free. You know we have not taught them to read or write."

Lilith looked down at her phone like we all weren't in the middle of a shit storm. She waved her hand, and another door appeared. Samael came marching through with two demons slung across his shoulder. He dumped them at Lilith's feet, and she conjured ropes to bind them.

"These two got squirrely when I was giving my speech. If they aren't in on it, they agree with him and are plotting a jailbreak."

"Now that we have that information, I think I'm going to go melt Dorian's brain. If I leave his necklace on, it won't kill him. You'd better have something epic for these two because Dorian kidnapped my witch, and Akul turned Bram's twin into a monster. I have opinions about that," Reyson said, stalking off.

"Keep going through Dorian's phone, Balthazar. Kaine, keep in touch with your people. I doubt we will get much from Akul and Dorian, but Hell hath no fury like a woman scorned, and we might get more information from the witch they manipulated. Akul might have sympathizers, but I'm sure he kept this to himself. Even other extremists would draw the line at giving those sigils out, knowing how people on Earth distrust demons. Humans have their own misconceptions about this realm. Someone with a grudge could partner up with humans to try to wipe everyone here out, even if they don't work in deals."

I doubted that. I knew everyone was capable of evil no matter what realm you lived in. I saw pure evil when I looked at Akul. I saw it when I looked at my twin brother. If Akul could turn someone who shared my DNA and *should* look at him like an oppressor, I was guessing he could spin this to other extremists.

Balthazar slung his arm around my shoulder and led me out of the room.

"These assholes aren't going to say anything else today if they say anything at all. Ripley misses you, and so do all the Hellhounds. Felix gave them a pep talk, but he's a cat and might be their mortal enemy like cats and dogs on Earth."

This was what I wanted this entire time, but it didn't feel like we were done. But they were right. Akul and Dorian weren't going to talk. Their silence was the only thing keeping them alive. Reyson was holding back because of Lilith, but something told me what she had planned was even worse.

They didn't need me, but the Hellhounds did.

CHAPTER 35
RIPLEY

I couldn't help it. As soon as I saw Bram again, I flung myself at him and nuzzled his neck. I missed that fucking Hellhound. I knew Reyson had gotten something out of Dorian and took his phone. Balthazar had deleted his blackmail material, and Felix left to go wail on him.

Felix came back in spattered in blood shortly after, but where was Reyson? We were all finally together except Reyson. Reyson finally strolled in and tossed his long hair over his shoulder.

"My theory was correct. If I melted his brain while he was wearing the locket, it didn't kill him. He did scream like a little bitch. I got what I needed. Dorian and Akul had a conversation about how they thought this would play out. Akul intended on murdering everyone who didn't agree with him and then framing a demon named Mastrang as the traitor. Does anyone know that one?"

Talvath started laughing.

"Samael knocked him out and brought him in here. He

was one of two demons that were acting like they were going to try to rally an army to free Akul. If you tell him that, he'll fill in pieces on Akul's other crimes."

"We can do that tomorrow," Lilith said. "It's late, and everyone is tired. We should go to bed. We can pick this up in the morning."

Reyson started nudging Bram and me closer together. What was he up to?

"Ripley and Bram will share a bed tonight," he announced.

Ah. That. He was playing matchmaker. May stepped forward and looked a little uncertain.

"Can the rest of us share beds if we want to?"

I hoped she had a *really* hot Hellhound threesome tonight. I hoped the rest of them got some lovin' too. They deserved it. All the Hellhounds looked like they had someone they wanted to pair up with. I might step on Lilith's toes, but I didn't care. I poked Ravyn in the side, and she nodded at me.

"My twin and I can do birth control magic, so you don't get pregnant. It will wear off in six months unless it's replaced. So you can have all the happy fun bangs you want tonight and not worry about pups."

All the Hellhounds started nodding, and Lilith just stepped forwards.

"It's already taken care of. I did it as soon as you said you wanted it. Ladies, who do you think wrote that spell?" she said, winking at us.

Everyone left to the rooms Lilith gave them. Balthazar pinched my ass and nipped at my ear.

"Don't do anything I wouldn't."

I noticed Balthazar and Reyson leaving together. I was glad. I was getting good at noticing when he needed blood.

He always got this little tic below his left eye. He hadn't fed since he bit Reyson during our little orgy, and we'd been working nonstop since then. Reyson was perfectly happy to let Balthazar bite him, and I was sure they'd be having a grand kinky time tonight.

I sighed when I saw Ravyn and Killian going towards separate bedrooms. She turned to watch him as he walked down the hall. Once this was over, I was planning on having a come to Lilith talk with my twin. What was she waiting on? She clearly liked him. This had better not be about Valentine. Since when had she waited to go after a guy she liked?

Bram came up behind me and wrapped his arms around my waist.

"I missed snuggling with you when we left."

I whirled around and kissed him. Now that he had kissed me, he couldn't take it back. I expected a lot more kisses.

"Then we had better do it again just to be safe."

Bram gently scooped me up and carried me down the hallway. He nudged a door open with his foot and kicked it closed. Bram walked straight to the bed with me and set me down.

"This is the room Lilith gave me. It's not like mine, but it's nice."

I snuggled into his chest. He just felt so nice.

"Are you kidding me? I make good money at the library, and just that chandelier costs more than ten years of my salary. Thank you, Bram. I'd still be in that cage if it weren't for you."

"I did nothing, Ripley. Talvath was the one who got us to Lilith's house."

I pinched his nipple to get his attention because he

totally did. Bram let out a little growl and nipped at my nose.

"Don't start something you can't finish, Ripley."

"Who said that wasn't also in my plans tonight, Bram? You can't introduce yourself to a girl by telling her your cock is pierced and not follow through. But I did want to talk first. How are you dealing with all of this? I called you because I was hoping you would team up with the guys at the library to get me out. I wasn't expecting Lilith and a Hellhound revolution, but I'm glad it ended this way."

"It's honestly fucked up. I was at Lilith's place, but I wasn't in the meeting she was having with Talvath. So when I saw your number on the caller ID, I knew the only way you could be calling me was if you had gotten your hands on the app that let you call between realms. I was sure Dorian had it, but there was no way for *you* to get it without being here. When you told me Dorian kidnapped you and brought you here, I just lost it. I kicked the door in. She could have killed me."

"I've lost track of how many times I've prayed to Lilith. I have candles and offerings to her on my altar. After you told us she was in Hell and retired, it kind of shattered my faith. Still, old habits die hard, and I fired off a little prayer that you'd pick up before I called. I'm pretty sure she was expecting you."

Bram chuckled.

"That wouldn't shock me because she didn't seem surprised in the slightest. We have seers here that Lilith created. I know Reyson can see possibilities because of what he does as a god, but it wouldn't shock me if Lilith knew all of this would happen and let it play out the way it did because it was the only way to free the Hellhounds without a civil war. Reyson has been angrier about this than Lilith is. I think the only reason he hasn't killed anyone is mutual respect."

"Reyson's possibilities have never been wrong. I thought he was insane when he told me I would be his wife when I first raised him, but he's probably right about that one. He's mine now. He was the one whispering in my ear to keep everyone who showed up and got all-access library cards long before I realized the library was trying to tell me something. He kept saying he had a bad feeling about splitting up when they went to grab Dorian. We were worried about Talvath coming back with an army of demons because of what happened to him. I had been texting you, but I didn't know about the app."

"Seriously? Talvath is against war, even in situations like what Dorian and Silvaria did to him. He thought *we* were in danger from *you*. I kept trying to convince him to go back and work with you, but I honestly think he was afraid of you. The only thing that would have gotten him back was a vision from his seer telling him it was necessary. Visions can't be forced, so he managed to get an audience with Lilith."

"I'm pretty much big mad about the fact that a vain human was able to get the jump on me and put me in a cage, but witches know everything happens for a reason. It had to play out this way, and maybe the cosmos decided I was getting a little arrogant with that many sexy men in my life and decided to give me a little perspective by sticking me in a cage. Still, it rewarded me because it made *this* possible."

"What do you intend to do with this possibility?"

Oh, Bram was taunting a witch. Did he think since he

was a Hellhound, I would let him get away with that? I graduated top of my class in high school and at the Academy of the Profane, but I would totally fling a little sexual goading at a Hellhound if it got me what I wanted.

I shifted my body so that I was straddling Bram. I yanked his shirt up and raked my nails down his amazing abs. Bram groaned as I ground myself into his cock.

"Keep it as long as I can. I know you'll be needed here with the Hellhounds. We'll all help as much as we can because *you* deserve happiness too. You're one of us, and I'm claiming you as mine. If I have to make this work long distance, I will, but I'd love to have you in the library with us, and so would everyone else."

"This isn't over yet, Ripley. Let's table that discussion when I don't have a hot librarian on my junk."

Bram grabbed my hips and flipped me on my back. He ran his nose up my neck and nipped at my jaw.

"I'm an apex predator. I hope you didn't think I was going to let you be on top our first time."

"Dude, apex predator yourself all over my vagina," I growled, pulling him down for a kiss.

"I might break you, little witch. The god would get mad."

"Pssh. I've had several threesomes with Reyson and Balthazar, and nothing got broken. I loved every minute of it. I like it rough," I purred, reaching between us to rub his cock. There was *a lot* of promise there.

"Oh, really?" he asked, nibbling on my collarbone.

"It would mean a lot to Reyson to have a threesome with you and me."

I was just throwing that out there. It wasn't just that Reyson asked me about it and was obsessed with it since reading the entire fiction section in the Library of the

Profane. I knew Reyson really cared for Bram the same way he did Balthazar. He cared for Felix and Gabriel, too, just in different ways. Was Bram even into that kind of thing? I was usually good at picking up vibes, and so were Reyson and Balthazar.

"Reyson is insanely attractive and an excellent kisser."

"Wait, you kissed Reyson?"

Where the fuck was I when that happened? It was probably sexy as hell. Why wasn't I invited?

"Reyson missed me when I was gone, and he was grateful I made it possible for him to get here and help rescue you. He showed his appreciation with a big wet kiss."

Oh, yeah. I was in a fucking cage when that went down. As if I needed another reason to murder Dorian Gray. I didn't want to think about that. I wanted Bram naked. There were many different options for cock piercings. I was *dying* to know what he had.

I snapped my fingers and removed our clothes so that they were neatly folded on the dresser.

"That's a handy trick," Bram said between furious kisses.

"You've never been with a witch before?"

"Once, but she preferred me ripping her clothes off. After I got my cock cursed trying to collect payment from a witch, I decided not to risk it again."

I bit his bottom lip.

"When I have access to my closets and am not just existing in the clothes they kidnapped in me, it would be sexy as fuck to have you destroy my clothes just to fuck me."

"Shut up, Ripley," Bram growled.

He took my nipple in his mouth and bit down. His

thumb found my clit and started making slow circles. Oh, Lilith, he knew what he was doing. I wanted him to keep going, but he was the one that announced his cock was pierced, and I couldn't see it. He was covered in tattoos, and I wanted to see those too. Bram was beautiful. I just wanted to take him in for a minute.

"Wait, wait," I said. "Let me look at you for a minute and appreciate you. I know now those aren't just tattoos on your skin. You're beautiful, and I want to stare."

Bram sat back on his haunches, and I sat up. He was beautiful the way sharks are beautiful. He had this air of danger about him, and I'd seen him kill. But I'd also seen his soul. I saw it when we stayed up all night talking, and he offered to bake Felix a cake when I forgot his birthday. I saw it the way he got the Hellhounds to rally and fight back.

He was covered in tattoos. They differed from the demon women at Akul's estate. They just put their sigils anywhere. Bram's were hidden in this amazing artwork. You had to look twice to find them. Bram's entire body was a work of art. I traced my hand down the dragon on his chest until my fingers rested on his nipple piercings.

"I'm guessing you didn't get these in Hell. There are probably some shitty rules about it."

"There are, but Talvath doesn't care about those. He's a gifted artist. I told him what I wanted, and he did them. Do you really want to talk about my tattoos?"

"No. I wanted you to look at me so I could tell you how special you are. I knew it that night we spent together just talking and snuggling, and you offered to make Felix's cake. I'm a beast at making any potion or salve, and I'm a decent cook unless it involves baking. I would have ruined that cake. Felix shows affection by being a dick. I can't remember if he was mean to you or not, but you offered anyway. It meant a lot. Now, show me your cock piercing."

Bram fell out laughing and gripped his cock.

"Talvath gives me inspirational speeches like that, but he never asks to see my junk at the end. It would be weird if he did. I like it when you do it."

"Oh, shit. You didn't just get your cock pierced. You went for the full Jacob's Ladder ribbed for her pleasure mother of all cock piercings. I rarely see one of those out in the wild. I'd give you ten stars on Yelp just for getting your cock pierced that many times just to please a woman. Get that over here and put it inside me."

Bram winked at me.

"Don't forget the knot Reyson is so obsessed with."

"You might be my new favorite sex toy, Bram."

"Then, I'd better make this good."

Bram pounced. I felt every single barbell that lined the underside of his cock as he slid into me. Man, did that boy have some girth. I was humming with pleasure when he was finally fully inside me. Bram gripped my hair, and I was all about the hair pulling.

Bram started thrusting hard and fast. I felt the pressure and pleasure as his knot grew. Between the knot and the barbells, it was hitting my G spot in all the right places. I clawed his arms and bit his shoulder. I wasn't fucking in my library where no one could hear me. I needed to muffle that shit, so I didn't traumatize the Hellhounds. Something told me Lilith wouldn't mind.

Bram made that really hard. He was a total beast in bed. Talvath clearly gave him a lot of vacation time on Earth to experiment sexually. I came so hard, I nearly blacked out. Bram's knot grew to its maximum, and he stopped moving.

He grunted and crushed his lips on mine. We were

going to be stuck like this unless he came soon. I clamped down on his cock and shifted my hips. Bram buried his face in my neck and bit my shoulder as he came. We stayed like that for a bit while his knot went down. He collapsed on his back and yanked me to his chest. I snuggled in and sighed.

Now more than ever, I was going to fight as hard as I could to make this work with Bram.

RIPLEY

I was still on my library schedule, so I was awake early. Bram woke up when I did, but we were still the last people awake. Everyone seemed to be waiting on us? Lilith handed Bram a smoothie and gave him a look.

"We have work to do. The rest of you turn on the television. Reyson, with me."

Lilith conjured another door. Reyson and Bram just shrugged at me and stepped through. Talvath and Samael followed. Lucifer was still with us. He slung his arm around Gabriel's shoulder and started leading us out of the room.

"Right this way, babies. Ripley, there's a smoothie for you on the table."

I had no idea what was going on, but I grabbed my cup and followed them. Felix and Ravyn flanked me.

"What's happening?" I whispered.

"No idea," Ravyn said. "We all ate breakfast alone, except Lucifer was here. Lilith and Samael were missing until about five minutes before you came in. She wasn't fucking around."

"Don't we still need to be beating information out of Dorian and Akul?" Felix said.

"No," Balthazar said. "Samael went back and got me Akul's electronics. Reyson and I have been awake all night going through them and Dorian's phone. Between that and what Kaine's minion got out of Silvaria, we don't need them."

"I still want to beat on Dorian," Felix grunted.

"I owe Dorian too. He kidnapped my twin."

"I get the feeling Lilith has something worse planned," Killian said. "Even worse than you, Ravyn."

"Not possible. I've never been this pissed before. Pity all my toys are back at the museum."

"Hello? I'm the one he gassed and stuck in a cage. I'm more pissed than any of you."

"If it makes you feel any better, Silvaria is pretty pissed at him too," Kaine said. "Reyson told me most of what Dorian said about her when he threatened to melt his brain. I made sure it got passed along. She didn't just rat him out about everything she knew about this plot. She told us about every other shady deal she knew about."

"Please tell me that wasn't part of a plea bargain, and it's going to get her a lighter sentence," I said.

"Silvaria may have been greedy enough to make a deal with a demon and dumb enough to be taken in by Dorian, but she's not completely stupid. A lot of prominent supernaturals went down with her because she brought attention to that warehouse. She'd get eaten alive if she got a lesser sentence than they did. Silvaria knows she's safer in jail. Her only demand is to be in a different prison than all her colleagues that were arrested at the bank."

"That miserable cunt corrupted my library. I don't care if she gets stabbed with a toothbrush in prison," I growled.

"Take it out on Dorian because you aren't getting anywhere near Silvaria now that she's in my custody. The only reason I'm not demanding Dorian come back with me is that it's a jurisdictional nightmare because of him being human. Everyone knows he made a deal because he blabbed about it to a writer and everyone knows you can't get out of them. I put it out that I went to Hell to rescue Ripley, but I think pretty much everyone expects me to leave Dorian to the demons."

"What was on those electronics?" I demanded.

"A lot of blackmail material on demons, a weird manifesto explaining his actions where he tried to take sole credit for this mess and painting himself the hero. I wanted to take a shower after reading it. Lilith has a copy. As soon as she read it, she said she had a plan, but she didn't exactly tell me what it was."

"Well, she has Reyson and Bram with her, so it had better be safe."

"It is," Lucifer said. "Sit down and watch a goddess at work, babies. Lilith called a press conference."

We all piled on the couches in Lilith's entertainment room. I snuggled with Felix and Gabriel. Several of the Hellhounds were cuddling and looked totally into it. I sighed because my sister and her familiar were sitting about as far apart as possible, but they kept sneaking glances at everyone else like they wanted to move closer, but their stupid heads were getting in the way. Since when did my sister let her brain get in the way of a guy she liked? It was going to be explosive when those two finally got together.

And a press conference? She was going to put Bram and Reyson in front of a bunch of demon reporters who didn't like outsiders? I hoped she knew what she was doing. They couldn't hurt Reyson, but he would get pissed if they tried.

The sigils tattooed on the Real Housewives of Hell seemed to bounce off Bram, and I could thank Talvath for that. Reyson would be just as protective of Bram as he was of me.

"I hope Lilith knows what she's doing because two of my guys are out there with her."

Lilith didn't tell any of *us* what she was up to, and she didn't tell Bram when she roped him into this, but Lucifer seemed to know.

"You didn't read Akul's manifesto, Ripley," Lucifer said. "It was terrible. It was the rantings of a terrorist trying to justify betraying their people, murdering anyone who didn't agree with them, and abusing living beings. Even if someone agreed with keeping Hellhounds as slaves, they aren't going to agree with that tripe. All the reporters have it. Every politician in Hell has it. Any influential demon who might want Hellhound slavery to continue has it in their inbox. Add to that, Lilith doing a press conference is a major event. Everyone will be watching. She knows what she is doing."

"She'd better because I'm just as protective of my men as they are of me. And if you think Reyson just goes all psycho alpha over me, that extended to all of us. If anyone there tries to hurt Bram, you aren't going to have to worry about him shifting and killing anyone because Reyson is going to do it on everyone's television screens."

"It's not going to come to that, Ripley. Lilith knows what she's doing. I get you haven't known her as long as you've known Reyson, but I've known her for a very long time. Lilith is a cunning strategist. She knows when to fight and when to walk away. If she's fighting now, it's because she *knows* she's going to win."

Lucifer had a lot of faith in Lilith, but many of us in this room had every reason to doubt her. Yeah, she answered one prayer of mine, but I was in my thirties. That was a lot of prayers she *didn't* answer. I'm sure every Hellhound here prayed a lot more than I ever did and for much more terrible situations. So yeah, she was stepping in *now,* and we all appreciated it, but after everything I had learned so far, my faith was just a bit shattered.

Lucifer started flipping through the channels. I could see an empty podium or a newscaster on every single one. What was he looking for? Any one of these would do.

"Sorry, they pay some of these stations to be shitty. They don't report *all* the news. They pick and choose what's going to rile up their base the most. You can bet your ass if *anyone* but Lilith called a press conference about that manifesto, they wouldn't be there covering it."

"The news is like that on Earth too, but people like to put their own spin on it."

"That's illegal here. News is supposed to be presented propaganda free, but people get around it by only focusing on certain news. This one is a good station. They cover everything."

If we weren't getting shitty commentary from any of these people, then any station would have done. I got why it bothered him, but was that really what we needed to be worried about right now?

I saw Lilith take the podium. Reyson, Bram, Talvath, and Samael flanked her in the back. I'd been throwing shade at her in my head like she wasn't perfectly capable of wiping me from existence. She had just been so relaxed about this entire situation, even when the Hellhounds were ripping apart all those demons.

Lilith looked pretty damned frightening right now as she glared at the cameras. Remind me never to mouth off to her like I did to Reyson. The way she was giving the stink eye to the camera, I got the feeling she wouldn't give a shit what Reyson would do to her if I made her reach the level of pisstivity she was at right now.

She opened her mouth and just unloaded. She graphically described what happened to Talvath that I didn't know because he was passed out at the library, and I didn't ask Bram when I finally had him alone. I should have asked because no one deserved what Silvaria and Dorian did to him.

I wanted to kill Dorian. Everyone who cared about me wanted to kill him for kidnapping me. Aside from a lot of discomfort from the gas and trying to use me to manipulate Reyson, he hadn't harmed me at all compared to what he did to Talvath. He needed me alive and unharmed if he had any hope of his plan working. Both Dorian *and* Akul wanted Talvath dead, and they treated him as such while he was their captive.

"Talvath would still be in that kind of torment if it weren't for his Hellhound. Some of you are aware of why Talvath has one in the first place. Bram is right here. You can see that he's clean, dressed how *he* likes to dress, and he's decorated his body how he sees fit. Bram differs from most of the Hellhounds here. He's not a slave, and he's not a pet.

"He was raised like a family member. So, when Talvath didn't come back after a routine soul collection, he did what family does. He used every resource available to him to get Talvath home safely. Unfortunately, none of your Hellhounds would give you the same courtesy because you treat them like garbage.

"Bram allied with people on Earth, and it was needed because of the sigils Akul gave Dorian. They would have weakened him too. So a Hellhound not only saved the life of one demon, but he also saved countless lives here in Hell.

"Akul had a hit list. He fully intended on murdering anyone who wanted the Hellhounds to be free. But, I want you to know something else. Demons mistrust people on Earth, and they mistrust us because of our deals. Akul had every intention of turning on Dorian Gray, and Dorian knew that.

"Every sigil Akul gave him that could trap a demon and hurt them was uploaded to a cloud server, which would have made anyone going to Earth a target. It would have eventually killed Hell and everyone here.

"I didn't create Hellhounds to be slaves. I didn't create demons to be slave masters and abuse my other creations. This *was not* my vision for any of you when I created Hell. It stops now. I know several politicians have tried, and we found Akul's blackmail material on you. I expect it to be done as soon as possible."

Oh, shit. Lilith wasn't just dropping she found Akul's blackmail spank bank to let them know that information was now safe. She was letting them know that if they didn't do the right thing, she would use it.

That was evil, and I loved it.

"Another thing that will change is the deals we make. Bram found us another ally. The witch Dorian kidnapped is a lover to a god who has no intention of bullying me or my creations. Reyson helped create the universe, and between the two of us, we can fix Hell's sun so that deals are no longer necessary.

"People will always try to get out of deals because of the misinformation that has been spread about Hell. We let it sit because the balance on Earth would be skewed if everyone was supercharged with demon magic.

"This is a wake-up call. Dorian Gray's deal seemed harmless at the time. He was human and wasn't viewed as a threat. He didn't care how many demons died as long as he got out of his deal. I'm not risking anyone else like that again. The cloud drive with the sigils has been destroyed by a vampire hacker Bram met on Earth.

"Hell is going to be moving into a new era. You can keep up or be left behind. The Hellhounds *will* be free. Talvath has already offered to teach as many as he can. As a result, many of you in the soul collection business will need to find a new vocation. I realize that is a scary prospect, but it doesn't have to be. This is the perfect time to help people or follow your dreams. That is all."

All the reporters started screaming questions and waving microphones in the air. I was pretty sure some of them had shit opinions about all of this. They knew *a lot* more about Lilith than I did and had more reason to fear her. I saw the look on her face, and I heard her speak. I wouldn't be questioning a fucking thing she said, even if it was my job. I'd done some stupid shit in my life, but not that stupid.

Lilith must have the same ability to magnify her voice as Reyson did because she broke it out.

"Enough! This was a terrorist attack by a prominent demon so that he could continue profiting off the abuse of one of my creations. You don't have to like it, but I suggest you get on board because it's happening. So is fixing our sun. The souls were a Band-Aid to a bigger problem. We'd be stupid not to take Reyson up on his offer. I'm looking at this long-term. That is all."

Damn. Lilith dropped a whole bomb on Hell, told them to deal with it, then just opened a door and disappeared into it with everyone she brought with her. She magically appeared in her entertainment room in a blaze of red-headed glory. Samael came up behind her and wrapped his arms around her waist.

"Think the politicians are going to get it done?"

"They will if they knew Akul. He didn't just have black-mail material he'd already used. He had backups in case he needed them in the future. Notice I never said I deleted it like what was on the cloud server. They aren't stupid. Every politician, on any realm, no matter what century it is, is adept at reading between the lines."

"Not to step on your toes, but why didn't you answer their questions?" Reyson asked.

"Sometimes, creations get a little naughty and need to be spanked into obedience. If you have to play the god card, it's best just to tell them what's happening and not allow questions. I hate it, but it's not the first time I've had to do it. They'll hate it and complain endlessly, but it'll get done. A few decades will pass, and it will be an unfortunate history lesson taught in schools."

"Aren't you worried about the Hellhounds speeding up the process by killing the demons that abused them?" Felix asked.

"Not at all because I don't intend to give them time. There is also the worry that demons will hurt the Hell-hounds. I'm meeting with the government after lunch, where they *will* make the appropriate changes. I expect some pushback. Bram and May, I'd love for you to come with me. I can tell them all day that I didn't create Hell-hounds the way they teach nowadays, but you can tell them for yourselves. You both had different upbringings, and you are both perfect."

"I'll do it," May said immediately.

"So will I. That was the point of all this, wasn't it?" Bram said.

Kaine ran his fingers through his hair.

"Not to be a bother, but we technically caught the bad guys. I'd love to stay and watch a revolution go down, but I've got a teenage witch at home with two broken feet and magic that was awakened early. Since her parents raised her human, they had some human friends around her. The assholes have human child protective services after me like I'm some pervert for taking my best friend's child in. I really need to get back."

Lilith clearly didn't know that.

"You took in one of mine?"

Kaine puffed up his chest proudly.

"Yeah. She's going to be a famous ballerina one day. Mark my words."

"Why would her parents raise her human?" Lilith asked.

"I don't pretend to know all that witch crap, but something about the stars and a tarot reading the night she was born, which is all the more reason for me to get back. If it scared her parents enough to take her birthright away, then I need to make sure she has an excellent support system."

"Bring her to the library. Ravyn and I will teach her how to use her magic."

"And, you know, girl stuff?" Kaine said, looking at us in a panic.

I suppressed my giggle. Kaine was perfectly happy to charge into Hell, change into his dragon, and yeet a demon forty feet in the air, but Lilith help him if he had to talk to a sixteen-year-old about tampons. It was kind of adorable how purple he was right now.

I thought about my twin. I knew how much she wanted

to see Dorian Gray die. I knew she had more people at the museum than I did at the library, but I also knew they weren't as good as she was with cursed objects. She had a good bit of them coming over from the Cult of the Aether Sisters. Maybe she needed to get back too. I put my hand on her shoulder.

"Do you need to get back to the museum? No one will get mad. I'm not in trouble anymore. You have that shipment coming in from the Cult of the Aether Sisters, and I'm worried about how dangerous the items will be."

"It's not coming in for another three weeks."

"Did you say the Cult of the Aether Sisters?" Lilith asked. "They were after we left, but I heard about them. They summoned countless demons trying to get more powerful. The first demon refused the deal and reported back. We had to put a stop to deals until the Earth dwellers took care of them. The demon reported they had the same powers as witches, but they weren't. They were more. The Cult of the Aether Sisters weren't my creations."

Ravyn frowned, and so did I. Everything passed down about them was that they were dark witches.

"How is that possible?"

"Someone must have bastardized my creation. I'm not sure, but they were extremely dangerous. If you're getting items from them, I'd be very careful. Not a single demon would agree to make them more powerful."

Shit. And my twin was about to get everything they kept in their secret basement. I didn't like that in the slightest.

"Still, there's nothing I can do until the ship gets here with the items. I'd rather be here with my twin."

"Of course. Kaine, it was a pleasure. Get back to your young witch and take care of her. There's still work to do. I need to leave and get in front of our government. Reyson, I'm going to make sure that it's a public ceremony when we fix the sun. Bram, you're perfect as you are. May, what would you wear if you could put on anything you like?"

"I've always wanted to wear a pretty dress and makeup with my hair fixed."

Lilith could have waved her hand and done it because I could. Instead, she wrapped her hand around May's shoulder.

"Come with me. There's probably something in my closet. I can do your hair and makeup. We have enough time."

I got that on a deep emotional level. Lilith was going to spoil May because she needed it. No one had cared for her before. I dug it. Before Lilith could leave, Ravyn cleared her throat.

"Is anyone going to get mad if we go beat on Dorian while you're gone?"

Lilith flashed her a devious smile.

"Just leave his necklace on so you don't kill him."

CHAPTER 37
BRAM

I knew why this was needed. Talvath had been preparing me for my entire life for this, even if he hadn't told me and might have changed his mind about it. I honestly just wanted to go back to Ripley and the guys from the library. I had a feeling they were going to be awful when I testified in front of parliament.

May looked absolutely terrified when she stepped out of Lilith's bedroom. Lilith had put her in a lovely dress, done her makeup, and curled her hair. I noticed she had disappeared with two Hellhounds last night, and I was happy for her. I tucked her hair behind her ear and smiled at her.

"Solomon and Duke are going to *die* when they see how pretty you look."

"You think? I always wanted to wear a dress, but I thought they would be uncomfortable. This one is nice."

"You look great in it. We're going to knock them dead. They will try to trip us up, but we just have to tell the truth and keep our cool. They will try to prod us into shifting so they can say all Hellhounds are vicious killers who must be under their feet, but we both know that's not how it works. It's okay to get angry about what Akul and Oscar did to you. Just don't lose it."

Talvath rounded the hall and looked at me with tears in his eyes. He pulled me into a hug. He was so much smaller than me. His arms barely fit around me.

"I'm so proud of you. I want you to do something for me, Bram. Ripley and Reyson make you happy. So do the rest of the people at the library. When this is over, go be with them. Keep in touch, but be with the people you love. I've always thought of you as more like a son, and part of having a son is letting them find their new family when they fall in love. That wasn't an option before, but it is now.

"You too, May. I hardly know you, but I can see you have affection for Solomon and Duke and them you. I realize you've been fighting your entire life, and this is the big one. You can have a different life. You can have love. Demons submit saliva samples to websites and trace their ancestry. They can find fourth cousins in different parts of Hell. I know how Akul made his money. If we can pull this off, nothing is stopping Hellhounds from using it to locate their parents or any pups that were torn away from them at the breeding farms. I want Bram to have a family because I love him, but I want the rest of you to have one because you deserve it."

Talvath had spared me the breeding farms. It wasn't a requirement if you owned a Hellhound, but most people did it because there was money in it. I only ever had sex when I wanted to, and if I even suspected they weren't totally into it, I called it off.

I was nervous, but I *needed* to do this. Not just for every Hellhound back at Lilith's, but every Hellhound here. Enough was enough. If Lilith needed me by her side as proof, I'd be right there with her. She came through when Ripley needed help. She could have rescued Ripley and dealt with Akul, but she decided to use this mess to free my people.

Lilith stepped out of her bedroom and gave May a gentle smile. Samael joined us.

"You really do look quite lovely. I knew my clothes would fit you. We're almost the same size."

They really were. They were both petite women hiding a lot of power. Talvath raised me never to think less of the opposite sex, especially since female Hellhounds were perfectly capable of kicking my ass, and none of us would be here if it weren't for a woman, no matter who created you.

Samael kissed Lilith's hand.

"Shall we go, my love? I'm more worried about you losing it than the Hellhounds."

Thank you! Reyson and Lilith could do *a lot* more damage than any of us Hellhounds could, and now they were besties. Lilith conjured a door, and we stepped through. There were rows of demons at tables just staring at us. Lilith strolled to a table at the front, so we all followed her. A pinched-faced woman at the front glared down at her.

"I'm sure you understand laws just can't be passed in a day, Lilith."

"I created demons, witches, and Hellhounds in a day. It took me five to create Hell. Every day, I created plants and animals so that you could survive here, and after four weeks, Hell was ready for you. You *can*. You just don't want to. You can certainly pass other laws fast enough. Anyway, you don't have to start over and write new laws from scratch. You just need to repeal the ones that turned Hellhounds into slaves and took away all their rights. They *used* to sit among you writing laws. They were your spouses and family. All of *you* might be too young to remember that, but I'm not."

"No offense, but you are asking us to free vicious killers," a man said.

"Bram, how many people have you killed?" Lilith asked me.

"None, until Talvath got kidnapped. I killed the shifter guarding the door to his prison so we could get him out. We were only at Akul's to arrest him and Dorian, which we did. Akul's wife showed up with her friends and was trying to hurt Lilith. We fought back in self-defense. It's not something we enjoy."

"May, how many people have you killed?"

"None, until the fight at Akul's house."

"Yes, and how many times were you raped and beaten while you belonged to Akul?"

"There was no point in keeping track. It happened all the time, to all of us."

"I would hope all of you had a chance to read Akul's manifesto and the sheer number of people he was planning on having killed. May's story isn't unusual. Neither are the injuries Reyson, and I healed from her. I have Hellhounds at my house from many different demon families. They all have scars and bruises where they've been beaten and whipped. You have a very different definition of vicious than mine because the way I see it, anyone who would beat one of my creations, force them to mate with a stranger, then rip their pup away from them for a profit is the very definition of cruel. I didn't create any of you to lord over the Hellhounds. Honestly, if you look at the statistics in our jails, demons have killed more people than

Hellhounds, but you treat prisoners more humanely than them."

"You point out we are young and don't remember everything about the past, but you were alive during the civil war that led to those laws. We passed them for good reason."

"Yes, I was alive during the civil war and can tell you that half the history they taught you is false because the victors wrote it. It wasn't Hellhounds versus demons, and the demons managed to beat them back. It was over a political issue. It's not in your DNA to have specific political beliefs.

"There were Hellhounds *and* demons on both sides. When all was said and done, not only those involved in the fighting died but also many innocent civilians. People wanted someone to blame, so a group of politicians placed all the blame on the Hellhounds, even though they didn't start the war and fought by their side to help end it.

"It horrified me when they were rounded up and subjugated. Their rights were stripped away. I should have stopped it then. The only reason I didn't was that so many people had died, and I thought my creations were better than that. I thought you would see reason, and you wouldn't come to *this*. That was about the time I stopped being involved in your affairs, but I always intended to right this wrong. I was waiting for the opportunity to present itself that it could be done without another civil war.

"You know the truth. I've told you the *actual history* behind the civil war and not what the victors taught you. You know how far Akul was willing to go with this. He has blackmail files on everyone here. If your name wasn't on his hit list, you still weren't safe. Trust me. If you voiced the opinion to do better by my creation, you would have been blackmailed into silence.

"Just to let you know, I've read what Akul has on all of you. Some of you have *no right* to make any assumptions about the morality and temperament of another one of my creations."

The room got uncomfortably silent, and I could smell anxiety and the start of people sweating everywhere. That was the second time Lilith mentioned she had that. This time, she said she knew the contents. She also never said she deleted it. Damn. Lilith brought receipts. If Akul's manifesto and plot, May and I's testimony, and her retelling of the history of the civil war that not even Talvath knew weren't enough, she was fully prepared to blackmail these fuckers to get the laws repealed.

"I fully support this," a woman said. "I always have. I ran for office on that platform. There are plenty of demons out there that agree with it. Akul tried to ruin my campaign by leaking news of my husband's affair, but we have an open relationship, and people got that when I said it when it made the news.

"He didn't give up. He had nothing on me, and he knew it. As soon as I proposed my bill to change things, he manu-factured something. The frame job was tight. Everything could be traced to me, and there was no way I could prove it was him and not me.

"I had a choice. If I left the bill as is, he would have revealed it, and I would have been arrested. I wouldn't be here to argue when the time came. If I withdrew it, I could stay in office and work on this in the shadows. I've seen the same thing happen to literally everyone who proposed a bill to make things better for the Hellhounds. I just want to say to everyone that has doubts about this that there are plenty of us sitting among you who support it but have been blackmailed into silence, and there are plenty of demons we were elected to represent who want them free too."

"What about the economy?" a toad-faced man said. "You'll be taking income away from many demons. You'll be taking away their household help. How are they to run their estates and make a living now? There are not enough jobs to go around for everyone. The Hellhounds will need food and shelter. How are they to do that with no jobs? They can't even read or write!"

"Bram can," Talvath said. "He was a fast learner as a child and a voracious reader now. Even if the sun wouldn't be fixed, after what Akul did to me, I have no desire to return to Earth and collect souls. I intend to open a school. The Hellhounds can come and learn what they need to transition. They will be taught to read and write. They will learn the skills they need to get jobs. My estate is just as big as anyone else's. I run it with *paid* demon servants. If your estate requires people to keep it up and running, you can pay them like a civilized person."

"I also run my estate with paid servants," Lilith said. "I'm a god. I created this entire realm. I have people on two realms that pray to me and leave offerings out. Not even I expect people to work for free, and I outrank all of you. As far as the money people are making at the breeding farms, it's paid rape. There's no gentle way to put that, but it is. We have strict penalties for rapists here in Hell, and prisons are full of them. So why should we allow *anyone* to profit from it because their income is more important than a living being? And remember, I've seen Akul's files. I know exactly who is okay with it and why."

If a few men in the room could have begged the

universe to open a crack in the floor to swallow them whole, they would have. The hair on the back of my neck was standing up from the level of anxiety that just got ramped up when Lilith just dropped that.

If some of these men were rapists, they needed to be in jail, not parliament. I had a lot of opinions on that subject. I drew attention to myself on Earth, getting into a few bar fights if I saw something getting slipped in drinks. I'd pretended to be a few women's boyfriends to get some creeper to leave them alone, then walked them to their car.

I really hoped Lilith didn't intend to sit on that information.

The woman who had initially spoken first was chewing her bottom lip and seemed to think this over. However, she was the speaker, and she would be the one to organize the vote.

"I do agree with you on several points. It's beneath us to do these things to another living being, especially if everything they have taught us is lies. I do have concerns, though. Do you have plans for integrating them back into society to avoid another civil war? Won't they want revenge? Some of the demons aren't going to react well to this. Where will we put them while Talvath is setting up his school?"

"As you know, I own several properties. I have resorts and hotels all over Hell. I'm not hurting for money, either. They can stay at one of my properties for free. The soul collection business was vital to continuing Hell itself, but it brought no money to the economy. The salaries were all paid with heavy taxes.

"Now that era is over, and we will have to move into a new one. Everyone employed in that line of work will have to find new jobs. Here's something for you big economy grumps. We're about to have a whole bunch of previously underrepresented consumers entering the market.

"Instead of getting butt hurt they aren't working their asses off for free anymore, think of them as consumers with needs. There are no Hellhound bars. There is absolutely zero representation for them in television and movies. We tore away them from their parents and their pups taken away. Apps that would allow them to reconnect would be beneficial and make money. They want love just as much as you do. Make a dating app for them.

"You are about to free up a good bit of your budget with the sun fixed. Hellhounds need help, and plenty of demons do too. So put those tax dollars to good work."

"Will there be a Hellhound elected to speak for them when needed?"

"Bram was my champion. He wasn't too scared to kick down my office door and tell me Dorian Gray and the traitor kidnapped someone he cared about and were currently in Hell. Bram connected me with Reyson, which is how our sun is getting fixed. He also rallied the Hellhounds and prevented a lot of death at Akul's place.

"Still, Bram has done enough, and he never asked for this. He found a family on Earth when he was trying to find Talvath, and I won't deny him that. I'm not going to deny any of my creations love or family. May is also a leader. She kept the faith and defended the witch Dorian and Akul kidnapped at the risk of her own life. I think May would make a lovely representative for the Hellhounds."

That was... surprising. Lilith gave me an out. I was pretty sure no matter what my soul truly desired, I'd have to stay here and help. She had pretty much accounted for everything I had been worried about, and May would be much better at that than I would.

I was a Hellhound like they were, but I didn't live the same life they did because of Talvath. I could imagine what they went through, because I hadn't experienced it. Not like May had. May had been protecting the Hellhounds where she lived long before I showed up, at her own expense.

She honestly looked terrified and shot me a panicked look like she wanted me to get her out of it. I put my hand over hers and leaned in to whisper in her ear.

"You're going to be great at it. Ask Solomon and Duke for help. You can understand them in ways I can't. You're so brave, May. You just need to be brave a little longer, and things will get better."

She let out the breath she was holding and nodded. The speaker pounded her gavel on the table and called for a vote to abolish all the laws that hurt Hellhounds. Most people looked like Lilith had convinced them, and they were happy to do it. A few were scowling like they hated every minute of this.

I didn't trust anyone unhappy about abolishing slavery. I hoped Lilith was noting that and intended to break out Akul's blackmail files if they sowed insurrection about it and hurt my people.

CHAPTER 38

RIPLEY

I was worried for Bram and May, and I couldn't even amuse myself tormenting Dorian. Reyson's theory was correct. Dorian survived the brain melting with the necklace on, but he was this drooling, crying mess while his body tried to heal that. His body kept convulsing, and he was crying in pain.

He deserved every minute of it, but Ravyn and I didn't have a go at him. We wanted him conscious and knowing it was us when it happened. Reyson offered to heal him so we could have our vengeance, but we both said no. Why? He had no problem torturing Talvath.

We were all piled in the living room. Gabriel and Lucifer were buddied up, and I was so happy for him. It was odd how much they looked alike, considering how far removed Gabriel was from Lucifer. That angel must have potent genes.

Solomon and Duke were pacing. They were worried about May. I *really* hoped Lilith pulled this off, and they got to be a little happy family when this was over.

"Do you miss your library, my witch?" Reyson asked.

"Yeah, but what's happening now are the things that are written in the history books in the Library of the Profane. It's nice to be here witnessing it. I'm not super fond of the fact that my role was the damsel in distress. I know we'll have to get back soon because I don't trust my library in someone else's hands, but we can stay a bit longer."

"What do you think Lilith meant that the Cult of the Aether Sisters weren't witches?" Ravyn said. "Some of their curses are still known and forbidden today. They can *only* be done by witches."

"I don't know, but I don't like it. I would prefer you put those objects back where you found them."

"I don't pretend to know what was going on with every single person in every part of the world, but wasn't that particular group associated with bears?" Reyson asked.

"Everything that is known about them was that they were dark witches with bear familiars, but I'm starting to doubt that. Not every witch gets a familiar. It would be odd for an entire coven to get the exact same one and for every member even to have a familiar," Ravyn said.

"I'd be wary of it too," Gabriel said. "The demons were so afraid of them, they wouldn't give them more power, and something tells me they aren't afraid of much."

"Demons are afraid of lots of things," Lucifer said. "The only reason we're in this mess now was that some demons feared the Hellhounds after the civil war and turned them into the villains, even though plenty of them fought on their side. Don't let anyone's bravado fool you. What Akul did frightened them too."

A magical door opened in the living room. May walked through first. She ran straight to Solomon and Duke, who scooped her up in a hug. May looked beautiful. Lilith had put her in one of her dresses, done her makeup, and curled her hair.

I was staring at them so long, I nearly missed Bram coming through. He was unharmed and beaming. Bram picked me up and kissed me.

"We did it! Lilith got all the old laws repealed. There's going to be another press conference in two hours. Lilith will be there. She's offering her properties to house everyone. It was great. One of the politicians owns a transport company. He offered his buses to get everyone there. Another owns a popular grocery store chain and said she would make sure they were fed while they were getting settled. The police are being dispatched all over the realm to make sure no one gets hurt in the transition."

"Parliament wanted a representative for the Hellhounds," May said. "Lilith asked me to do it. Can you imagine?"

My gaze flew to Lilith. She had been all about Bram this entire time. Lilith had been relying on him to rally and lead the Hellhounds. It had worked so far. I was shocked she hadn't put him forth when parliament wanted a Hellhound representative.

All she did was wink at me, and I got it.

Lilith gave Bram his out to come back to Earth with us. It was in his court now. May would be wonderful at it. I smiled at her and pulled her into a hug.

"You look beautiful, and you're going to be boss at this."

"I'm so nervous. I thought for sure it was going to be Bram!"

"One of my end goals is to reunite Hellhound families. I'm not going to start that off by ripping Bram away from his. He's on his own journey. Perhaps this is the start of Hellhounds occupying two realms. The choice is entirely up to Bram, but I'm not putting anything in his path where he thinks he's obligated to do anything.

"May, you are actually perfect for this, and I picked you for a reason. Akul was the worst of the worst. I can't imagine what it was like living with him. But, you never gave up hope things would change, even as Oscar and Akul tried to rape and beat it out of you. You're *exactly* who we need representing the Hellhounds."

"She's right," Solomon said. "We joined the fight because you stood up to Oscar. Between the two of you, it was a no brainer."

"No one is going to get angry if I go back to the library with the others?" Bram asked, worrying his bottom lip.

There were countless Hellhounds in Lilith's living room. Some of them heard his speech at Akul's, and some just joined in when they saw him shift and attack Akul's wife. They didn't get to talk to him until later and not very much because he'd been involved in the interrogations of Akul.

They saw how Lilith looked to him for this entire plan. He was her right-hand man for a lot of this, even once Reyson got here. Every Hellhound in the room was encouraging Bram to be happy, and it was a beautiful thing. They could have said they still needed him. If anyone knew how to be a mostly free Hellhound, it was Bram.

Talvath pulled him into a hug with tears in his eyes.

"Go, Bram. Be happy. We'll handle it. Just keep in touch."

Bram looked at me with hope in his eyes. I think that was the first time I ever saw that look.

"Will you have me?"

I growled and pulled him down for a kiss.

"Shut the fuck up. You're *mine*. I'm never letting you go again."

"I love happy endings," Lilith said, clapping her hands. "We still have a bit of work to do before the rest of the Hell-hounds can get theirs. May, you're going to need help with your new position. This isn't over yet. One more press conference, then we can start moving the Hellhounds out. Come with me. We need to prepare. Reyson, we will have a ceremony to fix the sun at one of my resorts on live television. Is that okay?"

Reyson bowed his head.

"I'd be honored."

"Good. Get some rest. Eat something. We have plans to get Hellhounds out immediately after the press conference to prevent any violence. So I could use some help with that."

She got my guys here so they could get me out of that cage. Lilith made sure we got to keep Bram. She was changing things for the better in Hell.

If she needed me to knock some demon heads around to make a smooth transition, I'd be happy to help.

CHAPTER 39
BALTHAZAR

Deleting that cloud server was child's play since I had Dorian's phone. Akul's laptop wasn't passcode protected, and he didn't even encrypt his blackmail files or that manifesto. It was *right there* on his desk. Idiots with no care about computer cooties who pirated porn instead of streaming it like a civilized person hid their porn better than he hid that whack ass manifesto. I hid my nudes better than that.

It was probably the easiest hacking job I'd ever done, but also the most important. I helped Kaine catch criminals plenty of times, and I liberated tons of money from people who were doing evil things with it. I never helped liberate an entire group of people and start a revolution.

It felt good.

While everyone else was eating and celebrating, Lilith gave me a little side project. She didn't create me, and I certainly never prayed to her, but it meant a lot that she trusted me with it when there were probably perfectly capable hackers here in Hell.

Lilith had learned some of the blackmail files had been fabricated. He started with framing people before he moved to mass murder and betrayal. I'd never used my hacking skills to frame anyone. That was never my MO. I did have *some* morals.

I could, however, unfuck a frame job if there was an electronic paper trail, and with a little digging, I could find out if most of these claims were legit or not. Digging into rape allegations wasn't beyond my scope either. There was usually money involved in that. Lots and lots of hush money to make sure it went away if your victim ever spoke up.

I had a *big* problem with guys like that, and Lilith apparently did too because she told me to take an extra hard look at those. I'd met plenty of fuck boys who didn't know what no meant and thought if they tried to pin me, I was just going to let them when I wasn't into it. I generally beat the crap out of them and stole all their shit. They weren't about to admit to anyone the cute vampire at the club who was wearing glitter beat their asses and stole all their valuables.

I was glued to the laptop Lilith gave me doing my thing. I was happy for everyone eating and talking, but I had work to do. Bram sat next to me on the couch. I knew this *totally* wasn't the time, but he smelled amazing, and I kind of wanted to bite him.

"I'm guessing you're doing your thing with computers again. Anything I can help with? Talvath might be of assistance."

"That actually would help. I'm going through Akul's nasty blackmail files. Lilith said some of them are frame jobs. I can undo that if they did electronically it if anyone else knows about it, but she also wants to know if any of these are true. There are some pretty serious allegations in here for people who are supposed to run an entire realm."

"Talvath! Can you come over here a minute? Lilith has Balthazar digging into the blackmail files, but he doesn't know these people. I know their policies and what they say when cameras are rolling, but you're friends with them."

Yeah, I definitely needed his insight. I wasn't super fond of Talvath at first and had only been busting my ass to help rescue him because it meant a lot to Bram, and we kind of needed him to get to Dorian. But I liked the demon now. He'd always been #teamBram, and he didn't deserve what happened to him. He'd been fighting for this revolution this entire time.

I usually worked alone unless I was helping Kaine. Shit was always much easier when I knew what I was digging for. I turned the laptop around so Talvath could look at the document.

"Okay, the first thing you should know is that parliament in Hell differs greatly from what you are used to back on Earth. Donations to politicians aren't allowed, even when they are running for office. It's not a career where you make more money and have better health insurance than the middle class.

"Everyone here has the exact same health insurance, and our politician's pay is based on the median income of the people they represent. So it keeps them honest and working for the people.

"Most politicians in Hell are inherently good. They take the job because they *want* to help people. But, like anything, some bad people get elected. People get elected with good intentions, then the power goes to their head, and they turn to the dark side.

"I could tell you my suspicions of everyone on this list,

but that's all they are. Some of these people are my friends and have been for a very long time. I'd love to be able to say that what's in this document was fabricated, but I saw their reaction when we stepped into the chamber, even after reading the manifesto and hearing the press conference.

"Some of this could very well be fabricated, but there's a different truth out there. If you want to find corruption in the government, start looking at money. They aren't going to be living lavish lifestyles. If a large sum of money randomly appeared once and was left there, there's a big chance someone moved it there, knowing it could get them kicked out of office.

"People get inheritances and sell vehicles and property all the time. Politicians are no different. It's generally spent or invested. If they are regularly taking bribes, it's going to be good and hidden. If a large sum of money randomly showed up in their account with a blackmail threat, it's going to sit untouched. They'll know the paper trail looks bad but trying to hide it looks worse. The only hope they have of saying they were framed was that they left the money untouched and unspent. I'm honestly not sure how you're going to verify the rape allegations, but I've always gotten bad vibes about the ones who have them."

"Oh, that comes down to money too."

"Hacking the bank is going to be difficult," Talvath said.

"Oh, please. I hacked both the supernatural and human government just for funsies."

Bram draped his arm around my shoulder, and I was so here for that. Would he mind just a little nip to his neck? I'll bet he tasted amazing.

"We never would have found you if it weren't for Balthazar. I *know* he can do it."

I felt someone rubbing my neck. I'd know that wonderful smell and those smooth hands anywhere. Ripley was behind me. Reyson, Felix, Gabriel, and Lucifer joined us.

They were all chiming in about my abilities. It felt good, but it also didn't. I was insecure about many things, but not about things I *knew* I was good at or what I saw in the mirror every day. There wasn't a bank in existence that could keep me out, and that included demonic banks.

But I hadn't been able to tell them exactly where to find Ripley. I had a general location, but I would have needed more time to get an address. If Reyson wasn't Reyson and Felix couldn't sense Ripley, something bad would have happened. It might not have been to Ripley, but they could have hurt May. Akul and Oscar wouldn't have taken May standing up to him for trying to rape Ripley lightly.

They may have needed Ripley unharmed, but May was expendable to them. I knew Ripley. She wasn't fighting because she knew we were coming, but she would if someone tried to hurt May. Dorian was unkillable with that necklace around his neck. He certainly should have been dead after we all took turns with him. Apparently, demons were pretty hard to kill unless you knew how, which Ripley didn't. Her safe status could have changed real fast.

I *knew* I could do this, but how fast? Could I do this before anyone got hurt? Also, Ripley and Ravyn were both in love with their jobs. They worked their asses off to get them and took pride in it. The twins were staying to watch history be made, but I knew they were worried about what was going on at the library and museum with them gone.

Lilith got exactly what she wanted when she took on parliament, but I was there at Akul's house when his wife and all her friends thought they were capable of killing gods. Some of these allegations were no joke, and these people had followers.

I knew I was good but was I good enough to crack this before any violence started?

CHAPTER 40
FELIX

I'd been alive for historical events before. I'd been reborn as a familiar and seen how they were talked about centuries later. Most of the time, it was accurate, but some of it was revisionist history, like what happened with the Hellhounds after the civil war in Hell.

Everyone always says they'd like to be able to go back in time to see history being made, but honestly, the entire thing is nerve-wracking. There are always two sides with various extremists. Some people wanted change so badly, they didn't care who they killed to get it, and then some feared it and were willing to massacre anyone trying to bring it.

It was usually humans killing each other over religion or their fear of the supernatural back in my day. Of course, most of the things they thought were witchcraft were pretty far off, and they murdered plenty of their own.

There had been no violence so far aside from that mess at Akul's, and you'd have to be pretty stupid to go against two gods, but I'd already witnessed an entire group of housewives try. Every time there was another press conference, or I thought about us helping with the transitions, I was transported back in time where we were all expected to go out and witness someone burning alive or being drawn and quartered.

And that happened pretty often. It wasn't like there was television back then, and many people looked at actors like they were degenerates. Plenty of people viewed public violence as their entertainment because they thought they were safe from it. I always knew it could be me up there and would have gladly skipped it, but it was a surefire way to draw attention to yourself. Plenty of people pretended to like it while feeling sick to their stomachs.

I felt like that every time there was another press conference. Bram wasn't with Lilith this time, but May was. I didn't know her as well as Bram, but she had all of my respect. She never stopped fighting, and she protected Ripley at her own expense. She *deserved* happiness.

Lucifer did his strange thing with the channels again. If it was going to be on every channel, and we wouldn't have to deal with propaganda in the commentary, any channel would have done. I wondered if questions were going to be allowed this time.

Lucifer finally settled on a station, but there were plenty of people on the podium this time. A woman stepped forward, and it looked like she was going to be the one doing the talking this time. Lilith was standing close by like she was her bodyguard. I didn't think Lilith would allow anyone to speak for her. Her witches certainly didn't allow that.

"Who is that woman?" I asked.

"The prime minister," Talvath said. "She's a good woman and has long told me she wanted this. She would have put her support behind a bill if it wasn't withdrawn before all this happened. The best part is that she's a very powerful demon and most people are terrified of her. Sozath is actually quite lovely if she likes you."

I'd never met her, but I was a little terrified of her as she glared at the camera. I'd seen what the tattoos on the women at Akul's were capable of. Sozath had way more tattoos than they did. She even had them on her face. She was not fucking around. She cleared her throat, and the entire room went silent.

I didn't have thumbs for a long time, but I made Ripley put on the news and pull up news articles from my home country. Sozath certainly didn't speak like any government member back home.

"I'm not going to bullshit any of you. You know that's not me. You all heard Lilith's press conference before, and you will hear me now. I agreed with everything she said even before she told parliament the truth about the civil war. We are above this.

"To sum up what we were told by someone who lived through it, the civil war was never Hellhounds and demons fighting for dominance. There were Hellhounds and demons on *both* sides. It was a terrible time, and we decided it someone needed to be made a villain.

"In turning the Hellhounds into villains that long ago, we've become them ourselves. Parliament has revoked every law regarding owning Hellhounds as property. It's also now just as much a crime to harm them as it is a demon.

"There will be busses coming around to move them to Lilith's properties during the transition. You will let them leave *without* harming them. You *will* go to them and explain to them and explain they have been freed them like they are intelligent beings since I know they weren't allowed to watch this press conference.

"Two gods are here in support of this. Parliament voted for it. I know some of you would like to keep your free labor and money coming in from the breeding farms, and you're willing to risk defying two gods and break the law. Every single member of the police and military will be out, ensuring a smooth transition. If they find your Hellhounds locked up instead of ready to get on the bus, you'll be arrested for kidnapping. Don't be stupid. You've beaten your Hellhounds until they did what they were told. Now, it's your turn. That is all. Thank you."

Yeah, I was definitely scared of that woman. But she wasn't allowing questions either. She just said this is how it's going to go, so do it. Sozath reminded me *a lot* of Ripley's mom, and she raised two brilliant, wonderful witches.

"I take it she doesn't have Hellhounds?" I asked.

Talvath shook his head.

"Many demons don't. Some of them would, but can't afford to purchase one. A lot of them don't agree with the whole thing and hire demons if they need help. Not all demons live how Akul lives or have estates like Lilith does. They have modest homes and do everything for themselves. We do have townhouses, condos, and apartments like you have on Earth. You've only seen how the ultra rich live here. There are perfectly lovely people here who don't agree with this. It's the ones that do that you need to worry about."

Reyson cracked his neck and glared at Talvath.

"I haven't killed anyone in this realm yet out of respect to Lilith, even though it was perfectly within my right to slaughter Dorian and Akul for taking my witch and trying to manipulate me. I have no problem going out there and making sure everyone gets to safety unharmed, but I care about every single person who came here with me. I *will* end anyone that tries to hurt them."

Lucifer just leaned back and laughed. I got that he was distantly related to Gabriel. Like, super distantly related even if they looked like brothers. Lucifer was kind of a weird mother fucker. I guess one would have to be.

Everyone on Earth thought he took on his creator or the creator of all things, depending on your belief, fell from grace, and got turned into the devil running Hell. He wasn't running a damned thing here. Lucifer was kind of the third wheel to Lilith and Samael's love fest. He seemed to really miss the family he left.

"Happy hunting, man. Before today, it was acceptable to murder a Hellhound if they kidnapped or attacked a demon. Hellhounds are full citizens now, and the same laws apply. They might not live here, but witches and warlocks are Lilith's creations too. We have laws about them too. They are never to be harmed unless it involves payment for a deal, and it's their time. Sorry, Balthazar. Vampires aren't a protected race here, but something tells me you can handle yourself just fine."

I got that vibe about Balthazar too. He put a ton of effort into his look, and we all thought he looked amazing, even if I gave him a hard time about it. I didn't mean it, but I was pretty sure there were people out there that meant it. I was also pretty sure Balthazar beat the shit out of them if he needed to, and he won every fight he was in.

"I can. I might not be able to shoot magic out of my palms, but I was created with other gifts."

I didn't even hear Lilith come in, but she was apparently right behind us.

"You're all capable, but I'm not sending you in blind. Sozath has always wanted this. I didn't know this, but she's silently been preparing for it in the background in case it ever managed to get up for a vote. She's been keeping records of who all owns Hellhounds and who she thinks is going to cause the most trouble."

"I'm all for the demonic NSA as long as it's judging people porn viewing," Balthazar said.

Lilith cocked an eyebrow at Balthazar like she had no idea what he was talking about. They probably didn't have that here. Balthazar was constantly getting into people's online activity without their permission, but he probably took offense at the government doing it. He probably hacked them and deleted shit just because he could.

"I can assure you that the government here in Hell is not looking at pornography on people's computers. They have other ways of locating that if it involves anyone underage. Can we move on?"

Only Balthazar could manage to distract Lilith during battle. After that, we all just nodded like it was us who got caught talking back to the teacher.

"Sozath thinks most of the problems are going to come from Akul's neighborhood. It's a pretty big one. Vegran didn't nearly bring all her friends with her when the house was under attack. The Hellhounds here probably aren't all the Hellhounds at those particular houses. People there are angry. They lost wives and friends. They saw Samael and Lucifer in the air with Kaine, so they knew I was involved.

"Most of them closed their curtains and hoped they weren't next, but some were foolish enough to follow Vegran. They will want to blame someone, and it will be the Hellhounds since they aren't dumb enough to take most of the government or me on. I'll be out there with you."

"If they touch my people, I'm going to kill them," Reyson said.

Lilith just gave Reyson the stink eye.

"If they don't do what they are told and free my creations, I'll kill them myself."

CHAPTER 41
RIPLEY

I had no problem magically kicking some asses to get the Hellhounds to safety. Honestly, I didn't, but no one was talking about what would happen to Akul and Dorian. They weren't even in jail. We chained them up in Lilith's plush mansion, being fed the rich food everyone else was eating. I was fine with the Hellhounds living it up on gourmet food, and they got so excited about every new dish. Personally, I thought they should feed Dorian and Akul dog food since they thought it was good enough for the Hellhounds.

What *were* we going to do with them? Kaine didn't even want Dorian, or he would have taken him with him. I got it. Some opportunistic lawyer would have made the case he couldn't be tried in supernatural court because he was human. No one was about to bring this to the attention of the humans. They all thought Dorian Gray was fiction, and the real Dorian Gray was just some pretty social media celebrity who took that name for likes.

Hell wouldn't need their souls once Reyson did his thing with Lilith, but I sure hoped no one intended just to throw them in jail where they could spread their vile nonsense. Then again, killing them could turn them into martyrs for extremists. I just wanted to know what was going on, and Lilith was only revealing things a little at a time as she went.

She certainly wasn't clarifying now. She opened one of her doors and sent the Hellhounds here to one of her resorts. She opened a second for us, and we all marched through.

Samael and Lucifer went first. They could hide their wings, but as soon as we stepped out on the street, their wings were out, and they were holding flaming swords. Where did those even come from? Their trousers looked painted on. I wasn't complaining about the view of tight angel ass, but where were they hiding the swords?

I'll give it to Lilith. She moved fast. There were all these demon party buses lining the street. The Hellhounds deserved to be taken to those resorts in style. I was all for that. Tattooed demons in uniform were going around knocking on doors. There were dazed and confused Hellhounds following them out that didn't know if they should be hopeful about this or not. Some were already waiting at the curb, holding a trash bag with the few rags they were given to wear.

Most everyone seemed to cooperate, but we had addresses for people that might not. I got horrifically lost in the place I lived and worked without the GPS on my phone if I'd never been there before. Hell was totally unfamiliar territory for me.

This neighborhood reminded me of the places rich supernaturals lived that they inherited, and the house had been in their family for generations. I had way more rooms than I needed at my apartment at the library because they took up the entire top floor. The people in this neighborhood probably had rooms just for antiques.

Talvath went straight to the front. I got that in terms of demon magic, he was probably strong, and he tattooed Bram with some pretty potent sigils. Ravyn and I were taller than Talvath was. Killian was thin with wiry muscles, but he still had more meat on his bones than Talvath did. He was dressed in a pinstripe suit, for Lilith's sake. How was he going to fight in that? Lilith stepped up and joined him.

"You have the list, Talvath. Lead the way."

Oh, yeah. Talvath was the only one who knew where these cunts lived. Bram was with us. The Hellhounds making their way to the buses all saw him. Their eyes would draw to us, and he would wave. Even though I was sure they hadn't been allowed to watch the press conference, they all seemed to have heard of him. They looked at him with awe. Bram would give them a reassuring nod, and their spines would get a little straighter.

Talvath led us to a cul-de-sac at the end of the neighborhood. There was a bus there, but no one in uniform had made it back there yet.

"This is where the HOA lives. They are going to be the ones we might have a problem with," Talvath said.

There were a lot of things about Hell I didn't like, but some of the things I'd learned so far, I really did like. I was a little shocked they had demonic HOAs. The supernatural community tried to adopt that from humans, and it epically failed. Most neighborhoods were mixed now, and any rules for one species were going to be totally against the nature of another. So we got rid of them.

"Who do we start with?" Gabriel asked.

Talvath pointed to a large stone house with spires. It looked like a fucking castle. It was a little ominous. A few of the neighbors had poked their heads out. When they realized Lilith was here with Reyson, Samael, and Lucifer, they went back inside, and their Hellhounds started filing out.

I saw the curtains part on the creepy castle, and then they slammed shut. The door didn't open, and no one came out. Okay then. I guess they wanted a fight. I was ready for that too. So was Lilith, apparently. She did that thing where she magnified her voice.

"Hellhounds, step away from the door!"

She gave them exactly one minute before she flung her hands out. The front door blew in, and every window shattered. A demon woman with a whole lot of balls peered her head over the shattered window frame.

"You're paying for that!"

Holy shit. If a god just destroyed my front door because I was breaking the law, that would *not* be the first thing out of my mouth. I'd be worried she was about to treat me like that splintered, smoking door.

Balthazar came out of nowhere and tackled me just as magic flew out of the house and landed right where I was standing. Did that bitch just attack me? I wasn't even the one that wrecked her damned house.

"Oh, fuck no," Ravyn growled.

My sister flung a killing curse at the window, but we were kind of at a standoff at this point. They were hiding in the house, and we were out here hiding behind Lilith and Reyson.

"Don't be stupid," Lilith yelled. "Release your Hellhounds."

"Fuck no!" a man yelled. "Do you know how much I paid for them? One female is pregnant. I've got a buyer lined up for that pup that is going to net me a lot of money."

That was enough for Reyson. I knew he didn't have any

kids running around out there, but he'd mentioned a few times he always wanted them if he met the right woman. He'd mentioned our little demigod children with this dreamy look on his face like he could see it clearly in his head.

Reyson could be a big, scary Chaos god, but he could also be a big teddy bear. He had a soft spot for babies and pregnant women, and that demon just signed his own death warrant. He'd been restrained so far and not killed anyone in Hell, but he couldn't be well behaved forever. Reyson was the God of Chaos, and he had his limits. I was pretty sure he was going to have big opinions if Dorian and Akul didn't meet a gruesome end.

Reyson started stomping towards the house. Lilith didn't stop him. She followed him. That was when I noticed Bram was missing. Where the fuck was my Hellhound?

Magic was flying in every direction out of that castle. The residents were trying to fling it out of the window and duck in case someone fired back. Felix dragged me behind a car.

"Where's Bram?" I yelled.

"I don't know, but he has tattoos that make him immune to some of this shite, and you don't."

"Lucifer and Samael must have gone with him because they disappeared too," Gabriel said.

"Where the fuck did they go? Bram might not be immune to come of those sigils!"

"I can shift and do aerial reconnaissance," Killian said. "They aren't going to notice a bat, and I can fly above the magic."

My twin looked panicked, and I got it. I desperately wanted to know where Bram was, but Talvath did everything he could to make sure Bram could come to as little harm with demon magic as possible. He had two angels with him, and I was guessing Lilith made them demon proof if their creator hadn't.

I knew Killian was a powerful warlock, or he wouldn't have been paired up with my sister as her familiar. She'd be devastated if he died. It wasn't just how I saw her looking at him now that he had a body. Killian had been with her just as long as Felix had been with me. He was her best friend. Killian knew just as much about my sister as I did, and he accepted her.

I wanted to know where Bram was, but I wasn't risking Killian to do it.

"No. It's too risky. What's going on at the house?" I asked, peering over the side of the car.

Balthazar yanked me down just as a stray bit of magic slammed into the side of it and shattered all the windows. Balthazar shielded me with his body like a crazy vampire, but I didn't want him getting hurt either. When the glass stopped falling, I crawled from underneath him and started checking him for injuries. I got that he had speed healing abilities because he was a vampire, but I was *pissed* he was bleeding.

"Reyson better make it hurt because that is *not* okay."

Bram was missing, Balthazar was bleeding, and we were all cowering behind a car because these assholes inside thought they could take on two gods and live. This was *not* how I liked to fight. My battle magic teacher at the academy would be so ashamed if he knew I was hiding from a fight. So I looked to my sister.

"Want to wonder twin some magic at them? This is the second time they've almost hit me, and Balthazar is bleeding."

Ravyn was always ready for a fight. She probably got

into more of them growing up than I did. We'd both fight to the death if the other were hurt. But she bit her lip and hesitated.

"You know I'd love to, right? I'm pissed, and no one will let me kill Dorian Gray. Killing those demons in there would take the edge off, but you don't know where Bram is. He could be inside, and so could the Hellhounds. Reyson and Lilith could survive that castle coming down on them, but no one else could."

Gabriel and Balthazar hadn't really seen Ravyn and me in action when we combined our magic, but Felix and Killian were quite familiar with what we could do.

"I know you want to, but hold off. Listen. Lilith and Reyson must be inside because I don't hear magic out here anymore," Felix said.

"I'm guessing you two are pretty lethal together," Gabriel said.

"Oh, you actually have no idea," Killian said. "If you're going to date Ripley, you should know she has a twin, and the two of them together can turn you into a pile of man goo if you hurt her."

"I still think we should have done that to Valentine," I said.

Especially since he was about to make a reappearance in my sister's life and if she was going to dye her hair red, she *did not* need to be doing it because that serial cheater never could tell us apart, even though we made it pretty obvious if you bothered.

"I agree with Ripley on Valentine, but we need to table that for later. I think it's safe to take a peek," Killian said.

I conjured a gust of wind to blow all the broken glass away. The last thing we needed was all of us cut and bleeding. We all peered over the car, and the house had gone deadly silent. What were my god and my creator doing in there?

A male demon came flying out the door so hard, he crashed into the car we were hiding behind. We had to jump back because the car actually moved with the impact. Reyson appeared in the doorway, glaring at the corpse.

"That's for almost hitting my witch with your magic and refusing to let a pregnant woman leave to deliver her baby in safety!"

A magical blast hit the house so hard, the ground shook. A crack appeared on the front stone wall, and bits of roof shingle fell to the ground. What was Lilith doing in there? Bram might be inside.

I saw Reyson's gaze move to his left, so I followed it. Bram was coming around the back of the house with Lucifer, Samael, and several Hellhounds. Oh, thank Lilith. He hadn't been in there when all that magic was being flung around, and the Hellhounds were safe.

Lilith stepped out of the house and brushed some ceiling plaster off her shoulder.

"Well, that was certainly uncalled for. The entire family tried to fight me. I would have spared their son, but he thought it was wise to hold a knife to a pregnant Hellhound's throat. You're safe now, Jena."

A very pregnant Hellhound who looked terrified joined Lilith in the front yard. One of the other female Hellhounds took off running and gave her a passionate kiss. I didn't know who the father of her pup was or even if she did. I didn't know if he wanted children. But based on the way they were kissing, and her hands were caressing Jena's belly, that little pup was going to be lucky enough to have two mommies when they were born.

One bus pulled into the cul-de-sac. I guess it was a good

thing they waited because the car in front of this house was totally destroyed. I hoped it belonged to the family Lilith and Reyson killed. I knew back on Earth, some things weren't covered by insurance because it was considered an act of god. Technically, two gods were involved in destroying this car. Would insurance even pay for that?

The people in uniform finally showed up too. They went straight to Lilith.

"I'm guessing they decided not to cooperate?"

"They had their Hellhounds locked in a greenhouse outside except for Jena. They thought they could get me to back down by threatening a pregnant woman, but it just pissed me off. How are things going?"

"There has been plenty of bitching, but no violence except for what happened here. We're all trained in de-escalation, so we let them have their say so they don't get violent. Some of my people had to stand there a little longer while people worked through some shit and got it off their chest, but everyone should be on the buses now."

That was it? Akul had twelve and made so much money forcing them to the breeding farms, he started this mess. There were six of them at this house, and there was a good bit of them at Lilith's place. The party buses were big, but there wasn't a ton of them on the street, and I couldn't imagine there being enough of them in Hell to transport an entire race of people. I was also sure Lilith had several nice properties, but not enough to put up that many people.

My people flocked around me. Reyson was still furious but seemed to calm down once he was near me. Bram said something to the Hellhounds before they made their way to the bus, then jogged over.

"Is this it?" I asked. "I thought they made a lot of money

at the breeding farms. Shouldn't there be more Hellhounds?"

"No, because they don't want us to outnumber them. It costs a lot to buy a pup. They paired us up based on size, strength, and what they perceived as trainability. They think they've created powerful beasts but bred our nature out of us. They didn't. They just beat us into submission. There are way fewer Hellhounds than there are demons, and that's on purpose. That will change now."

"Yes, it will," Lilith said. "Now, we have a demon and a human back at my place that need dealing with and a sun to fix, so we need to get back."

She just opened a door and ushered us thought. I was glad we were finally doing *something* with them, but what exactly were we doing?

CHAPTER 42

BRAM

I'd never wanted to kill anyone as much as recently. Who threatened a pregnant woman? That was low. That family was dead, and we were finally taking care of Dorian and Akul. Lilith didn't say what she planned on doing with them, but she hadn't really said much about what she had planned. She just revealed it as she went.

We stepped into the door into Lilith's place, and we were in the room Dorian was in. He finally wasn't a drooling mess because Reyson melted his brain. Dorian was filthy and chained to a chair. Unfortunately, he still had the nerve to be an utter turd when he saw us.

"You can't keep me here like this. I have rights," he spat.

Lilith just threw back her head and laughed.

"Oh, sweetie, what rights do you think humans have in Hell when they plot the murder of my creations? Honestly, the witch who got you into that deal in the first place should have had you killed for knowing about the supernatural."

"If I had known you were going to take it this far, I

would have killed you then instead of giving you that deal," Talvath said.

"You hurt my witch. I'd be less worried about your rights and more worried about what I'm going to do to you," Reyson growled.

"Yes, that's the problem. You *all* want to kill Dorian Gray. He had Talvath tortured, hurt someone you all care about, and he plotted to kill my creations. Should we draw straws?" Lilith asked.

"I didn't hurt the librarian!" Dorian yelled. "I was never going to hurt her. I was going to release her as soon as I got what I wanted."

"I'd stop talking, you utter cunt," Felix said. "I was there when you gassed the library. That shit hurt. And you put her in a cage."

"For her protection! I had excellent reason to! Akul's Hellhound tried to hurt her, but he wouldn't have gotten past my blood lock. It was the only way to keep her safe from Akul and his Hellhounds!"

"Oh, shut it, Dorian. I was there, and I remember everything you said to me. You *are not* the hero in this story."

Reyson just grunted and glared at Dorian.

"He took my witch, but he didn't put her through what you went through, Talvath. He had you for much longer and tortured you. Of course, we all want to, but honestly, his death is yours."

"Don't I have any say in this?"

Balthazar smacked him on the back of the head.

"I'd shut up because people here hate you *way* more than someone who went viral getting recorded doing something shitty. So you're getting permanently canceled, bro."

Talvath stroked his goatee. He had every right to kill

Dorian Gray, and none of us would judge him for it. He had just never been a violent person, and I didn't think this experience changed him. I didn't even think being tortured while two assholes tried to raise a god to kill him and all his friends were enough to make Talvath violent.

Talvath worked in soul collection, but his deals were fair. He never showed up to collect until someone had lived a full life. He gave Dorian Gray much longer than he should have, and look how he was repaid.

"I don't think this human fears death so much as he fears growing old and losing his looks. Supernaturals live longer than humans do, but we still age and eventually die. Dorian not only wanted the lifespan of a supernatural, but he also didn't want to age. He wanted to be frozen at that point in his life.

"That was only doable if I got creative. I did a magical painting of Dorian and tied his life to it. As long as the painting is intact, he couldn't die and wouldn't age. I channeled all of that into the portrait. It should be horrific to look upon by now. If you destroyed the painting, in a matter of hours, Dorian would age and die. My plan had always been to destroy the painting and make it quick, but no one says any of *you* have to do that."

Oh, shit. Talvath was *pissed*. I knew he'd never raise a finger to commit violence to Dorian's person, but he'd always been a master at deals. He could get his revenge on Dorian Gray by just completing the contract he agreed on in the first place.

And based on the tantrum Dorian was throwing as he begged for a quick death, Talvath's solution terrified the shit out of him.

"I like that idea, but is it going to stink up my house?" Lilith asked.

Dorian let out a wail and started weeping. I only knew two gods, but they seemed to worry about the strangest things. Dorian's brains were all over what looked like a very expensive rug, as well as a good bit of blood. Dorian hadn't showered since we grabbed him, and he was getting pretty ripe. I was pretty sure him slowly rotting in her basement was *definitely* going to leave behind an odor you could smell even if you weren't a Hellhound.

"I'll take care of that part," Reyson said with a wink and a smirk.

Oh, he was reveling in this. Remind me never to piss him off when I went to live at the library with them. I was still processing that bit but looking forwards to it. Reyson had already come up with his own revenge in his lizard god brain. He wouldn't say a damned thing about it. Reyson was going to surprise us.

Still, I'll bet it was going to be epic. Dorian hurt several people I cared about. I knew he wouldn't, but if Talvath said he wanted me to shift and rip his head off, I would have happily done it.

Reyson rubbed his hands together with sadistic glee. We were all just ignoring Dorian as he cried and begged for a quick death. I was listening a little. It took him *way* longer than it should have, but he finally realized he played his hand and lost. He had no friends here.

Reyson got right in Dorian's face and smashed his finger against his mouth.

"You wanted the God of Chaos, Dorian Gray. Your simple human brain thought taking someone I loved would get what you wanted, and you'd live through it. Did you know I once destroyed a man for kidnapping a king's wife, and I couldn't stand either of them? We created humans with one of the greatest gifts we had as gods. We gave you the ability to love and find soulmates.

"The *worst* thing you can do with that gift and the gift of life is to steal someone's soulmate for your own gain. You could have spent your additional years with a pretty face trying to find love. Instead, you manipulated women who *thought* they were in love with you, and you tried to steal my soulmate. So, stop begging and sniveling. You *earned* this."

Whatever Reyson had planned, I imagined none of us were going to be able to conceive it until we saw it. Did I even want to watch?

Dorian Gray tortured Talvath and hurt Ripley. Yeah, I did.

CHAPTER 43
RIPLEY

Reyson was sexy as fuck in my kitchen, wearing nothing but trousers and one of the ridiculous aprons my grandmother got me for Solstice. He was pretty sexy, ripping the head off a revenant because he didn't like it looking at me. All that was *nothing* compared to him going full God of Chaos on the man who kidnapped me. Holy shit, this wasn't even remotely the right time to get horny, but he looked magnificent in his rage.

Reyson tore Dorian's necklace off and stalked over to me like a cat. Then, he fell to one knee and presented it to me like some knight.

"This man hurt you, my witch. He assaulted your library with noxious gasses and had a witch corrupt the spirits. You deserve your vengeance. You should be the one to destroy the portrait."

How did he manage to just be so fucking perfect? He could have easily destroyed Dorian, and I would have happily watched, but he acknowledged that even though he was a god and I was a witch, I needed this too.

"Wait a minute," Ravyn said, snatching the necklace out

of my hands. "Dorian likes to use witches. If this necklace is the only thing keeping him young and pretty, it's probably cursed up the ass."

Good thinking. I wouldn't put it past this fucker. Ravyn and I went out of town for spring break at the academy and ended up somewhere with flying attack cockroaches. You couldn't just throw a shoe at them like civilized cockroaches. Even flinging magic at them didn't kill them, then you had to pay for the damage to the wall. They'd fly at your face trying to attack you with roach cooties and get stuck in your hair until you could get them for good. Dorian was a flying cockroach, and I was never going back to Florida.

I was good at breaking curses, but I wasn't at the same level as my twin sister. We both knew our limits and looked to the other if one of us was stronger at something than the other.

"Do we need wonder twin powers to break them?" I asked.

"I could break them, but honestly, I've heard so much about the two of you and your abilities. I'd love to see you in action," Lilith said.

Ravyn just puffed up. We were both humble when we needed to be, but we weren't above showing off at what we were good at. My twin nearly lost her shit when Professor Krauss singled her out for independent study, and she worked her ass off to learn everything she knew. Our creator just complimented her and *asked* her to show off, so she would be over the top with his.

Ravyn held the locket in her hands and let her magic seep into it. I was guessing whatever curses were placed on it were only activated if we opened it since Dorian wore it around his neck. Ravyn was good at this. I'd seen her do it countless times, and it always impressed me. Killian peered over her shoulder. Their magic was just as in tune as mine and Felix's was.

"He certainly found a witch who was thorough and had knowledge of a lot of forbidden killing curses," Killian said.

Reyson walked over and punched Dorian in the face.

"That wouldn't have killed me, but you said nothing when I handed it to my witch. That was foolish."

Reyson waved his hand. Suddenly, Dorian was completely clean and no longer a little stinky. He was dressed to the nines and looked like he usually did in his selfies. Reyson had also conjured a big ass mirror right in front of him.

"I made you beautiful again. Ravyn is perfectly capable of disabling those curses, and then my witch will destroy your painting. So you can sit and watch yourself age while you think about what you did."

Dorian started thrashing and shrieking again. Dorian was a creature I just didn't understand. He wasn't scared of dying. He was still begging for someone just to kill him. The idea of sitting there and watching himself grow old scared him more than that. I was cute. Everyone usually told me that. I had a whole magical skincare routine to make sure I stayed cute as long as possible. I also knew damned well there was beauty in wrinkles and gray hair too.

Ravyn waved her hand and sealed Dorian's lips shut. He turned purple as he continued trying to make that awful shrieking noise.

"He's such a fucking *whiner*. I can't think with him doing that. If he acted like that and asked me to curse some stupid locket, I'd curse him instead. So anyway, we're going to have to wonder twin this shit because it's overkill on this thing."

I grabbed Ravyn's hand so she could share my magic. I felt my magic swell as it joined with hers. I could have easily kept holding my twin sister's hand and made a mess of Dorian Gray once the locket was destroyed, but that was exactly what he wanted. I liked Reyson and Talvath's idea better. I was still pissed about being gassed and put in a cage.

Ravyn and I were Gemini twins, so we were uber effective and powerful when we combined our magic. Ravyn was right that whoever cursed the locket put *way* too many killing curses on it because when we destroyed the curses, the locket was done. It sprung open, and the painting inside caught fire. Ravyn dropped it when the metal started melting.

"And *that* is how you break curses, bitches," Ravyn said, bumping me in the chest.

Okay, that was a little bit of overkill, and she didn't need to assault my boobs to make her point. Lilith clapped her hands in glee.

"I do love my witches, but we still need to take care of Akul. I don't want him in my house any longer than needed. We don't have time to sit here and watch Dorian slowly age. Since they made the locket with magic that came from me, I'm going to speed up the process a bit."

Felix jumped behind Dorian and grabbed his head when he attempted to look away from the mirror. I knew Reyson was mad. We all were, but I knew exactly what Felix was feeling. He was with me when I was taken. Even if he hadn't gone outside to scout, he would have been just as helpless as I was when the gas hit.

Dorian needed me alive, but he understood friendship about as much as he knew how to locate the clitoris. He would have had Felix killed after the gas hit because he just couldn't understand that even though Reyson and Felix didn't have a sexual relationship, Reyson still cared about him just as much as he did me. His vengeance would have been just as severe if Felix had been killed.

Felix blamed himself for me getting taken, but he couldn't have stopped it. I was still pretty pissed about it, but I was certain it was *supposed* to happen this way. I was supposed to be brought to Hell against my will because it would mean my people came too. Reyson could fix their sun, Balthazar was an impartial hacker Lilith could trust, and Lucifer and Gabriel needed to meet. This was all needed to free the Hellhounds.

Felix had a death grip on Dorian's head so that he couldn't look away. When he realized Dorian was trying to clamp his eyes shut, he pried them open with his fingers. Dorian Gray was getting older right before our eyes and having this whole existential crisis about it. Ravyn hadn't unglued his mouth, but it was plastered all over his tear-stained face.

Even if I couldn't hear him, he was being a whiny little bitch. How long did he have to prepare for this? He went out of his way to make a deal with a demon. Dorian Gray thought he was this special little snowflake who would do what literally countless people had tried and failed at. I'm not sure how he thought he would get out of his deal when his superpower was being forever pretty.

Dorian looked to be about ninety years old now, and he wasn't handling life well. He'd probably be dying of old age soon, but Reyson wouldn't let him slip off quietly. He flung his hand out, and Dorian's entire body went rigid on the chair. Don't ask me what kind of magic that was, but I could literally *see* Dorian's skeleton glowing underneath his skin.

Felix took a big step back, but he didn't move in time. Dorian Gray exploded in what looked like a massive cloud of pink glitter. Felix was coated in it. Reyson did that on purpose. He totally did. He smirked at Balthazar and held out his fist for a bump. Balthazar snorted with laughter and bumped it back.

Felix was less amused.

"Seriously? You did that on purpose, you utter cunt!"

I was trying so hard not to laugh at Felix's expense. He just looked so mortified in pink glitter, and while Balthazar always pulled it off, it just wasn't a good look on my familiar. Lilith just sighed.

"Glitter is so much harder to get rid of than blood. Did it really have to be glitter, Reyson? Pink doesn't even go with my decorating."

Felix fell out laughing, and I allowed myself to lose it now that he was. Dorian Gray went out in a cloud of pink glitter, which was just about as ridiculous as his social media feed. No one cared. Everyone was worried about how stupidly hard it was to get glitter out of anything.

"I can get glitter off my hair and body no problem, but you're going to have to toss that rug," Balthazar said. "It's now possessed by ghosts of sad floors at raves held at buildings with carpeted floors. You're going to have to burn it."

"I was going to do that, anyway. Even if I had it professionally cleaned, I'd always *know* Dorian's brains were on it."

"One of you gods with superpowers better clean this shite off of me. Not even Balthazar would be seen in public wearing this much glitter."

"Set the scene. Have I been drinking, and are there

people there taking photos of the party that could make me famous?" Balthazar said.

"That's enough," Lilith said. "The warlock has been poked enough. There's still a traitor in my house I need to deal with."

Lilith waved her hand, and Felix was clean. Then, she stalked out of the room without telling us a damned thing about what she had planned next.

CHAPTER 44
RIPLEY

I admired the effectiveness at which Lilith got shit done, but she was just so bad at keeping us in the loop about anything. I got that we were peons compared to her, but I didn't think even Reyson knew what the fuck had happened. If he did, he would have told us. He was pretty open about literally everything.

Akul was pretty mouthy and ballsy when we went into his room, considering we were there to kill him. He'd been stuck in this spare room with no television and no one giving him any attention while a revolution was going on. This dumbass right here still thought his friends were going to rise up and free him. He was just sitting there with this smug look on his face like he wasn't staring at his creator, and she was pissed.

"Just so you know, while I left you sitting in here to rot, I've been busy. Parliament revoked all laws subjugating Hellhounds. It's now illegal to own them, force them to have sex against their will, and it's a crime to hurt them in any way. They've all been liberated and moved to my properties. Only one family attempted to disobey, and they are dead.

"Literally none of your friends backed you on this, Akul. The family that tried to keep their Hellhounds didn't do it out of loyalty to you. One woman was pregnant, and they didn't want to lose that money. We thought two of them might have ideas about joining your little murder crusade, but we informed one of them you intended to frame him for your misdeeds, and the other wanted nothing to do with you after that. So you're all alone in this, Akul."

"So, what? You've come to tell me I've been a naughty boy for trying to keep inferior, violent creatures in their place? People will eventually realize I was right all along when the Hellhounds slaughter people again."

"Are you mansplaining my creations to me, Akul? Do you think to know what Hellhounds are capable of more than the woman who created them? I may have stepped back for a while, but I'm still quite protective of my children, and you hit the trifecta. You plotted to kill demons so you could continue to abuse Hellhounds, and you dragged one of my witches into it. I have no doubts you would have betrayed Dorian and killed Ripley when this was done to protect your own ass. So, no, Akul, I'm not here to tell you that you've been a naughty boy. You're about to find out what happens when you try to hurt a goddess's children, asshole."

I wouldn't want to be Akul right now. Shit, Akul was looking like he didn't want to be Akul right now. He was trying to fake it, but he shifted in his seat like his asshole was about to swallow him whole, so he didn't have to face Lilith's rage. A bead of sweat slowly trickled down his face.

This was the second time today I'd seen a grown ass man come to terms with the fact that no matter how big and powerful they thought they were, there was always someone bigger and badder out there. I had a healthy ego about my skills, but I wasn't about to piss off a god. Fuck, it was probably pretty stupid to tell Reyson I wouldn't be his wife when we first met, but he was a patient god and let me get to know him first.

"What do you intend to do to me?" Akul asked. "My friends might not be coming for me, but if you kill me over those filthy Hellhounds, the demons will rise up and avenge me."

Oh, man. He just *did not* know when to shut up. I was worried about that too, but we'd gotten this far following Lilith without knowing what her plans were. She knew her creations much better than I did, and I was certain she had already accounted for that. Lilith was *pissed*. Now was the time to shut the fuck up, so she didn't change her mind and think up something worse.

"Samael?" Lilith said, giving him a curt nod.

Samael and Lilith seemed desperately in love, even after all this time. He probably knew what she had planned. Samael had this ornate woven bracelet with a silver talisman on it. He pressed the rune on it, and a sword just appeared in his hand. So *that* was where the swords came from.

Samael just clubbed Akul over the head with the butt of his sword. There wasn't really a gentle way to beat someone with a sword, but Samael wasn't holding back. He flung Akul over his shoulder and nodded to Lilith. She opened another one of her doors, and he stomped through it.

Were we invited to this? I never quite knew. I didn't know until Lilith gestured to the door that we should step through it. I never really knew where I would end up when I stepped through one of these things. I just did it and trusted my creator. She hadn't led us wrong so far, but I was a little shocked to walk out on a stage with an entire audience of demons.

There were reporters here like there always were, but there were also many well-dressed demons who looked crabby as fuck sitting out there. I had plenty of tattoos in strategic places, but none of them would protect me down here like Bram's tattoos. I could hear grunts and displeasure from the crowd when Samael walked Akul to the center of the stage and just dropped him.

Lilith stepped out, and those people didn't immediately shut the fuck up. She waved her hands, and six more magical doors opened. May stepped through one with Duke and Solomon. Other Hellhounds stepped through the other doors. The little bitchy grunts got a little louder.

Lilith stepped to the center of the stage, and everyone was smart enough to shut the fuck up as she stood up there and glared at everyone.

"Unlike the last few press conferences, every Hellhound here has access to watch this one. Parliament asked for a representative for the Hellhounds, so they have one. They are scattered across all of my various properties and have chosen someone from each property to bring their needs to May and then to me.

"I could have done this privately or even among the Hellhounds, but all of you needed to see this. Akul planned to murder any demon to didn't agree with him and then frame one of his friends for it. What do you think he would have done if he had gotten away with it? Do you think *any* of you who disagreed with him on anything would be safe after that?

"If you counted him as a friend and agreed with his

stance on the Hellhounds, do you honestly think he wouldn't have betrayed you too? Giving those sigils to Dorian Gray would have damned everyone here. Two of Akul's friends moved like they were going to try to free him. They were *loyal* to him. One of those loyal friends was the demon he intended to frame for all of this. I want you to take a minute to think about that. All of that so he could continue to abuse one of my creations."

Throats started clearing, and people got really uncomfortable. I was pretty sure they had heard all of this before, but maybe they needed to hear it a third time before it actually sunk in that one of them was way worse than any of the propaganda they spread about Hellhounds.

"All of my creations are sacred to me. I might not have met some of you personally, but you are important to me. I'm just as angry about what Akul would have done to *you* as I am about the treatment of Hellhounds.

"Dorian and Akul kidnapped one of my witches and brought her to Hell. I think Dorian Gray always intended to return her to Earth unharmed because it was the only way he could survive Reyson's wrath, even if that idea were completely misguided. I think Akul always intended to kill Dorian and my witch.

"They might not live here with you, and there might be distrust between the lot of you because of the deals, but the witches and warlocks are just as much your siblings as the Hellhounds are.

"All of you are precious to me, but we must make an example. I don't want to deal with this again. I don't want a single resident of Hell to think something like this is okay because it's not. I want you to think about this incident if you think you want to commit violence against one of my creations. That goes for all of you. I don't care if you're a demon, Hellhound, or witch. I made you. I can easily unmake you."

Lilith turned and pointed her finger at Akul, and he lifted off the ground. He finally woke up from that head knock and realized he was in front of his friends. He had to have a pretty shitty headache, but he started screaming for people to fight back and save him.

It was pretty beautiful. Yeah, these people counted him as a friend, and they were probably still pissed they lost their Hellhounds, but I think it *finally* got through to them that he'd never been their friend at all. They quickly drowned him out with chants calling him a traitor.

He didn't explode into pink glitter. I was pretty sure Reyson would trademark that if he could. Instead, Akul's body just sort of crumpled in on itself as he screamed in pain and terror. It didn't take long at all for Akul to just disappear in a flash of light. The entire room went silent.

"In case you were wondering, that was agonizing for both of us. I didn't enjoy it, but it needed to happen. Be kind to each other. I will be moving to my main resort to fix our sun with Reyson next. You are welcome to join us, all of you. This is a big moment in our history. The Hellhounds are staying there. Mingle with them. Talk to them and get to know them. You'll see they are no different from you are. That is all."

Everyone was clapping this time instead of shouting questions. I was sure some of them were still against freeing the Hellhounds, but they at least acknowledged Akul was a bigger monster.

When the clapping died down, Lilith opened more doors. I saw plenty of demons with tattoos disappear, but I didn't know if they were going to be at the ceremony.

It was progress.

CHAPTER 45
REYSON

had been slowly reading my way through books at Ripley's library. I enjoyed the books about werewolves having sex, and that opened a million questions for me, but after I had settled on a name, I moved to the history books.

I didn't pay attention to the creatures on Earth while I was in the Aether, even when my services were required to bring balance. They really had come a long way, and not just in their inventions. Of course, they still did terrible things and thought it was the will of one of the gods. But they did plenty of remarkable things too.

Many of the things that people got away with the last time I walked the earth were now illegal, for a good reason. Supernaturals usually stayed out of the affairs of humans to keep their secrets. Still, if a particular human or group of humans was becoming so dangerous that several countries came together to end the threat, the supernaturals were enlisting and fighting right alongside them.

I missed all that while I was playing in the Aether, but it was quite an honor to be invited to Lilith's realm to help with this event and to fix their sun. I was glad my witch got to be here to see it too. This would be written about like the history books in her library. I was still *furious* that Dorian and Akul assaulted her library and kidnapped her, but they were dead, so I dealt with it.

Lilith's resort was something else. She put the Hellhounds up in style. They must do theatre out here because they constructed a large stone stage in an extensive field where people could sit and watch. Lilith must have provided clothes for all of them because there were a ton of Hellhounds sitting on blankets in the grass in much better outfits than the demons gave them.

They had picnic baskets and were snacking and drinking wine. I was happy for them. Plenty of demons started appearing using the means of travel Lilith had gifted them with her sigils.

I stood on that stage and glared at them. They rooted for Lilith to end Akul's existence, but that didn't mean they saw these Hellhounds as people. I only killed Dorian out of respect for Lilith and her creations, but they needed to get over the fact that they couldn't buy and sell people anymore.

This ceremony was also a monumental moment in their history. We weren't thinking of these people when we created the universe. Lilith was thinking about her creations when she made Hell, but none of these people personally. Not even some of the gods who came later got to see what they were about to see. They were about to witness two gods channel their powers to fix a dying sun.

They could at least show some fucking respect by being nice to the Hellhounds.

Demons who worked at Lilith's resort came out to meet the newcomers. They started handing out baskets to each group. They'd better get one of those to my group because I wanted to show off. They'd only seen some of what I was capable of. My witch had seen me kill and use my more destructive gifts to protect her and her library, but she'd never seen me use them to create anything.

I knew that everyone at the library knew I helped create the universe, but they couldn't even conceptualize that in their heads. Yet, I was there, and not even the best poets and storytellers in history could put into words what the experience was like.

But I could show them a little by helping Lilith and her realm. It was also just the right thing to do.

Lilith's employees came on stage and handed baskets to the Hellhounds and my people. Felix took the basket, and Ripley wrapped her arms around my waist.

"Thank you for doing this," she whispered.

She also snuck in a pinch to my bottom when she hugged me. I'd always loved aggressive women, and Ripley was just perfect. They disappeared to find the perfect spot of grass with a good view of the stage.

Lilith was created after me with different gifts. I didn't presume to think she was less powerful than me because she was younger. I didn't consider her less than me because she was a woman either. I was pretty sure Lilith was created around the same time as the god who bullied her, and he was trying to make himself look more powerful by being an ass.

This was her realm. Lilith created it and kept all of us out unless she wanted us here. She used unique magic than we did when we created the universe. As a result, there were several of us pooling our powers and contributing something different. I was happy to do whatever she needed me to do to heal her realm.

Samael appeared with another basket. He kissed Lilith's forehead, handed her the basket, and went to join Lucifer and the others on their blanket.

"Tell me what you want me to do."

Lilith pulled a jar of what looked like blood out of the basket. She painted a sigil in the middle of a circle and stepped back.

"There are candles in the basket. Can you help me put them on each point of the sigil? I'm going to need to share your magic the way Ripley and Ravyn do."

I wasn't even angry about that. Ripley and Ravyn did it all the time, and it was beautiful to watch. If Lilith just needed me to stand there in this circle painted from blood while she used me like the device Balthazar always had on him to keep his cell phone charged, I'd be honored to do it.

It didn't take long to place all the candles. Lilith snapped her fingers and lit them. Was that sandalwood and lavender? It was lovely. Lilith stood at the center of the stage and addressed the crowd.

"Everyone, this is a significant moment in our history. Samael and Lucifer are the only people here who were alive when I created Hell. Today, all of you get to see Reyson, and I fix a dying sun. All of you are now free citizens. Enjoy the moment, but look at us, not the sun. There's bound to be an occurrence that hurts your eyes. One shouldn't look directly into the sun, even if it were dying like ours. Just feel the warmth on your skin and enjoy it.

"Use this moment to move past anything you were holding onto. That goes for Hellhounds and demons alike. I know plenty of you want vengeance. Some of you deserve it. I'm asking you to please, for the sake of this realm, to put it aside. Let this new sun usher in an era of prosperity and peace."

The demons looked uneasy at first, but all the Hellhounds started clapping. I wouldn't have blamed them if they wanted to kill their oppressors, but all the Hellhounds were here, and demons vastly outnumbered them. The demons I'd met might not want to admit when they had lost, but the Hellhounds seemed to not even want to risk anyone for the sake of revenge.

The demons looked around like they had just hit the plot twist of a gripping novel. They looked like they couldn't believe the Hellhounds were clapping for peace instead of shifting and trying to fight them. That must have been quite the propaganda slam when they started smearing the Hellhounds here.

The demons got into the clapping too. I was betting some of them knew full well what they were doing was wrong and was against all this because they thought there would be a reckoning if we freed them. If there was, it was going to be from Lilith. The Hellhounds just seemed to want to enjoy their freedom and find their families for now.

Lilith let the applause die down and stepped into her circle. She held out her hands and nodded to me.

"Are you ready?" she asked.

I was always ready to help out most of the other gods.

CHAPTER 46
BRAM

I pulled Ripley into my lap and winked at Balthazar to snuggle close. I wrapped an arm around her waist and used my other hand to play with Balthazar's hair. Talvath was sitting on the blanket with us. Talvath's seer Anod rarely left the house because he said people gave him bad vibes that sometimes triggered visions, but he was here too. Everyone I cared about was here to watch this with me.

I looked around with a small smile. I wasn't the only one. You just didn't go through what these Hellhounds went through with each other for that long and not start developing feelings. Some of the younger Hellhounds had paired up and were snuggling.

None of these Hellhounds knew who their parents were or where their children were, but that didn't mean another Hellhound hadn't stepped up. There were older Hellhounds on a blanket looking proudly at some that were snuggling, and there were some pups out there that didn't know if they were allowed to play or not.

Two elderly Hellhounds had a blanket with four pups laying on it. While Lilith and Reyson were setting everything up, they took them by the hand and introduced them to all the other pups out there. I was hoping to see them wrestle and play, but it didn't take long for Lilith to set up what she needed and address the pile. The pups were adorable as they dog piled on their adoptive parents. They were still young enough to not quite have everything beaten out of them yet.

I didn't think I'd ever see this day. Hellhounds were sitting among demons as equals, and the demons weren't doing a damned thing about it. They weren't even scowling at them. Instead, they were enjoying a picnic in Lilith's amphitheater while something pretty major happened. Some of them even shot smiles to some of the younger Hellhound pups when they got a little loud.

Lilith gave her speech, and Reyson stepped into the circle with her. They joined hands, and the hair on the back of my neck stood up at the power pulsing from the stage. I'd seen Reyson use some of his gifts before, but I knew that was nowhere near the extent of what he was capable of.

It was pretty much an honor for everyone here to be witnessing this. There were countless different religions on Earth right now, and some had some pretty devout followers. They prayed, asked for guidance, and gave those gods credit for every good thing that happened in their life. There was all this devotion, and I was certain Lilith wasn't the only god who had briefly retired. Likewise, Reyson wasn't the only god who spent ages in the Aether not listening.

It was honestly a total mind fuck meeting both of them. Yeah, they were powerful, but they were also... normal? Reyson fiercely protected those he cared about like I did. He could be passive aggressive when he wanted to be, and he had a twisted sense of humor. There were countless ways to kill Dorian that didn't involve coating Felix in glitter, but he went there anyway. I'd been in the room when Felix and Balthazar were trading barbs, and it was pretty fucking funny.

Lilith had been flexing her powers without telling us much of her plans, but she had plenty of love to go around. It was obvious when she looked at Samael. She could have asked me to stay and be her representative. I would have done it because it was the right thing to do. Instead, she found a better alternative because she wanted me and everyone at the library to be happy. She didn't give birth to me, but she still considered me her child.

The black candles surrounding Lilith and Reyson flared several feet in the air, then the two of them started glowing with an almost blinding light. I could only see their outlines and couldn't look directly at them without hurting my eyes.

I could see their heads flung back as a large ball of magical light exploded from their chest and into the sky. I didn't look directly at it because I wasn't an idiot, but it went straight into our sun.

Ever since I had been alive, Hell's sun differed from that of Earth. It warmed us, and it wasn't dark out, but it was always a redder color than the sun on Earth. I let my gaze travel up in the general direction of our sun. The sickly red color was gone, and it was now a healthy ball of fire.

They did it! Holy shit, they just healed an entire realm. Even the young pups knew how amazing this was. They started jumping up and down, howling. The adult Hellhounds weren't about to let them feel left out. They flung back their heads and joined them. I did too.

The demons weren't even judging us. They didn't try to silence them like they would have when the Hellhounds were their property. Instead, they were clapping, hooting, and even the wealthiest Hellhounds out there weren't worried about manners and decorum right now.

Ripley spun in my lap and flung me on my back. She didn't want sex in front of all these people, right? I was okay with putting on a show in front of everyone at the library, but Talvath was kind of like my dad, and two of these Hellhounds might be my parents. And there were kids out there.

She kissed me, then snuggled into my side.

"That was fucking amazing, and I don't even live here."

I squeezed her. All this entire group had seen so far were the bad parts of Hell. They saw the rich neighborhoods and people abusing their Hellhounds. They didn't see all the good things about my home.

"I know we need to get you back to your library, but Lilith made it possible for you to come back. Everyone knows your face and that this wouldn't be possible without you. No one will attack you if you come back. You do get weekends off. We could come back here as a vacation, and I could show you around."

Did she even want that? Would any of them? I had always intended to come back and visit with Talvath, but would they want to come?

"Definitely," she said. "You and Talvath are close, and Lucifer and Gabriel have a whole thing now. So we'll be back here often."

"You'd better visit me too," Lilith said.

I didn't know she had left the stage, but she was standing right on top of us.

"All of you. I'm out of retirement now, and I want you to keep me up to date on my witches on Earth. None of this would be possible without you. I consider you friends now. I *want* to hear from you. Bram, I expect updates on your new life at the library. I want to know if anyone gives you problems because you're the only Hellhound there. I'll make a visit and set them straight."

Did Lilith just threaten any supernatural bully that had a problem with me? That was certainly interesting. I was used to fighting my own battles, but having two gods at your back was never a bad idea.

Lilith waved her hand, and another one of her doors opened.

"I'm not clueless about Earth, even though I haven't lived there in a very long time. I know the twins have important jobs that a substitute can't really do. It's time to go back because I know people are missing you. I do, however, expect you back here for visits, and I may turn up for a visit myself."

All the witches and warlocks had eyes the size of saucers that Lilith might just pop up and visit them. I thought it was pretty fucking cool too. There were plenty of times I doubted her because of how my people were treated down here, but she'd just been biding her time waiting for the right moment.

She was pretty damned cool.

Reyson scooped Ripley up.

"Let's get back to your library, my witch. I'm sure whoever they have running it while you were gone did something you didn't like. We'll help you fix it."

"The sentient books are probably having a total meltdown because no one has gone in there to talk to them," Ripley moaned. "I *know* whoever they had fill in for me didn't because they get violent if you don't do it right."

Lilith looked amused as Reyson carried Ripley through. I turned around, and Talvath and Anod were standing there with tears in their eyes.

"I knew this day would come, eventually. Go, Bram. I'll bring your things to you once I've packed them up."

I grabbed Talvath and pulled him into a bear hug. My life would have been totally different if it weren't for him. I felt bad leaving him behind, but he *wanted* me to go.

I hugged Anod and stepped into my new life at the library.

CHAPTER 47
RIPLEY

Lilith's door brought us straight to my desk at the library. It was mostly dark except for the safety lights. I closed my eyes and inhaled the comforting scent of ritual incense and old books. I was home. That lasted about two seconds. Felix turned the lights on, and I saw what they had done to my library.

I threw back my head and screamed. I scared Balthazar, and he shrieked too. I hadn't been gone *that* long, and my library was a hot mess. Whoever had filled in for me hadn't even attempted to re shelve anything. Instead, they pulled every book cart in the library over to my desk and just shoved ancient tomes on it.

"They drank something on my desk *without a coaster.* There are rings now. This desk is an antique. It belonged to the first librarian that ran this place after it was completed. If they ruined the fucking desk, what did they do to the books?" I shrieked.

Reyson peered over my shoulder and frowned. Was he seeing this shit? Was he willing to make someone explode in a cloud of pink glitter over it? Because I certainly didn't know how to dispose of a body without getting caught.

Reyson waved his hand, and there was suddenly an ornate pot covering the rings on my desk with a beautiful, healthy Queen of the Night planted in it. The flowers only bloomed at night for a few hours, but they had a ton of medicinal purposes in potions and salves. Unfortunately, the flowers and plants were super expensive in witch markets, and most people didn't want to deal with a cactus you had to babysit to get the flowers.

Many people preferred to buy the potion or salve already made because they were lazy, but I'd always loved my garden witch classes. Ravyn leaned over my desk.

"Now, you can't even see the damage to your desk. The leaves on these would make pretty potent curses if you wanted revenge on your substitute."

"They sent a fucking degenerate in my library! If they just threw these books on the cart and ignored all the coasters on my desk because you're all here with me now, then they *definitely* looked at porn on my work computer. I'll bet they didn't even clear it when they were done. They are probably into weird shit like lesbians with men in T-Rex costumes."

"I still can't believe you felt the need to send that to me when you found it," Ravyn groaned.

"You're not innocent in this either, Ravyn. You made me watch it too," Killian said.

"I demand to see this video," Balthazar said. "And hello! Computer genius here. I can do an exorcism on your laptop like it's never seen porn during work hours. Unfortunately, I can't fix sticky keyboards. You might want to burn it if they are a work jerker."

They'd better not have! Not only was it gross, but just because you *thought* no one was here watching you didn't mean there wasn't. The spirits here lived with the Puritans, but some of them were perverts. I had to reinforce the wards in my apartment when one of them haunted my bathroom and only appeared when I was naked.

I heard the bell from the front door as it opened. It was late, and the library was closed. The last time I heard that bell, Dorian Gray tossed a canister of gas in my library and kidnapped me. I called magic to my fingertips and sprinted to the lobby.

We ended up scaring the shit out of some kid, who jumped so hard, he fell flat on his ass. He was a warlock, and his hands were empty.

"What the shit are you doing in my library?" I demanded.

"Oh, thank Lilith, you're back. I just came back because I left my phone charger. My mom is on the board here, and she was so mad at me when I got a C on my Arcane Magic exam at the academy. So she pulled some strings, and if I watched the library while you were gone, I'd get extra credit on my exam that would bump me up to a B.

"I didn't *want* to. I have no idea what I'm doing. I don't even have a library card here. My first time in this library was when I showed up to work. I don't know where *anything* is, and people got mean about it. I begged her to take over for me, but a C just isn't good enough when you have my last name."

"You knew where the coasters were on my desk, but you still didn't use them."

"What? I'm sorry! No one told me shit about what I was supposed to do. They said to just sit at the desk and let people do their thing. No one told me everyone was going to want to bleed on the desk. I'm only a freshman. We haven't even gotten to blood magic yet at the academy!"

"Get your charger and go home. I'll take it from here."

I wasn't even mad at the kid, even though he was old enough to know how to use a coaster. I was, however, really mad at his mother for abusing her position on the library board to put her eighteen-year-old son in my job while I was kidnapped.

She wouldn't have been able to do a good bit of my job either, but she knew the rules here and how things were run. Fuck, she'd at least been around blood magic and didn't get squeamish about the system here. If I was going to get revenge for this, it wouldn't be against some kid who just had his magic awakened and was in over his head.

But I'd totally drop a little hex on his mom because she should have known better.

He was super nervous as he came back with his phone charged.

"Am I in trouble?" he squeaked.

"That depends. Were you looking at porn on my work computer?"

I think I just murdered that kid from sheer embarrassment. Even his hair was blushing.

"I didn't! My family arranged a marriage with a prominent witch, and we are both saving ourselves until marriage. I don't look at porn!"

Oh, man. That was quite a mouthful. This kid was *way* too innocent for his own good, and I could say without fibbing that his fiancé was definitely enjoying her academy experience and getting plenty of dick.

"Dude, I'm going to do you a favor and give you some

advice, even though you damaged my desk. Don't deny yourself *anything* because you think she is. Witches and warlocks are sexual creatures. Most of us have moved into the modern world and stopped arranging marriages, but there are a few holdouts.

"You probably don't even want to marry her and are doing it because your parents want you to. I can guarantee she feels exactly the same. Watch all the porn. Find out how sex works. Experiment with your classmates. If you do go through with marrying her, she'll appreciate having a husband who knows how to please her. Now, go forth and fornicate, young Jedi."

I mortified that kid, and he scurried out of my library. So now, I was left with the mess he left behind. Felix wrapped his arms around my waist and hugged me.

"I was there through all your training. I was here every year you ran this library. So I can help you fix this."

"And bonus points, there's no jizz on your work computer," Balthazar said.

"You don't just need to put books away and deal with the sentient books," Ravyn said. "Silvaria and Dorian made promises to the spirits of this library to corrupt the system here. So you're going to have to deal with that."

"Allow me," Reyson said, giving me a little bow.

I told Ravyn all about how Reyson addressed spirits, but she'd never seen it in person before. She hated dealing with them just as much as I did. There was so much prep work and ass-kissing involved any time you were dealing with ghosts. Reyson just skipped all that. Ravyn was going to lose her shit.

Reyson didn't even so much as light black candles or put a protective circle of salt around us when he got to work. I had seen him do this before, and it was still amazing. He used that sexy voice that bounced off the walls and commanded respect.

"I need every spirit in this library to listen to me! A witch and a stupid human sold you a false bill of goods. Dorian Gray used the witch for his own purposes, then betrayed her. That witch is rotting in jail with a good bit of the wealthy supernatural community wanting her death.

"Dorian betrayed many people, and he kidnapped the caretaker of this library. I killed him myself. Whatever they promised you would never have happened. They aren't capable of doing the rites on any of you. If they promised you I could do something about it, I can't.

"None of you are my creations. I can't do a damned thing to your souls. I can't force them from this place and move them to the Aether because I didn't make any of you. But, if I *could* do something about it, I would for those of you that want it.

"There are plenty of spirits out there that weren't given the rites or a purpose with their afterlife. I'm not saying you don't have to be bitter about your lot, but I am demanding you put the library back the way it was. My witch was hurt because you manipulated the system here and allowed Dorian Gray into this library. I can't move you to the Aether, but I can't be killed. I can make your eternity miserable if you hurt my witch and her library."

Ravyn was just sitting there with her mouth open. Everyone knew better than to talk to ghosts like that. That was when they went full poltergeist. They'd start flinging shit and wailing if you so much as offended them. They never did that with Reyson.

The same drowned puritan boy who addressed us the

first time came back. Plenty of adults had died in the massacre, but he seemed to be their spokesperson.

"We heard you, ancient one. Many of us are happy with the jobs they gave us on these unholy sites, but some of us are very tired of not touching or tasting. They gave us an option, and we took it."

"Let me tell you all something. You might not be able to touch or taste, but you can communicate. What do you think happens when you leave this site? You move to the Aether. You still won't be able to touch or taste, but you lose the ability to communicate with anyone. You just are.

"You'll be that way until the Aether decides it's time for you to be reborn. You'll remember nothing of your previous lives. Anything you might have learned will be forgotten. You'll have all the senses you lost when you are reborn, but that also includes pain and heartbreak. You could experience a violent death and not be given the rites again. This time, you wouldn't have the buildings on this site.

"I get what you want. I do. I'm just saying life is hard and unexpected. People are violent no matter what century you live in. It might not make things better. Do we have a deal?"

"We do, but only because we have no other option, ancient one. We've always liked our current caretaker and never intended for her to be harmed. This will not happen again."

The spirit disappeared, and Ravyn fell out laughing.

"Holy shit. The next time I need to deal with the ghosts at the museum, I'm calling Reyson."

Reyson squared his shoulders and tossed his hair over his shoulder.

"Now that's settled, I think I'd like to get my nipples pierced like Bram."

That was just so Reyson. After everything we went through in Hell, me flipping out at the state of my library, and him spanking the ghost into cooperating, he was just ready to move on.

With nipple piercings, apparently.

CHAPTER 48
RIPLEY

My first day back at work wouldn't be a huge one. It was Friday, so I'd be off for two days after this. When I woke up, everyone was gone except Balthazar. He was rubbing his nose and erection into me. I rolled over and kissed him.

"Hello, my love. Can I say how much I adore waking up next to you?"

"Reyson is cooking breakfast, and Felix, Bram, and Gabriel snuck downstairs to get a head start on putting your library back in order."

I bit his collarbone.

"Thanks for the update, but I have you all to myself right now. Do you need to feed?"

He didn't have that little twitch like he needed to, but sometimes, I thought he wasn't comfortable asking Reyson or me to bite us, so he put it off until he got uncomfortable. But I had a feeling Reyson liked it just as much as I did and had no problem with Balthazar sinking his fangs in us whenever he needed.

"Reyson let me when you were with Bram. The magic in

his blood is so fucking potent, I nearly pass out when I feed from him."

"Balthazar, Reyson and I aren't *allowing* you to bite us, and it's this enormous chore. It's extremely erotic, intimate, and an *honor* to have our blood sustain you. Take it when you need it. Don't wait until you get that little twitch. I'm going to get big mad if you don't bite me every time we fuck. Reyson probably feels the same. You can also sneak in a little bite when we are snuggling. Just don't do it in the library because I've had to kick a few vampires out for doing that. I'm supposed to be responsible and shit as the librarian, and they would definitely bitch about it if they saw."

Balthazar chuckled.

"Noted, but I don't feed in public. I've bitten a few people to make a point, but I made it hurt."

"Be honest. Do you need to feed right now?"

"Can I admit something?"

"No judgment here."

"I pretty much *always* want to bite you, but I don't really need to right now."

I rolled over and looked at my alarm clock. Damn. Not being on a set schedule while I was in Hell really threw me off. Balthazar had epic lasting time and a refractory period they liked to promise in dick pill advertisements, but I was guessing he could also fuck me silly with a pre-work quicky.

If I hadn't been super gracious with my snooze button and slept through four people exiting my bed, I could be getting super dicked by a vampire before work.

"We don't have time for a quickie, but *please* bite me."

His fangs popped out, and he traced them down my neck. If anyone else tried to rub their teeth on me, I would have blasted them out of my bed with magic. When Balthazar did it, I broke into goosebumps and instantly got wet.

I moaned and tangled my hands in his hair to pull him closer. Getting bit *should not* be this sexy.

I felt his fangs sink into my neck. He explained it to me he could control the type of venom that hit my system. It could either be agonizing or erotic. I was pretty much furious about the vampires I took to bed before him that had me thinking all vampire bites were painful. Fucking sadists. That was *way* different from getting tied up and spanked. I had safe words for that.

Balthazar removed his fangs and licked the wound closed. Mother fucker. I was now hornier than that time Ravyn paid a greased up shifter to crash our birthday and give me a lap dance, and not even my trusty Hitachi wand was fast enough to get me to home base before I had to go to work.

I grabbed Balthazar and kissed him.

"That should be illegal, and I have plans for you later, but I really do need to get some coffee in me before work."

"You need sustenance too, my witch," Reyson said from the door. "I made breakfast to fortify you while you are putting things right in your library."

How was he so perfect? The man gave Dorian Gray the death he feared so much for coming at me like that, and he'd do it again. And he made me a fucking souffle for breakfast and my coffee just the way I liked it. Ladies, if he doesn't know how you take your coffee, he's not even trying. Walk away.

I utterly destroyed Reyson's souffle because he was an amazing chef, and I was running late. I threw on my clothes and was downstairs to unlock the doors with just a minute to spare. I got a whole standing ovation when the regulars realized it was me unlocking the door.

Camilla, one of my favorites, pulled me into a hug and

nuzzled my neck. She was this shifter granny, and they tended to be on the tactile side. She was her pack matriarch and had several alphas in her line. Camilla was constantly in here researching her family history. She'd already gone back many generations, but she was trying to trace it to one of the original wolf packs Selene created.

"We are so grateful to have you back. Dennis was sweet, but he had no idea what he was doing. He nearly shat himself when we showed him the bowl on your desk and how the library works. I think the wee lad briefly fainted when he saw the blood, and all we did was prick our fingers. Should you really be back at work so soon after your abduction? We missed you, but we were having fun messing with the young warlock."

I snorted and led them inside. What was Dennis's mother thinking? Most of my regulars were senior citizens and utter savages when it came to burns. They regularly gave *me* a hard time just for helping them. I liked it and flung it right back at them, but a nervous young warlock out of his element? They would have eaten him alive.

"Please tell me you didn't make him cry."

"Pssh. We aren't cruel. We just enjoyed making him blush. It's not like you have any shame. That's impossible with you. Did you know he's a virgin still?"

"He let that slip when he came back for his phone charger."

"Oh, my. Is that a Hellhound?"

Bram came around one of the stacks, and he looked magnificent.

"That one is all mine."

"Lucky girl. He looks like a total beast in the sack."

"Ripley?"

I turned around, and Professor Krauss was standing there.

"Someone posted on the library's social media page you were back at work. Shouldn't you be taking some time off to deal with your trauma?"

I motioned her over to my desk. I think we inflicted way more trauma on certain residents of Hell and Dorian Gray than I got. I motioned her over to my desk and fired up my electric tea kettle on the shelf behind me. I pulled her favorite lemon cookies out of my drawer and filled her in on what happened.

"That's quite a journey. I always knew you and Ravyn were destined for greatness. I still do tarot readings for Ravyn because I'm quite fond of her. Something big is headed her way."

"It had better not be a stupid, cheating wolf."

"If Lilith ever visits, I'd be honored to meet her."

"I think she'd love to meet you too."

Professor Krauss's eyes went to all the carts by my desk. Felix, Bram, and Gabriel had gotten through some of them, but only Felix knew where those books went. That was going to be a slow process, and if I didn't get in there and talk to the sentient books, they would go feral.

"I see Dennis left you a mess."

"I'm still not sure how his mother pulled strings to get him in here. She should have been here herself."

"She probably couldn't. Your friend Kaine held a press conference after he got back from Hell. Everyone knows Silvaria and several prominent members of the supernatural community were arrested. A lot of them were board members. Some of them were very close to board members. People have gotten fired if they weren't arrested, and anyone who wasn't is trying to do damage control. I don't think they could spare anyone to run the library."

"What else happened while I was gone?"

"Well, plenty of people are trying to pretend they didn't know Dorian Gray, but he practically posted a selfie every time he used the toilet, so it's all out there. You'll be glad to know Kaine made your Gabriel out to be a vital part of rescuing you and freeing the Hellhounds. I'm sure he was, but Kaine talked him up. I'm guessing you'll find the magical community will be a lot nicer to him and his family from now on. Especially since they now realize even powerful, respected families can fall."

I looked to Gabriel as he came back for another book. I was happy for him, and I desperately wanted that for him. He gained a lot when he met Lucifer, but Lucifer was in Hell and would probably stay there.

"They'd better because Reyson has opinions on that."

"I hope he does if they don't shape up. It looks like Dennis left a mess. I'll leave you to get your library back in shape."

By the time my day was done, all the books on the carts were on the shelf, they put away the carts, and Reyson had to heal three bites from the sentient books. They were calmed, though. My library was finally back in order.

We ordered delivery and headed to my bedroom, but I had other ideas. Reyson had been talking about it for so long, and Bram was on board. I curled up in the Papasan chair in my bedroom and looked at my guys.

"For tonight's entertainment, I want to watch Reyson and Bram."

They both let out a little growl. Yeah, they were totally into it. I couldn't *wait* to watch.

CHAPTER 49
REYSON

I was so in love with my witch. She pointed me towards a genre of fiction that wasn't so prevalent the last time I walked the Earth to pick my name. It raised so many questions for me because every writer took different liberties with their cocks. I'd sampled nearly every supernatural creation of every gender in my time, but a willing male shifter had never come to me to warm my bed.

Based on some of the literal infant arms I read about, neither had some of those writers.

She could have hit me and pitched a tantrum when I asked her to find me a wolf. I think it amused her when I asked. When she started collecting men, I put the idea out of my head, and I loved them like brothers. It would have been weird to bring an outsider in, then Bram joined us.

Big, strapping, tattooed Bram with rings in his nipples. He was beautiful, and he promised to pierce mine for me when Talvath brought his stuff over from Hell. Bram had been flirting with both Balthazar and me, and I heard him admit he didn't care about gender when it came to sex, but the man looked a little nervous about this.

"What's wrong?"

"It's a Hellhound thing."

"Have you not heard me talking about how much I want to experience your Hellhound thing? So let's talk it out."

I had a feeling Bram was about to tell me something those books got wrong. There was plenty of gay shifter fiction. There were even some where men got pregnant and carried the babies in the books. I was fairly certain Bram wasn't about to tell me he would impregnate me with this encounter, but wouldn't it be wild if he did?

"Well, it's a dominance thing. My Hellhound wants to fight you and *make* you submit, but you're kind of a god. You'd kick my ass. I rolled Ripley on her back, and she wrapped her legs around me. That was enough."

He looked unsure, but wrestling was also a fun form of foreplay, and I didn't *have* to win at everything. Balthazar didn't seem too into it, but I had a vampire lover in the past who was into hunting his prey, and it got pretty kinky. So I let him win, of course, but I put up enough of a fight that he still earned it.

"I know my limits, Bram. However, I also think that sounds like a lot of fun."

"I think it sounds hot," Ripley said. "I'm here for it."

"Me too," Balthazar said. "I think you should both cover yourselves in lube first to make it interesting."

Ooh. Balthazar was always the source of the most delicious ideas. We were going to need lube anyway, and some of Ripley's lube was flavored. I would *adore* licking something strawberry flavored off a very sexy Hellhound.

"I've got spare sheets in the drawer," Ripley said. "I vote for two hot, lubed up men wrestling, but one of you is going to volunteer as tribute to do laundry and wash it out of my good sheets."

That was all I needed to hear, and washing clothes in this century was fascinating. I was out of my clothes in seconds and rifling through her toy drawer. There were so many options here. This was an important moment in my long life. I'd never done this before. It was shocking to me too. I couldn't ruin this with the wrong flavor lube.

"Is the mango good?"

"Oh, Lilith, no. That one is vile. I should have tossed it. But, if you use the pineapple and Bram uses the coconut, you could make a kinky pina colada when you rub up against each other. Those two taste the best."

My witch always had the best ideas. I tossed Bram the coconut and got a good look at him nude. He was beautiful. He had metal barbells lining the entire length of his cock. That was also a first for me, but I imagined it was quite pleasurable. Did I want him to do that to mine? I'd take the pain if it added pleasure to my witch.

I squirted the lube on my chest and rubbed it in. I'd barely gotten myself oiled up when Bram came out of nowhere, and body tackled me on the bed. So, it begins.

I growled and flipped Bram on his back. I'd wrestled with men before, but never coated in different flavored lube. It smelled divine. I didn't know what a pina colada was, but I was going to have to try one. I tried to pin Bram with my arm across his chest, but it just kept sliding everywhere.

Bram used the opportunity to bring his knees between us and practically launch me off this massive bed. He was quite strong, and that was a massive turn on. Not everyone could do that, even if I was holding back. Things just got interesting, and I was hard as a rock.

I loved sleeping on Ripley's silk sheets, but they made lube wrestling nude a lot more difficult. Bram and I went for each other at the same time and slid straight off the bed. Bram landed on top of me with his knees in my ribs. I had super healing, but that didn't mean I couldn't get the air knocked out of my lungs.

Bram flung his body over my back. I could feel his erection pressing into my back, and I knew *exactly* where I wanted it. I heard him snarl, and then I felt his teeth pressing into my shoulder. He was trying to get me to submit. I didn't need a book to tell me that.

I could have kept this up and continued wrestling, but why? My cock was so hard, it hurt. I could feel how hard he was. I wanted, no, *needed* to be fucked.

"I submit!" I growled.

Bram was still interested in playing a little rough. He was off my back in seconds, but he wrapped his arms around my waist and flung me on the bed. He jumped behind me and spooned my back. I felt more lube and then his fingers.

I knew Ripley was doing this for me, but we were also putting on a show for her. Bram knew that just as much as I did. He pulled his teeth out of my shoulder as soon as he slid his fingers inside me.

"Balthazar, get over here and suck Reyson's cock," Bram said.

It appeared we all had good ideas today. I felt the need to contribute. Ripley was sitting there with hooded eyes and her hands down her thong. A beautiful woman should *not* be pleasuring herself with so many men in the room.

"Felix and Gabriel, you'd better get over there and pleasure our woman," I growled.

This was perfect. Bram was working me with his fingers and biting my shoulder. Balthazar seemed to have no gag reflex whatsoever. Gabriel had his face between Ripley's thighs, and Felix was playing with her nipples. She was looking me dead in the eye and moaning. I was so turned on right now.

Bram was an expert with his fingers, but I was ready and I wanted more. I curled my fingers into Balthazar's hair, and my eyes never left Ripley's.

"I want the knot."

Bram grabbed my knee and hoisted my leg up. I felt him guide himself inside me. Oh, my. Those piercings were something else. Would it be considering copying him if I got some of those for my witch? Maybe there were other options to please her.

I'd think about that when I didn't have a pierced, curiously growing cock in my ass. Bram was already situated and thrusting. I could *feel* him expanding inside me. Between the piercings, Balthazar's attention, and the Ripley show on the other side of the room, I might actually be losing my mind right now.

There was a time for gentle, sweet lovemaking, but it was pretty much never after that kind of foreplay. I had expectations going in, and my blood was pumping after that wrestling match with Bram. He was giving me *exactly* want I needed and wanted.

There was an entire multitude of different shifters walking this planet created by different gods. My friend Loki thought it would be funny to terrorize the world with spider shifters. It was so amazing that they kept some of their animals when they were having sex like this. Their creators were *clearly* thinking about their bedroom partners when they did this because it felt amazing, especially with

Balthazar's attention to my cock and Ripley's cries of pleasure.

It was sensory overload, and I wouldn't last much longer. Bram locked into place and sank his canines in my shoulder right when Balthazar squeezed my balls. I came as hard as the fictional orgasms in the books I read that seemed to happen in under a minute, and people thought they saw a god in the aftershocks. None of us made appearances during other people's bedroom activities unless someone had specifically invited us.

I felt Bram let go, and there was just one thing missing.

"Bite me, Balthazar!"

He sunk his fangs in my thigh, and the pleasure from my aftershocks increased. This was perfect. Better than I could have imagined. I was grateful to Bram for inviting Balthazar, and that little show Ripley, Felix, and Gabriel put on was like the whipped cream and cherry on top of the milkshakes I'd grown fond of in this century.

Bram spooned my back, and I yanked Balthazar up to snuggle with him.

"I think in addition to my cookbook, I'd like to publish shifter porn under a pseudonym strictly for accuracy purposes."

Bram nuzzled my neck.

"I'm happy to do this again for book research."

"And I'm happy to watch and participate. Most people know those books aren't accurate. They read them because they are kinky and fun."

"Well, I just experienced accurate, and it was kinky *and* fun. So I'm making it a thing."

"Lilith help us all," Felix moaned.

CHAPTER 50
FELIX

I wasn't remotely into men, so I wasn't watching the Reyson show. My eyes and hands were solely on Ripley, and *she* was certainly enjoying it. I had plans as soon as Reyson got his arse out of our bed. Reyson got fucked up the ass, but I wasn't planning on it. I'd be damned if he was the only one who got a threesome tonight. I had way too much fun with the last one I had.

Reyson stood up and stretched like a cat who just got a can of tuna. Trust me. I knew that feeling. It used to be a treat when my life was nothing but cat food. He had that satisfied look on his face like he got the whole can instead of just being allowed to lick an empty one. Was I that smug when I was a cat? Did I have that stupid look on my face over tuna? I'd never ask Ripley because she'd tell me the truth, and I didn't want to know.

"Thank you for allowing me to bring my fantasy to life, my witch. It was better than I could have dreamed. I'd like to watch you now."

That was my cue. It was time for my moment. I stepped

around the chair and grabbed Ripley's hand to escort her to bed.

"Gabriel, get your ass over here."

Ripley flopped on the bed and blew a kiss at Balthazar.

"Remember this morning when I said I had plans for you? Unfortunately, I didn't get to have my wicked way with you because there wasn't time. I'm off for the next two days, and I intend to keep all of you quite busy. You'd better stock up on B vitamins."

Oh, shit. I wasn't remotely worried how Ripley would handle the four of us being what we were. I was worried about keeping up with *her* when she got this horny. I had all sorts of magical powers, but Lilith didn't really put any of those in my dick. I could only go so many times before it stopped working. Warlocks had been experimenting with potions since before I was born to make their cocks bigger or last longer. Ripley's spam folder made it seem like someone figured it out, but I'd seen men walking around with spots, and I had my doubts.

Ripley was ready to get started. She grabbed Gabriel, and me and yanked us into bed with her. Okay, we were starting this. I was so glad she hadn't gotten any ideas from Reyson and Bram and wanted to wrestle first. That could be sexy, too, just not right now.

We furiously kissed, bit, and touched until Gabriel grabbed the lube. We didn't even have to communicate on that after our last threesome. Gabriel was an arse man, and I would not take that away from him when the three of us were together.

Ripley flung me on my back and swallowed my cock while Gabriel prepared her. Oh, Lilith. This was my second time being alive, but she was definitely the best at this. I couldn't help but start purring. I was so mad when I figured out Reyson had done that to me, but it was still comforting, and Ripley liked it.

She squeezed my balls and then crawled up to rest her head on my chest.

"You're like my own personal vibrator," she sighed. "I'm ready."

Ripley crawled up and slid down me. I'd shout from the rooftops how much I loved this woman. She leaned forward and kissed me.

"I'm glad you're mine, exactly like this," she whispered.

I squeezed her to my chest because I was too. All because I knocked Reyson's cookies over. How weird was my life?

Gabriel situated himself into her with a groan. Ripley didn't even wait. She started moving and pulling my hair. I grabbed her hips and thrust up into her. This woman was going to kill me one day—what a way to go.

Ripley egged us on until the entire bed was shaking. I wouldn't last much longer. She was grinding herself into me, and I felt her clamp down on me. Holy shit. She started bucking on top of me, and I utterly lost it.

Gabriel let go, and we collapsed on the bed in a heap. Gabriel spooned her back, and I nuzzled her neck. I just loved her so damned much. She built us a powerful coven. We took on Hell and won. We even got to meet Lilith. I was still trying to get over that.

Hopefully, the rest of our lives would be less dramatic.

CHAPTER 51
BALTHAZAR

Vampires were solitary creatures that usually stayed in the shadows. In many ways, I was defective. We didn't die in the sunlight, but we definitely preferred the night. I did too, but only because that was when the parties happened. I loved being around people. You could say I craved it. I was a bit of an attention whore, and I had no regrets.

This arrangement at the library *should* be perfect for me. I didn't have to deny anything about myself, and I knew these people liked me for who I was. But, I just kept having this feeling in my gut that they just kept me around because I was good with computers, and they needed me to get to Dorian Gray.

No one had given me any reason to feel that way. They'd been nothing but great to me. They were perfect, but if I said that hadn't happened to me before, I'd be lying. I tried to give people pleasure when I was feeding from them only to have them throw it in my face that they found it disgusting. Then, there were the venom junkies who went around asking to get bit, but anyone with fangs would do.

Ripley settled my mind this morning when we both knew she was cutting it close to missing breakfast before work. She loved me. She loved my bites and everything about me. Reyson asked me to bite him all the time. He pretty much did whatever the fuck he wanted. I was guessing doing something he didn't like barely even crossed his mind. He knew Ripley offered, but he sure asked a lot.

I thought she would have been upset to wake up with just me in bed. Instead, Ripley was happy to have me all to herself. That meant a lot. She said she had plans for me later, and she totally did. I didn't know what, but I was here for it.

Gabriel and Felix crawled out of bed, and Ripley gave me this come hither look. She stopped me before I could join her in bed.

"Toy drawer. I want you to tie me up and give me the full vampire experience."

"Ooh. I'd like to request that too if we're going to spend this weekend fornicating," Reyson said.

"You are ridiculously horny," Felix said.

"No, I have needs. There's a difference."

I'd take all of Ripley and Reyson's needs because I was pretty ridiculously horny myself. And Ripley had a ton of options for restraints. How did I want to play this? The handcuffs would work, but I didn't want to chaff her beautiful skin giving her what she wanted. How did she have that many dildos and no fuzzy pink handcuffs? I was going to surprise her and buy her some. The entire room could enjoy those.

She had a lot of pretty silk scarves, so I grabbed those. This was going to be perfect. I jumped into bed and blew a raspberry on her stomach. Just because Felix and Gabriel didn't want a little fight after that show with Reyson and Bram, but I was also an apex predator.

Vampires were all about the hunt. I enjoyed it too, but sometimes, I was lazy and just wanted blood delivery, so I sank my fangs into someone without chasing them all over the place. Honestly, it could be exhausting sometimes. But watching Bram and Reyson got my blood pumping, and now I was in a mood.

I was going to do it my way, though.

I pounced and started tickling Ripley. Ooh, she was deliciously ticklish. She shrieked in laughter while I used my vampire speed and strength to tickle her and tie her up at the same time. I straddled her waist and looked down at my handiwork. Yeah, that would definitely do. Ripley stuck her bottom lip out in a mock pout.

"That's cheating. I love it."

I flew all over her body, giving her little nips with my fangs and sealing the wound with my tongue. She was moaning and writhing.

"Oh, my Lilith, Balthazar!" she gasped. "That should be a felony. You'd better get up here and fuck me."

Yeah, I'd happily do that. I'd always wanted to do the whole super biting thing to someone, but I'd never met someone who I thought would be into it. She loved it. I nipped my way up to her mouth and kissed her. I pricked her bottom lip with my fang and tasted her beautiful blood.

She wrapped her legs around my waist and bit me back —little minx. I guided myself inside her. I gave her enough of my vampire speed and strength that she had a good time, but not that I would hurt her.

Ripley was cursing up a storm and biting me just as good as I bit her. I loved every minute of it.

"Oh, shit. I'm close. Do it now!"

I buried my face in her neck and sunk my fangs in. I felt her clamp down on my cock right as her sweet blood hit my throat. I let go and groaned as my orgasm hit me. I withdrew my fangs and used my speed to untie her. I pulled her to my chest, and everyone started crawling into bed with us.

Bram spooned my back, and that Hellhound could certainly cuddle. I sighed. I was so content. This was my family now.

"Hopefully, this is the start of our lives being less dramatic," Ripley said. "Professor Krauss said something big is coming for Ravyn, so I know I'll get pulled into that. If I have to get rid of a stupid cheating wolf, I *will* figure out where to hide a body. I hope from here, all we have left to do is eat, fuck, and be happy."

I wanted that too. And any one of us would be happy to help her dispose of a corpse if it made her happy.

"I can see all possibilities, my witch. That shipment your twin sister is getting at the museum will cause trouble, but she'll be given help. She'll need you for support, but it's going to be her battle, just like this one was yours. As for us, I see nothing but happiness and little demigods."

"I'm *not* squirting anything out my vagina any time soon."

She also said she wouldn't marry him, but I was certain that would happen. If Reyson dropped a little bomb with his possibilities, something big always happened.

If he said happiness and babies were on the way, then he was probably right. We were all going to make amazing dads.

EPILOGUE

RIPLEY

The delivery room was chaos. Why did I bother even fighting Reyson when he said something was going to happen? I was pretty sure I wouldn't marry him when he crawled out of that casket covered in rags. Two years ago, we had a lovely handfasting ceremony, and now I was married to all five of them.

He said he saw babies in my future when we were celebrating being back at the library. I didn't think that would happen any time soon either, but I was here giving birth a second time... to twins, no less.

My first child was Gabriel's son. My midwife was a witch, and after so many months, there was a magical test to find out which parent the baby would take after in mixed couples. It couldn't be determined with my son Michael, so Reyson and Bram were excited because there was the possibility he was theirs since the midwife wasn't used to testing for gods or Hellhounds.

My son ended up being born with bony protrusions from his back. We had no idea what was going on until Lilith showed up and informed us Lucifer's angel genes were poking through, and those were his little baby wings. They'd eventually fill out with feathers, and he could hide them when he was out.

Lucifer was over the moon. He video called with Gabriel all the time and kept sending presents. When Michael was old enough, we brought him to visit all the time.

It wasn't a huge inconvenience. We were already in Hell a lot. Bram was able to find out who his mother was. We ate dinner with Talvath and his mom in Hell every Sunday, then stopped by to visit with Lucifer and Lilith.

Things were really shaping up in Hell for the Hellhounds. We got updates every time we visited. Talvath's school wasn't the only new business set up for them. Some of them were running their own now.

I fell pregnant with twins a year after Michael was born. Girls this time, and they would be Gemini twins like Ravyn and me. But, once again, the midwife's test was inconclusive, and Reyson and Bram were all over me.

Bram had been sending all my pregnancy symptoms to his mother and told me everything sounded textbook Hellhound. Reyson kept insisting he was getting vibes I was carrying his child. The midwife said it was unusual but possible for twins to have two different fathers, so they just latched onto that and went with it rather than fighting about it. The nursery was getting a little insane.

I just went with it because, honestly, who knew at this point? There weren't classes at the Academy of the Profane on giving birth to supernatural creatures when their daddies were the only representations of their kind on Earth. I wasn't even an expert on giving birth. I delivered a healthy son and didn't permanently damage my husbands for putting me in that position the first time. It fucking hurt, and here I was doing it again.

Reyson and Bram were both holding my hands as the midwife told me to push. All five of them had been totally amazing the first time I found out I was pregnant. They were at every appointment, went to classes, and read every book on the subject. They were amazing with Michael, even if we all knew Gabriel was his father.

I squeezed their hands and shrieked. I didn't understand why the various gods that made us had to make sex feel so good and childbirth feel like *this*. That was some fucked up trickery right there. These men put *two* babies in me. Why was I the only one in pain right now? I would like to speak to a manager.

"I can see the head. She's got a lot of dark hair. One more big push," the midwife called.

This was not just one more push. There was still another baby in there, and I just wanted to pass out. How long had I been doing this already? So I gave one more big push, and she was out.

The midwife took her to the basin to clean her.

"She's a Hellhound like her daddy."

"Ha!" Bram yelled.

He wanted to name her Matilda after his mother, and I was totally fine with that. I adored his mom. We were all just going with the fact that the other twin was Reyson's, and we all knew how he was with names. He refused to even entertain the notion of picking a name until he met his daughter.

Reyson jumped up and got all up in the midwife's personal space peering over her shoulder.

"*Do not* point your phone at my vagina, Reyson!"

"I have to record this epic occasion. I may need to show it to boys when she's old enough to date before I threaten to kill them."

"If you show my gaping vagina to anyone she brings home, we're both going to murder you."

"Okay, fine. But this is my first child, my witch. So I want to capture the moment."

Just then, pain ripped through my body, and the lights flickered in the hospital. A massive clap of thunder shook the walls, and a flash of lightning lit the sky. It had been sunny with no thunderstorms predicted when I came to the hospital, but a massive storm started as soon as that pain started.

"Get ready to meet your second daughter, Ripley," the midwife said.

"Look at that storm! My daughter is making her entrance."

If there was any doubt my twins had different fathers, that raging storm outside got rid of them. Matilda started shrieking as the lights in the hospital continued to flicker. Bram had her in his arms, trying to soothe her, but I already knew that wouldn't happen until she was back with her twin.

"Big push!"

Felix and Balthazar rushed to my side to grab my hand. I gave one big push, and she was out. I could see her glowing golden aura from here. Yeah, she was definitely like Reyson. Reyson trailed after the midwife as she cleaned off our child and swaddled her.

"Want to hold her, dad?"

Reyson had probably seen so much in his long life, but he looked down at our daughter in pure awe. Then, he looked up at me with this goofy look on his face.

"We made a baby, Ripley!"

"That tends to happen when you have as much sex as we all do," Felix said.

"What are you going to name her?" I asked with a small smile.

"Well, she decided to enter this world by causing a thunderstorm, so she can only be called Tempest."

Tempest started crying too, and the thunder outside roared.

"You'd better get the twins back together. Can I see them?"

"You need to do more than that," the midwife said. "You need to try feeding them."

Bram and Reyson brought my babies over, and I finally got a look at them. They looked very similar, like Ravyn and I's baby photos, but they got minor differences from their dads. Matilda had baby blue eyes that might change when she got older, but Tempest's eyes were silver like Reyson and Lilith's. I was thinking all gods had eyes that color.

Lilith scared the shit out of me when she opened a magical door and stepped through with a basket and Bram's mother. It shouldn't have shocked me because she did the same thing when Michael was born, but I just pushed two kids out of my vagina, and I was a little jumpy.

"Mom! Come meet my baby. We named her after you."

Something made a noise in the basket Lilith was holding. When a god crashes your delivery with a crying basket, you should ask *all* the questions.

"What is that?"

She pulled a fat little Dolrun puppy out of the basket and set it between the twins on my belly. The puppy yawned and snuggled in, and the twins let out contented coos. Why was Lilith gifting Hell puppies to my twins?

"I *know* they aren't witches, but they are still going to be powerful twins. One will be one of the only two Hellhounds on Earth, and the other is the daughter of a god. Naturally, people are going to feel threatened by that. It hasn't happened in a long time, but some gods haven't reacted well to us having offspring with mortals in the past.

"I pulled some strings, and Mags is their familiar. She was a witch waiting in the Aether to be reborn, and when I asked her, she was honored to be their familiar. She was a fierce warrior back in her day and is perfect for them. I also know how Reyson feels about giving my familiars their bodies back and how the two witches in that situation look at theirs. Mags is female to keep Reyson from getting a little murdery if he gifts her body back."

Balthazar snorted.

"You do know being the same gender wouldn't have stopped *either* of the twin's daddies, right?"

I started giggling because Balthazar was totally right. Neither of them cared what was between your legs. It was all about the person. And I knew they would raise their daughters to be open-minded. If they happened to be bisexual, too, Bram and Reyson would deal with it.

"Just try not to kill my familiar if feelings develop, okay? She agreed to do this rather than be reborn as a witch."

"Wait, are my daughters going to be in danger?" I demanded. "We're already worried about Michael and the other angels."

Lilith pulled a necklace out of the basket and handed it to me. It appeared to be some sort of crystal, but I couldn't identify it. I aced that class in high school. I knew every crystal and its magical properties. This one hadn't been taught here on Earth.

"I created this from a rock in my garden. As long as she's wearing it, it will hide her aura to look more like a witch's. People will always sense she's powerful, but they won't guess the truth. Also, it will keep people from bothering her."

"You expect me to lie that my daughter is not like me?" Reyson boomed.

"Kids are cruel, Reyson. What do you think will happen if they find out they are going to school with a little god? They are going to want to establish dominance. They will dog pile on her, and she'll never get a break."

"She'll be perfectly capable of kicking their asses. She's not going to have to wait to come into her powers like they are."

I got where Reyson was coming from. I didn't want any of my kids to deny who they were, but Reyson had never been to school with other kids. She would be damned if she did and damned if she didn't. Those kids would want to be top dogs by fighting the strongest person in the school. If she revealed she had magic, they wouldn't react well. Everyone knew witches didn't get their powers early unless something terrible happened to them.

"Reyson, just for school. Let her pretend to be a witch around other kids. It'll allow her to have a normal childhood. When she's at home, teach her what she inherited from you because I can't."

"We'll do it that way until she's old enough to *ask* what she wants. I also plan on reaching out to my siblings I'm friends with. We are going to spread the word. If you come for my daughter, you are coming for all of us. The twins are going to have a perfect, lovely life. I'm going to make sure of it."

"If anyone tries to come at Matilda for being a Hellhound, if I don't eat them, she will," Bram said. "She'll start shifting when she's a toddler.

"Mags will be there to help," Lilith said. "You don't *always* need to kill anyone who comes at them."

I didn't want to worry about bullies or angry gods. The twins were snuggled into my chest with their arms over Mags. Their hands were touching. I had a feeling they would be just as close as Ravyn and I. They didn't stop crying until they were close to each other again.

They were just so precious. Michael was a year old. Some of the feathers on his wings had started to come in, and we hadn't had a single angel show up at the library. Reyson said our life would be full of happiness and babies after we did our thing in Hell.

I knew that extended to my children too. I'd put the crystal around Tempest's neck until she could tell us what she wanted for herself, but I knew my children and any future children I might have were going to have totally happy lives.

If someone threatened that, Reyson could just make them explode into a cloud of pink glitter.